Darkest Actions

Darkest Actions

Cherith Baldry

Copyright © 2024 Cherith Baldry

The moral right of the author has been asserted.

Apart from any fair dealing for the purposes of research or private study, or criticism or review, as permitted under the Copyright, Designs and Patents Act 1988, this publication may only be reproduced, stored or transmitted, in any form or by any means, with the prior permission in writing of the publishers, or in the case of reprographic reproduction in accordance with the terms of licences issued by the Copyright Licensing Agency. Enquiries concerning reproduction outside those terms should be sent to the publishers.

This is a work of fiction. Names, characters, businesses, places, events and incidents are either the products of the author's imagination or used in a fictitious manner. Any resemblance to actual persons, living or dead, or actual events is purely coincidental.

Troubador Publishing Ltd
Unit E2 Airfield Business Park,
Harrison Road, Market Harborough,
Leicestershire LE16 7UL
Tel: 0116 279 2299
Email: books@troubador.co.uk
Web: www.troubador.co.uk

ISBN 978 1 80514 408 3

British Library Cataloguing in Publication Data.
A catalogue record for this book is available from the British Library.

Printed and bound by CPI Group (UK) Ltd, Croydon, CR0 4YY
Typeset in 11pt MInion Pro by Troubador Publishing Ltd, Leicester, UK

For Heather

Your darkest actions, nay, your privat'st thoughts
Will come to light.
>	John Webster, *The Duchess of Malfi*, I.i

All the quotations at the chapter headings are taken from
the plays of John Webster.

Prologue

Past sorrows, let us moderately lament them,
For those to come, seek wisely to prevent them.
The Duchess of Malfi, III.ii

"I hope you don't mind meeting me like this," Iris Grant said. "I know how busy you are."

Persephone Brown took a sip of her Chianti and waited until the server had set down two bowls of steaming pasta and withdrawn. The heat and chatter of the Italian restaurant swirled around the two women and their tiny table tucked into an alcove.

"It's fine," Persephone said. "Just tell me what it's all about."

Iris hesitated. Examining her across the table Persephone realised that her usual carefree air was notably absent. She looked worried; her eyes were shadowed as if she hadn't slept.

"I need your advice, Seff," she confessed. "And maybe your help."

Seff felt faintly surprised. Iris was usually independent and thoroughly sensible, except in the matter of the useless object she had got engaged to. "Is it about Jake?" she asked.

Iris shook her head. "I'm not with Jake any more," she replied. "But that's not what's bothering me."

For the first time Seff noticed Iris's hands, square, capable and paint-stained as always, with a pale band where once she had worn her engagement ring.

So she dumped the little creep, Seff thought. *Good.* Aloud she asked, "So what is it?"

Iris prodded her *spaghetti alle vongole* without enthusiasm. "You remember I told you about my Great Uncle Petroc?" she asked.

"The one who lives on the Cornish island?"

"Yes, Morgarrow. Well, last week I had a letter from his solicitor, telling me that he'd died."

"I'm sorry." Seff reached out to touch her friend's hand. "I know you were close to him."

Iris nodded. "We were just about each other's only family." She took a deep breath. "Anyway," she went on with an effort, "that's when the trouble started with Jake. When I told him Great Uncle was dead, the first thing he said was about what he'd left me. And I suddenly realised that I didn't like Jake very much, and I didn't much like the person I was turning into when I was with him. We had a blazing row, and in the end I gave him his ring back and told him to pack his stuff and get out of my flat."

"And he went?" Seff asked, reflecting that Jake was unlikely to give up his rent-free and comfortable existence without a fight.

"Oh, yes, eventually." A gleam of humour showed in Iris's face as she added, "With much wailing and gnashing of teeth, but he went." She paused again, taking a gulp of wine. "It's not Jake who's the problem."

"Go on," Seff said encouragingly.

"Well, you know that Great Uncle Petroc owned the

island? Some king or other gave it to one of our ancestors." Seff hadn't known, but she let it go. "That's not as grand as it sounds," Iris continued. "Morgarrow is really tiny. There's a village, a few farms, and an Abbey – St Cadoc's – with a religious community attached to it. The Abbey is run by a trust, and Great Uncle Petroc was one of the trustees."

Seff took a bite of her *pollo al forno*, listening intently. Her finely honed reporter's senses had given a sudden twitch, as at the first hint of a story.

"Jake and I went down there last Easter," Iris went on. "We visited Great Uncle, and I painted, and Jake…messed about, I suppose. That was when Great Uncle told me that he was leaving the island to the Abbey, except for the cottage and its contents, which were to be mine."

"And were you happy with that?" Seff asked.

"Very happy. What would I do with an island? But that's not really relevant. What matters is that a couple of weeks ago I got a letter from Great Uncle Petroc. He doesn't – didn't – do email, much less texting. He wanted me to go down there, because he thought there was something fishy going on at the Abbey, and he needed to consult me."

Seff's senses twitched again, more emphatically. "Did you go?" she asked.

"How could I? My students were in the middle of their exams, so I wrote back to Great Uncle and told him I'd go down as soon as term ended, which would be this weekend. And then I got the letter saying that he was dead."

Seff took a thoughtful sip of her wine and topped up both glasses. "He didn't tell you what the 'something fishy' was?"

Iris shook her head. "And that's the problem. I'll have to go down there and see to his funeral, and sort out the legal stuff, but I don't think I can ignore the fact that something was worrying him. I feel I ought to find out what was going on, and do something about it, but I haven't got the least idea where to start."

Seff frowned slightly, seeing an implication she didn't like at all. "Iris, do you think your uncle's death was natural?"

"You mean, was he murdered?" Iris stared at her in shock. "Good heavens, no! He was ninety-two, and his heart had been bad for years. I'm just worried about what he thought he'd found out. What do you think I should do, Seff?"

"I think you need a knight in shining armour," Seff responded.

Iris let out a short, humourless laugh. "I wish!"

Seff grinned, her plan of action unrolling in front of her without any effort on her part. "Is there a hotel on Morgarrow?" she asked.

Iris nodded. "Oh, yes. The Abbey gets a lot of pilgrims, and they have to stay somewhere."

"Then here's what we do." Seff reached out and patted Iris's hand. "You go down there and start your arrangements. And I'll bring you a knight in shining armour."

Chapter One

Virtue, where art thou hid? What hideous thing
Is it that doth eclipse thee?
The Duchess of Malfi, III.ii

David Powers nudged the scarlet sports car onto the ramp leading into the bowels of the ferry, and edged forward until he drew to a stop behind a supermarket delivery van. With a hideous metallic screech, the ramp closed up behind.

"It's hardly worth getting out of the car," David said. "We'll be there in a few minutes."

Gawaine St Clair, in the passenger seat, stirred; he looked half asleep, golden hair ruffled, blue eyes heavy-lidded, drowsy. "Do you feel a sense of impending doom?" he asked.

David flashed a look at his companion. "No. Should I?"

"Consider, my dear David," Gawaine responded with a negligent wave of one hand. "We are *en route* to an island whose tenuous link with the mainland will shortly be shattered, leaving us trapped with a maniac who will begin picking us off one by one. At least," he finished, "I believe that is what usually happens."

"Idiot," David said affectionately. "I know this ferry is pretty antiquated, but it seems functional to me."

"Ah, but there's always sabotage," Gawaine reminded him. "And don't forget the Abbey. There are invariably nefarious doings around a ruined Abbey. Eldritch screams and things that flit through the night."

"Flit?" David said. "Why?"

Gawaine shrugged elegantly. "There is no 'why'. It is enough that they flit."

"If I didn't know you better," David said, "I'd think you'd been watching too many late night horror movies. Besides, didn't Seff say that the Abbey is still in use?"

Gawaine repeated the elegant shrug, conceding the point. "But I gather it will *be* ruined, unless they can expand their restoration project. And that may be where we come in."

David considered. Gawaine's past encounters with crime had usually involved murder. The current unspecified iniquity, probably nothing more than a bit of bog-standard fiddling, was a long way out of his experience. And considerably less traumatic, which was all to the good.

"I hope you don't mind doing this." Gawaine sounded suddenly guilty, as if he had picked up something of David's thought.

"Of course not," David replied. "I've a few days' holiday. Where better to spend it than in Cornwall in summer? I suppose I can hire a surf board or something, when we've done what we came to do."

"It shouldn't take long," Gawaine said. "Not with your financial expertise, my dear David. After all, 'something fishy' at the Abbey is likely to mean someone has had their hand in the till."

"'Something fishy' anywhere is likely to mean someone has had their hand in the till," David agreed.

A gentle shudder told him that the ferry had reached its destination. Light flooded in as the forward ramp opened up. The van jerked into motion and roared off, leaving David to follow more cautiously, glancing around as he waited for the foot passengers to clear the slipway.

The bulk of the village, a picturesque collection of whitewashed cottages, lay to his left, straggling along the shoreline and half way up the hill. On the other side of the slipway a stone-built jetty jutted out into the sea, with a few small boats moored beside it. Beyond it the village petered out and the hillside rose to the grey bulk of the Abbey, its walls and tower soaring out of an encircling drystone wall. Sheer cliffs fell away not far from the Abbey's seaward side; gulls swooped and screeched around the rocks.

Between the village and the Abbey stood a long, low building, whitewashed like the rest, surrounded by trees. David could just make out several cars parked at one side.

"That must be the hotel," he said, driving forward.

"Seff emailed me to say that she managed to book rooms for us," Gawaine said. "She told me that she and Iris Grant would meet us for dinner in—" He glanced at his watch. "In about an hour. And then maybe we can find out what all this is about."

"Two knights in shining armour." Iris Grant's mouth quirked in amusement. "I'm privileged." More seriously, she added, "And very grateful."

David deposited a tray of drinks on the table Seff had commandeered in the bar of the St Cadoc Hotel and surveyed Seff's friend Iris. She was a small woman with a tangle of light brown hair and clear, direct hazel eyes. Her loose cotton shirt, striped like pillow ticking, had a smear of paint on one cuff.

"So tell us about the Abbey," David said as he distributed glasses.

"It's dedicated to St Cadoc," Iris began. "He established a monastery here, back in the sixth century, and it developed into a famous seat of learning." She broke off, smiling. "I sound like Father Magnus's information leaflet! Anyway, the original buildings are long gone; the current Abbey is medieval. It was abandoned between the two world wars, but there was always a trickle of pilgrims, and so several years ago now Great Uncle Petroc got together with Father Magnus and managed to persuade the Church to reopen it."

"Fascinating," Gawaine murmured. His social, slightly affected manner did not prevent him from listening intently.

"Yes, riveting," Seff agreed, with a grin at Iris that took the sting out of her sharp comment. "But bring us up to date. What is happening now, and what do you think might be going wrong?"

"The Abbey is run by a Trust," Iris explained. There are five Trustees – four now, since Great Uncle Petroc died."

"And who are they?" Gawaine asked.

"Father Magnus, who was the priest in charge at St Cadoc's before he retired," Iris replied. "He's our local hermit: he lives in a tiny cottage up on the moor. Then there's Jenny Morland, who's the current priest in charge. Great Uncle's solicitor, Bernard White – he chairs the trust. And the Abbey treasurer, Elaine Chatham."

"The treasurer..." Gawaine murmured, with a glance at David.

"Is she likely to be fiddling the books?" David asked.

Iris gave a reluctant grin. "I doubt it," she said. "She's quite elderly, and more than a bit dotty. I wouldn't be surprised if she makes mistakes, but I don't think she'd be deliberately dishonest."

"Are the accounts audited?"

"Oh, yes. By a firm of accountants on the mainland. As far as I know, there's never been a problem."

"All the same, my dear David..." Gawaine bore his usual look of bemusement when anyone was discussing finance. "I think you ought to have a look at the books, just to make sure that's not the 'something fishy' that Great Uncle Petroc wrote about." He blinked thoughtfully into his glass of Prosecco and added, "I'm sure we can assume that he suspected one of those four trustees was responsible."

"Why?" Iris sounded surprised.

"Because if your great uncle thought that someone else had... er... done those things which they ought not to have done, he would have addressed it with his fellow trustees, not written to ask you for help."

"I see..." Iris nodded slowly, giving Gawaine a look that suggested she had discerned the intelligence behind the frivolous exterior. "In that case, we ought to add Elaine's son, Roddy. Or 'Roddy darling' as his mother calls him."

"But if he's not a trustee..?" Seff began.

"He's not, but he would like to be. And he's always up in the Abbey's business, far more than he should be."

"You don't sound as if you like him," David said.

"I think he's a pain in the neck," Iris responded. "Only son, spoilt rotten by his mother. He looks at Morgarrow as a business opportunity."

"In what way?" Seff asked.

"Well, Roddy darling works for an estate agent and auctioneer on the mainland," Iris explained. "He'd like to cover Morgarrow with mobile homes and timeshare resorts. Make it a tourist hot spot, all with the view of getting extra income for the Abbey, of course. Great Uncle Petroc would have nothing to do with his ideas." She paused, frowning, then continued, "But now that Great Uncle is dead, and has left the island to the Abbey…"

"Roddy might get his way," Gawaine said.

"I hate it!" Iris's voice was vehement. "Morgarrow would be completely spoilt. I know the Abbey needs money – there's a massive restoration project underway – but not like that. I've always felt there's something… something sacred about the island, and Roddy's plans would destroy it."

"And you think he'll be elected trustee now that there's a vacancy?" David asked.

"Strictly speaking, he can't," Iris replied. "The trustees have to be resident on the island, and Roddy lives on the mainland, near where he works."

"Would he consider moving back in with his mum?" Seff asked.

Iris shook her head. "Elaine lives in St Morwenna's Community – that's a big, old house not far from the Abbey. The people there are a team to take care of the Abbey: fundraising, brass polishing, hassock darning, all that kind of stuff. Most of them are students; some are training for the ministry, and there are always a few historians. They just stay for their long vac, or maybe take a gap year, but Elaine is permanent. Great Uncle let her stay there rent free in return for looking after the place. There's no room for Roddy darling, and even if there was, it's definitely not his cup of tea."

"I suppose he wouldn't need to be a trustee, if the current lot like his ideas," Seff pointed out. "Are you absolutely sure that Roddy darling didn't put something nasty in Great Uncle Petroc's evening mug of cocoa?"

"Absolutely sure!" Iris protested, while Gawaine closed his eyes and gave a delicate shudder. "I said Roddy is a pain in the neck, but I'm sure he hasn't it in him to be a murderer."

She sounded quite certain, but David couldn't help wondering if she was right. Great Uncle Petroc's death had been very convenient for someone.

"So, what's our next move?" Seff's brisk voice cut across his thoughts. David had long ago tagged her as the most irritating woman in the world, but tonight she was clear and incisive, keeping everyone focussed.

"Great Uncle's funeral is tomorrow," Iris replied. "As a trustee, he gets to be buried in the Abbey graveyard. After that, Bernard White will read the will, and then maybe I can get into the cottage. So far he's refused to cough up the keys."

"I wondered why you were staying here in the hotel," Seff remarked.

"Yes, spending money I haven't got." Iris sounded annoyed. "Honestly, I could cheerfully strangle Bernard! I should think the whole island knows what's in that will, and it's not as if I'm going to start vandalising the place."

"Maybe Great Uncle Petroc left something in the cottage that would give us an idea of what his 'something fishy' was," Gawaine suggested.

"Maybe, if we could get at it," Iris agreed.

"I'll stay for the funeral, but then I have to get back to work," Seff said. "I'm going to write a piece about Great Uncle Petroc. He was well-known in his day, and I imagine my editor wouldn't say no to an obituary."

"What was he famous for?" David asked.

"He was a travel writer," Seff told him. "He even made a few TV programmes back in the sixties and seventies."

"And he ended up on Morgarrow," Gawaine murmured. "Port after stormy seas…"

"He loved it here," Iris sighed. "It won't be the same without him. And whatever happens," she added fiercely, "I'm going to find out what was worrying him."

Chapter Two

Much you had of land and rent;
Your length in clay's now competent.
The Duchess of Malfi, IV.ii

St Cadoc's Abbey was a huge cavern of a place, its roof lost in shadows. Rows of pews faced a carved wooden screen that looked as if most of it had succumbed to woodworm long ago. At the front a coffin stood on trestles, flanked on either side by candles on wooden stands. Though the first several rows of pews were already full, and more people were entering all the time, the church still had an empty, echoing feel about it.

"I can see why they need a restoration fund," David murmured to Gawaine as they found seats.

Gawaine nodded. "It must have deteriorated quite quickly once it was closed."

David wondered why anyone had bothered to start restoring it, though he didn't say so out loud. He sat looking around him, noticing a ray of light striking through a hole in the roof, and a spot high up on the wall where an over-confident fern had rooted itself.

"Let's hope the building doesn't collapse on our heads," he muttered.

The service was taken by an elderly priest in a long

black cassock. He had a seamed and craggy face like an ancient gnome, and a shock of white hair brushed back as if he was standing in a stiff breeze.

"That must be Father Magnus." Gawaine leaned over and spoke softly into David's ear. "One of the other trustees."

The priest had a fine, booming delivery that rolled out across the congregation. Iris, in contrast, seemed quenched; her formal clothes for the funeral suited her far less than her casual outfit of the evening before. When she spoke the eulogy for her great uncle, her quiet voice would hardly have reached the first row of pews except for the surprisingly efficient sound system.

"I thought they would have fixed the roof before they put in all this," David murmured, glancing up at a nearby loudspeaker.

"Priorities." Gawaine gave a tiny shrug. "You can't hold a service if no one can hear it."

"Great Uncle Petroc was famous once, and he travelled the world," Iris finished. "But he was happiest of all on Morgarrow. I know he would be grateful to see so many of you here today. Thank you."

When the service was over, most of the congregation left, heading through the gates of the Abbey precinct and down the track that led to the village and the ferry. A few people followed Iris and Father Magnus to the graveside; Seff stayed close to Iris, but David and Gawaine hovered at a distance.

With Gawaine apparently concentrating on the burial service, David occupied himself by trying to identify the rest of the Abbey trustees. A young woman in cassock and dog collar was obviously Jenny Morland, the current priest in charge. She was thin and pale, with limp fair hair reaching to her shoulders; David thought there couldn't have been a greater contrast to Father Magnus, who looked as if he would dominate any gathering he happened to be involved in.

Beside Jenny Morland stood a much older woman, her white hair looped up and escaping from its many pins. She was swathed in a voluminous knitted shawl; a hand heavy with rings clutched at the arm of the man beside her.

Elaine and Roddy Chatham, David thought. He hadn't liked what he had heard the night before about Roddy darling, and he didn't much like the look of him now. His pin-striped suit and open-necked shirt with no tie probably fitted right in at the estate agency where he worked, but they weren't appropriate here. Roddy looked terminally bored, too, completely oblivious of his mother, who was dabbing at her eyes with a wisp of handkerchief. David, spotting him as he took a surreptitious glance at his watch, wondered what was making him so impatient. *Maybe he wants to hear the will read, and get his sticky paws on the island.*

The only other man at the graveside was standing at the far end, a little way away from the others, looking as if he had a bad smell under his nose. He was tall and gaunt, with a fringe of closely cropped grey hair around an otherwise bald head, and unlike Roddy, he was correctly, even severely, dressed, expect for the unexpected frivolity of a rose in his buttonhole. *Bernard White?* David asked himself.

A rattle of earth on the coffin lid brought David back

from his musing. A couple of refugees from *Hamlet* moved up with spades, while the group around the graveside turned away and headed back towards the Abbey.

"Come on," David said to Gawaine, who was standing in a kind of daze. "This is our chance to find out what this lot are up to."

Gawaine looked up at him, startled. "Of course, my dear David," he responded. "I was just wondering about our observer over there."

He tilted his head towards the graveyard gate; for the first time David spotted another onlooker, standing in the shadow of a tall Celtic cross. The man was short, dark and stocky, with a slim document case under one arm.

"He looks somewhat… purposeful," Gawaine continued.

"Well, if he's more than your average gawker, we'll find out soon enough," David said. "Meanwhile, we need to find out what's going on in the Abbey."

With a last glance at the man by the gate, Gawaine followed Iris and the rest of the group. He and David caught them up in the narthex of the Abbey.

"I'll leave you to it," Jenny Morland was saying as they entered. "I have to prepare for the lunch-time Communion." She hurried off through the main doors, which had been left wide open after the mourners left.

"Gawaine – David!" Iris turned to them with a look of relief. "I'm glad you're here. We—"

"And you are?" The man David had identified as Bernard White moved forward, placing himself between Gawaine and Iris, who had to take a pace back to avoid being stepped on.

Iris exchanged an annoyed glance with Seff. "My advisers," she said firmly.

David introduced them both, information Bernard White received with an ill-tempered snort. "I can't imagine why you think you need 'advisers,'" he said to Iris.

"Maybe that's why," she retorted.

Father Magnus loomed up beside them; though Bernard White was tall, he looked undersized, even puny, beside the old priest. "Shall we proceed?" Father Magnus suggested. "I'm sure we'd all like to hear the will and then go about our business."

"Yes," Elaine Chatham agreed, bestowing a beaming smile indiscriminately around the group. "I've laid on a few refreshments up at St Morwenna's, and you're all very welcome."

"Very kind of you, Elaine," Father Magnus said.

Bernard White met the invitation with no more than an impatient sniff. "I've placed the relevant documents in the Chapter House," he announced. "If you'll follow me…"

He led the way through the main doors and up one of the side aisles until he reached a door studded with iron nails. Fishing in a pocket, he drew out a heavy bunch of keys, selected one and pushed the door open.

The Chapter House was an octagonal chamber with a vaulted ceiling and wooden pew-like seats lining the walls. Bernard White crossed the room to where a briefcase had been placed on one of the seats, and began to draw out papers.

Meanwhile, the rest of the group found themselves somewhere to sit. Elaine Chatham fussed herself into a seat with much rearranging of her draperies, drew out a bright patchwork bag, until now hidden under her shawl, took from it a long narrow strip of something purple and placidly began to knit.

"It's a stole for dear Jenny," she informed the company at large. "I'm making her one in each of the liturgical colours."

Seff, who had taken the seat beside David, leaned over to murmur into his ear. "I bet Jenny will be *really* grateful."

David, to whom a stole was an evening wrap, and who had no idea what liturgical colours were, merely shrugged in response.

"Here, don't I know you?" That was Roddy Chatham, plonking himself down on Gawaine's other side. "I've seen you in the papers. You're that bloke who fancies himself as an amateur sleuth. Do you think somebody topped old Petroc?"

Gawaine, at his most languid and affected, was leaning back in his seat, one hand caressing the boss at the end of the arm, which was carved into the likeness of a snarling feline. He fixed Roddy with what he probably imagined was an icy expression. "I don't 'fancy myself' as anything," he replied. "And there seems to be no evidence that Petroc Tremayne died of anything except natural causes."

Roddy let out a guffaw. "We've only just planted the poor old sod," he said. "You'd better not think of digging him up again."

Gawaine's only response to that was a look of controlled distaste. Any answer he might have made was cut off by Iris, who had crossed the room to stand beside Bernard White.

"I hope when all this is over, you'll be able to let me have the keys to the cottage," she said.

"All in good time." Bernard White couldn't have sounded more unfriendly if he'd tried. "Let's get the will reading over with, and then we'll see. Let me remind you, you don't yet know how your great uncle left his property."

Iris looked as if she was about to protest, then let out an irritated sigh and went to sit beside Seff. Her shoulders were bowed; David guessed that she was exhausted, and only wanted the whole thing to be over with.

"Very well." Bernard White finished fiddling with his papers and extracted a document on thick legal paper. Straightening up, he faced the company and began to read. "The last will and testament of—"

He broke off as the Chapter House door swung open and the dark young man who had stood beside the graveyard gate stepped inside. David's interest quickened; he exchanged a glance with Gawaine, who suddenly straightened, seeming uncharacteristically alert.

"I thought I might find you here," the newcomer said.

Bernard White was looking suddenly furious. "Tom Turnbull!" he exclaimed. "What are you doing here? This is a private matter, nothing to do with you."

"I think you'll find it has," Tom Turnbull replied; in contrast to Bernard White, he was completely calm. Glancing around the room, he added, "Ms Grant?"

"That's me," Iris said, half rising, then subsiding back into her seat.

"Allow me to say how sorry I was to hear of your great uncle's death, I only knew him for a couple of months, but he was one of the most interesting men I've met for a long time."

Iris nodded. "Thank you."

"Turnbull, if you just wanted to express your condolences," Bernard White said, "there are more appropriate ways of doing it."

"But that's not the only reason I'm here," Tom Turnbull said. He still remained calm, but there was a gleam in his eye, and David guessed that he was enjoying himself.

"Then why are you?" Bernard White asked. "Spit it out, man, and then we can all get on."

"Certainly." Tom Turnbull unzipped his document case. "I'm here to read the last will and testament of Petroc Tremayne."

Chapter Three

> Then the law to him
> Is like a foul black cobweb to a spider.
> *The Duchess of Malfi,* I.i

Iris let out an audible gasp and pressed one hand to her mouth. Seff leaned over and touched her on the shoulder.

"What do you mean?" Bernard White's pallid features were reddening with anger. "That's preposterous! *I* have Petroc Tremayne's will right here." He flourished the document.

Tom Turnbull extracted an exactly similar document from his case. "I think you'll find that mine supersedes yours."

"Let me see that!" Bernard White strode across the chamber and snatched the papers from Tom Turnbull's hand. He flipped both documents out of their folds; his gaze flicked to and fro as he compared one with the other. His rage intensified; David wouldn't have been surprised to see steam come shrieking out of his ears.

Eventually he shoved Tom Turnbull's papers back at him. "Outrageous!" he snapped, turning back to his own seat, where he sat with a face that wouldn't only have curdled new milk, but put an end to the cow as well.

"Fascinating…" Gawaine breathed out, his eyes bright with interest.

Tom Turnbull turned to Iris. "Ms Grant, I'm sorry for the… misunderstanding," he said. "As you've probably guessed, I'm a solicitor, though not of course in the same practice as Mr White over there. Your great uncle came to see me not long after Easter and asked me to draw up a new will. He told me that his original will was with White and Carslake, but he didn't tell me why he wanted to change, and I didn't ask."

"I see." Iris sounded as if she was just about holding herself together.

"We can guess why," Gawaine murmured. "That would be about the time he discovered 'something fishy'."

"So are we going to hear this will, or not?" Roddy Chatham asked, his tone aggressive as he glared at Tom Turnbull. "I can't sit here frigging around all day. I've stuff to do."

"Of course," Tom Turnbull replied, reacting not at all to the tone or the language. He laid his case down on a vacant seat, but remained standing as he read from the document.

David listened with interest. He guessed that there must be something explosive in the new will, for Great Uncle Petroc to have secretly engaged another solicitor to make it.

After the usual preamble, Tom Turnbull began with some minor bequests: a chess set to Father Magnus, a thousand pounds to the Abbey restoration fund, another thousand to someone called Annis Radford. David had never heard of her, but the approving murmurs of the others told him that they knew who she was and had no problem with her legacy.

"And all other property of which I die possessed," Tom Turnbull finished, "I leave to my great niece Iris Grant."

"Dear me!" Elaine Chatham exclaimed, proving that she was a good deal quicker on the uptake than David had given her credit for.

Her start of surprise dislodged her ball of purple wool, which rolled off her lap and across the Chapter House floor, to come to rest at Gawaine's feet. David hid a grin as Gawaine rose to retrieve it and carried the ball back, winding up the wool as he went, to restore it to Elaine with a small bow.

The momentary hiatus gave everyone else the chance to catch up with what Tom Turnbull had just announced.

Iris had gone sheet-white. "He left me… the island?"

Tom Turnbull tilted his head towards her. "He did indeed."

"Here!" Roddy Chatham surged to his feet. "He can't do that!"

"He could and he did," Tom Turnbull said.

Bernard White rose and crossed the chamber, once again snatching the will out of Tom Turnbull's hands. "Let me see that!" His eyes were venomous.

"You'll find it quite in order."

David watched Bernard White as he examined the document, obviously taking in every detail. Gawaine leaned over and murmured into David's ear, "If there's a comma out of place, he'll find it."

But apparently all the commas were present and correct. "I shall want a copy of that," Bernard White said as he passed the will back. Then he turned to Iris and continued, "You won't accept the legacy, of course. You know perfectly well that your great uncle intended to leave the island to St Cadoc's."

Iris opened her mouth to respond, but he swept on regardless. "Of course, my dear, I'm sure we could come to some arrangement about the cottage."

Tom Turnbull was staring at the rival lawyer, half amused and half incredulous at what he was hearing. Iris, on the other hand, didn't look amused at all.

"Absolutely not," she said. "Great Uncle's will shows exactly what his intentions were. If he wanted to leave Morgarrow to St Cadoc's, why would he have made a new will at all? And incidentally, Mr White, I am not your dear."

David saw that her pallor of a few moments before had been replaced by a flush of anger. Her eyes were bright as she gazed up at Bernard White with a look of defiance.

"Then we'll contest the will," he said, a cold, pinched expression creeping over his face. "It's quite absurd that Petroc Tremayne would let St Cadoc's crumble into ruins for lack of proper funding. The man was obviously senile."

"Petroc's wits were as sharp as a man's half his age." Father Magnus's voice was a deep rumble in his chest. "He thrashed me at chess on a regular basis. I shall testify to that, if necessary."

"You may, for all the good it will do you." Bernard White began gathering papers together and stuffing them into his briefcase. "Make no mistake, we're going to get this will overturned."

"Yeah, we'll see you in court," Roddy Chatham added.

"Er... if I might make a suggestion," Gawaine said diffidently.

Bernard White swung round on him, looking as

startled as if the carved cat on the seat arm had sat up and addressed him. David could have warned him it was never a good idea to discount Gawaine. "What?" he snarled.

"It seems to me that a Christian organisation – you do consider the Abbey trustees to be a Christian organisation, do you not? – should hardly be going to court to deprive a perfectly innocent person of her rightful legacy," Gawaine said. "There's no question, is there, that Ms Grant put any pressure on Petroc Tremayne to change his will?"

"I never said there was," Bernard White snapped.

"I wasn't even here on the island when he did it," Iris added.

"Then taking her to court would surely give the wrong impression?" Gawaine continued silkily. "Of the trustees' Christian principles, I mean. The press might take an… undesirable interest."

"You bet they would," Seff agreed, bestowing a feral smile on Bernard White.

"And quite right, too," Father Magnus agreed. "It would be an appalling thing to do."

The solicitor's only response was an ill-tempered snort, but he didn't argue any further. David guessed that any adverse publicity might affect the Abbey's other funding, and if he knew Seff, she would make sure that the publicity was as adverse as it could get.

"Well, now that's settled," Iris said, rising to her feet, "perhaps you could let me have the keys to the cottage."

"Certainly not," Bernard White replied. "Have you forgotten about probate?"

Iris looked disconcerted, but before she could speak, Tom Turnbull stepped in.

"Oh, come on, Bernard. You know perfectly well that in this case probate will be perfectly straightforward, and the only reason not to give Ms Grant access would be if you're determined to be bloody-minded. I'm sure if there hadn't been a new will, you would have been perfectly happy to hand over the keys. In fact, I'd lay a bet that they're in your pocket right now."

Bernard White gave him a look of simmering anger and fished around in an inside pocket, drawing out two keys dangling from a ring. "Here," he said, handing them over to Iris with ill grace.

"Thank you." Iris stowed away the keys in her bag. "I shall be needing a set of the Abbey keys, too," she added.

"What?" Bernard White snarled. "That's perfectly absurd. Why do you imagine you have the right to—"

"Every right," Iris interrupted. David thought she had got her second wind by now, and was coping very well with the lawyer's hostility. "As owner of the island," she continued, "I'm *ex officio* a Trustee. So – keys to the Abbey, please."

That obviously hadn't occurred to Bernard White before then. His shoulders sagged. "Have it your own way," he said, clearly capitulating. "But I haven't a spare set with me – they're in my office on the mainland. I'll get them to you tomorrow."

Iris nodded. "Thank you."

"Is there anything else I can do for you?" Bernard White sounded savagely ironic, and obviously expected the answer to be 'no'.

"There is, as a matter of fact," Iris replied, and continued with a glance at David, "I'd like my adviser here to take a look at the Abbey's accounts."

Bernard White looked as if he was going to start protesting again, but in the end thought better of it, and it was Roddy Chatham who spoke, with a glare at Iris.

"I hope you're not accusing my mother of fiddling the books?"

"Of course she isn't, Roddy darling," his mother responded. "I'm sure I've nothing to hide. The books are in my office up at St Morwenna's," she added to David. "You can come up any time and take a look."

David nodded acknowledgement. "Thanks, I'll give you a ring."

"Then I think we're all done here." Tom Turnbull took charge again. "Ms Grant, I suggest we have lunch together at the hotel. There's quite a lot we need to discuss."

"Oh, of course," Iris responded. "There's probate – oh, and inheritance tax! What am I going to do about that?"

"Your great uncle organised everything," Tom Turnbull assured her. "You have nothing to worry about. I have a letter for you, too, that he left with me."

"I trust you'll keep me informed," Bernard White said, poisonously polite as he hefted his briefcase and headed for the door.

"Naturally," Iris said to his disappearing back. For a moment she looked after him, and then turned to Elaine Chatham. "I'm so sorry, Elaine, but I don't think anyone feels like coming to your drinks party."

"Oh dear." Elaine Chatham blinked in disappointment. "And I made all those sausage rolls…" She bundled up her long purple strip of knitting and stowed it away in her patchwork bag. "Never mind, I expect the students will eat them."

Chapter Four

> Sir, this gentlewoman
> Entreats your counsel in an honest cause.
> *The Devil's Law Case*, IV.i

Tom Turnbull bore Iris off to the hotel for lunch, while David, Seff and Gawaine followed more slowly. About half way back, Roddy Chatham passed them almost at a run, heading towards the harbour where the ferry was about to leave. He ignored David and the others as if they weren't there.

"He's not happy," Seff observed.

"No," David agreed. "Pretty furious, in fact."

"You can see why." Gawaine blinked thoughtfully. "If Morgarrow belongs to St Cadoc's, then the Trustees control it. And if Roddy is in... er... is 'cahoots' the word I'm looking for?"

"Cahoots, yes," David said, rolling his eyes at Seff.

"If Roddy is in cahoots with Bernard White, then development plans for the island could easily go ahead. And I may be dreadfully cynical—"

"Surely not," Seff murmured.

"I may be cynical, but I can't imagine that all the profits would end up in the Abbey's coffers," Gawaine finished.

"Not cynical at all, just realistic," Seff said. "Bernard

White was quite enraged when he found out about the new will. He'll end up having a stroke if he goes on like that."

"So if Roddy Chatham and Bernard White are planning together to develop the island…" Gawaine let his voice trail off.

"Of course they are," David said. "But that doesn't get us very far. Iris knows that, and Petroc Tremayne surely knew it too. It can't be the 'something fishy' that Great Uncle Petroc wrote to Iris about."

"True," Gawaine agreed. "So even though that perfectly dreadful scene in the Chapter House was entertaining in its own macabre way, we haven't actually learnt anything."

After the drama of the morning, David felt a distinct sense of anti-climax. When lunch was over, Seff, who had to be back at work the next day, went to pack. Iris was still deep in discussion with Tom Turnbull; when they had eaten they withdrew to the hotel's small TV room, uninhabited at that time of day. David and Gawaine were left in the hotel lounge, gazing through the large picture window; the view of the garden gave way to a rough grassy area along the cliff top, and then the expanse of water separating Morgarrow from the mainland.

Stretching out in a cushioned armchair, Gawaine let out a long sigh. "I'm not sure what I'm doing here," he said plaintively. "Solving this problem, my dear David, will depend on your skills, not mine."

David thought that he was probably right. Whatever legal or financial scheme Bernard White and Roddy Chatham had dreamed up wouldn't be discovered by a familiarity with the old Italian masters, or a nicely turned epigram in Ancient Greek. Or, indeed, the unexpectedly precise logic that on previous occasions had exposed a murderer.

"I'm sure you can find something to occupy yourself," he said. "Go for a wander round the Abbey. You never know what you might find."

"Moth and rust have corrupted there, I fear," Gawaine murmured. "Leaving nothing for thieves to break in and steal."

"Don't be too sure," David said. "Thieves don't come along with a crowbar and a bag marked 'Swag', not in these days. They do it with computers."

"Which I leave entirely to you, my dear David."

"Gee, thanks," David muttered. "Tomorrow I'll give Mrs Chatham a ring," he added after a moment. "The Abbey accounts may throw up something."

Before Gawaine could reply, the door of the TV room opened and Iris came out, followed by Tom Turnbull, who was shoving a handful of papers back into his document case. Iris escorted him through the lounge and out into the hotel lobby.

Gawaine rose as she returned. "Did everything go well?" he asked.

Iris thrust a hand through her hair. "It's all a bit confusing," she replied. "But I'm sure Mr Turnbull knows what he's doing. I must say, I'd much rather deal with him than Bernard – especially now that I own the island." She forced a faint smile. "I won't be forgiven for that in a hurry."

"You haven't done anything to need forgiveness for," Gawaine pointed out.

David thought that a shadow swiftly crossed Iris's face before she responded, with a wry twist to her mouth. "Try telling Bernard that. And really, if he only knew, there's no need for him to make a fuss. The letter that Mr Turnbull mentioned when he read the will – Great Uncle Petroc wrote that he doesn't intend for me to keep the island. Once I've discovered what was worrying him, and put it right, I'm to gift it to St Cadoc's, and just keep the cottage for myself, as it was in the original will." She let out a gusty sigh. "I have to say, it's a great relief."

"Once you've sorted out the problem," David said. "Was there anything in the letter about that?"

Iris shook her head, clearly struggling with frustration. "I don't know why he wouldn't explain!" After a moment she went on, more calmly, "I suppose he thought he would be able to tell me about it in person. This will is only a… a stop-gap, in case he died before he found out what was going on."

"Then he could have cancelled it and reverted to the original will," David said.

"Yes. I wish I'd been able to come down and see him when he first wrote, but it didn't seem to be urgent." Iris's voice quivered on the last few words.

"You couldn't have known he would die so soon," Gawaine said with a sympathetic glance.

"The other thing Tom Turnbull said I must do," Iris continued after a moment, "is make a will." Again the wry twist to her lips. "I don't know if he thinks I'm likely to jump off the cliffs – or maybe Bernard or Roddy will push me over."

Gawaine shuddered. "Don't."

"Anyway, it's a good idea. I have a will already, but it's out of date, so it makes sense to have a new one. Mr Turnbull and I drafted it out, and he's going to come up tomorrow so that I can sign it. It's quite straightforward, so—"

Iris broke off as the lounge door opened and Seff came in, carrying her week-end case. "There you are!" she said as she saw Iris. "Is everything sorted out?"

"More or less," Iris replied. "Anyway, I've made a start."

"At least you can get back into the cottage now," Seff said. "I can't believe Bernard White was looking for excuses not to cough up the keys! Will you move in right away? I'd come and help you, but I have to be back at my desk tomorrow."

"That's okay," Iris responded. "I'm going to stay here tonight. I've no idea what state the cottage was left in, and I'm just too tired to start clearing up."

"Yes, you need a good night's rest," Seff said. "And tomorrow you have your two minions..." she gestured towards David and Gawaine "...to help you find out what you need to know."

"And I'm so grateful," Iris said. "I was dreading trying to cope with it by myself." She paused, then added, "What I'd really like to do now is go up to the Abbey for evening prayer." She glanced at her watch. "It's almost time. And after that I'm going to have room service bring me some supper, and get an early night. I'm sorry to be anti-social, but I've just about had it for today."

"No wonder," David said.

He stood side by side with Seff and Gawaine and watched Iris through the window as she took the path across the hotel garden and passed through the gate onto the road that led up to the Abbey.

"Come on, walk me down to the ferry," Seff said once Iris had disappeared.

"I'll run you down in the car, if you like," David offered.

Seff sighed and rolled her eyes. "Honestly, it's no distance. Why do you think you have legs?" She gave David a prod. "You can carry my bag."

"Wow, thanks." Seff, David had to admit, had not been as annoying as usual since they arrived on the island. But clearly she had not lost her talent.

"Now listen," Seff said when she, Gawaine and David were walking down the road that led to the village and the ferry terminal. "I expect you to keep me up to date with what's happening here. I've got a feeling there might be a story in it."

"You think so?" David said. "But surely it will turn out to be just a bit of minor fiddling? Way below your pay grade, I'd have thought."

Seff frowned. "I'm not so sure. There might be more to it – and though Iris hasn't said so, I think she agrees with me. She's been very edgy, ever since she came down here."

"That's hardly surprising," Gawaine said, "seeing what she's had to go through."

"Yes…" Seff seemed unusually thoughtful. "But somehow, that isn't *Iris*. She always used to be such a carefree, take-each-day-as-it-comes sort of person. Mind you," she added, after a moment's pause, "that was before she took up with the dreaded Jake Fletcher."

"Jake Fletcher?" David asked.

"You haven't heard of him?"

David considered, then shrugged. "Nope. Should I have?"

"Well, you're not a teenage girl, so no," Seff told him. "Jake is an actor, and not a very good one. He looks pretty, but he has all the emotional range of a teabag."

"Not your favourite person, then," David said.

"I can't stand him," Seff replied. "He's not with Iris any more, thank goodness, but I'm sure he was living off her, all the time he was 'resting'. But then he got his big break, in one of these teen werewolf movies. Now he's well on the way to being a celebrity, with girls fainting at his feet on a regular basis."

"How perfectly frightful!" Gawaine murmured. He, as David well knew, not only had never heard of Jake Fletcher, but had never heard of teen werewolf movies, either.

"So he dumped Iris for someone more glamorous?" David asked.

"No, though I'm sure he would have, given time. But before it happened, Iris dumped *him*. She didn't like the way he talked about Great Uncle Petroc's death." Seff walked on in silence for a moment, then added, "There was a time when I was honestly worried she might go completely off the rails if Jake left her. Thank goodness she finally realised what a worm he is."

"But she's still edgy?" Gawaine said thoughtfully.

Seff shrugged, halting at the top of the slipway. "You said yourself, she's been through a lot. And it's hard to adjust to being single, after you've been in a relationship for a long time – even when you know it's for the best. Iris will be fine. And if she's not, she has two knights in shining armour to console her."

Gawaine gave Seff an alarmed look, while David said, "I don't think that was in our job description."

Seff tilted her head, her eyes glinting mischievously. "I wish! It might even be worth a few lines in the gossip columns."

"Don't you dare!" David exclaimed.

Laughing, Seff took her bag from him and hurried down the last few paces to where the ferry was boarding. "Text me!" she called, climbing the gangplank and standing by the rail.

"In your dreams!" David called back.

Seff's only response was to blow him a kiss.

Chapter Five

He that can compass me, and know my drifts,
May say he hath put a girdle 'bout the world
And sounded all her quicksands.
> *The Duchess of Malfi*, III.i

A couple of hundred yards from the hotel the road forked; the left fork led to the harbour, where the ferry docked, while the right headed into the centre of the village. A stretch of rough grass divided the two.

Petroc Tremayne's cottage was the first house of the village: a modest end of terrace with whitewashed walls and a roof of local slate. The front door and window frames were painted a cheerful sky blue; the window boxes and the tubs of geraniums that flanked the front step were all flourishing.

"Someone has been keeping an eye on the place," Gawaine remarked as he, Iris and David approached on the morning after the funeral.

"That would be Annis," Iris said. "She lives next door. She did an awful lot for Great Uncle Petroc in the last year or two, when he couldn't really manage for himself."

"Annis Radford who was mentioned in his will?" David asked.

Iris nodded. "And she deserves every penny."

Gawaine parked Iris's suitcase beside the step while Iris fished around in a big tapestry tote bag for the keys. "The first thing we need to do," he said, "is search to see if Great Uncle Petroc left any clues to what was bothering him. Are you comfortable with David and me helping you with that?"

"Oh, of course," Iris replied, finding the key and fitting it into the lock. "I'm sure there's nothing to hide."

She swung the door open. Gawaine turned back for the suitcase, but Iris darted in front of him and picked it up. "I'll just take this up," she said, leading the way inside. "There won't be anything to find in the bedroom; Great Uncle couldn't cope with the stairs."

She disappeared, hefting her bag, up a steep staircase.

David glanced around the tiny entrance hall, spotted a single door on the right and pushed it open. With Gawaine following, he stepped into Petroc Tremayne's living room.

"Well…" he said after a moment's pause. "Good luck finding anything among this lot."

Gawaine murmured agreement. At first glance, the room seemed to be stuffed full of potential evidence. One wall was covered in bookshelves, with books stacked in double rows and overflowing onto the floor. Most of the books had paper markers poking out of them at odd angles. On the opposite wall a roll-top desk stood open; every pigeonhole was stuffed with papers, and more were scattered over the flat surface. A whole forest of post-it notes had taken up residence on the desk framework. The mantelpiece held a letter rack, and more letters had been shoved behind the clock. A saggy leather sofa and matching armchair had escaped the drift, but the occasional tables at either end were both piled with magazines.

Incongruous among the general miscellany, an up-to-date TV and a wicker basket overflowing with knitting wool rose like small islands in the sea of debris.

"Did he never throw anything away?" David asked.

"Evidently not," Gawaine responded. He let out a small sigh. "This could take months, if not years."

"Think of it as job security."

Gawaine frowned, considering. "Delightful..." he murmured. "Except that meanwhile our nefarious Trustee continues with his evil plots unhindered. I wish that Great Uncle Petroc hadn't been so reluctant to commit something to paper."

"The law of libel?" David guessed.

"Or just not knowing enough to be useful? Well," Gawaine said, "I suppose we should make a start. I'm going to tackle the desk."

He headed towards it, while David perched on the arm of the sofa and picked up the top magazine on the pile: a journal of some art and antiques society. But he had hardly begun to flick through it when the doorbell rang and a voice called, "Iris! Iris!"

The outer door had been left ajar. Moving to answer the bell, David saw a tall woman standing on the step. She was wearing a gipsyish skirt and embroidered blouse, with a brightly coloured knitted shawl flung over her shoulders. Curly auburn hair streaked with turquoise was tied up in a silk scarf. For some reason she looked agitated – even more so when she saw David.

"Hi," she began. "I thought—"

At that moment, Iris came clattering down the stairs and gave the newcomer a warm hug. "Annis! It's good to see you again. How are you?" Not waiting for a reply, she introduced David and Gawaine, who had come quietly up to stand in the living room doorway. "They've come to help me sort out Great Uncle's affairs," she explained.

Annis gave them a distracted smile. "Nice to meet you. Iris," she went on, "please could you do me a favour? There's a spider in my workroom, and you know what I'm like about spiders."

"Of course," Iris said. She gave Gawaine and David a mischievous look. "Unless one of my knights in shining armour…"

Gawaine, David knew, did not do spiders. "I'll go," he said.

"Oh, thank you!" Annis let out a gusty sigh of relief. "Go straight through the shop; the door's open. The vile beast is on the wall just above my desk. You can't miss it."

David headed for the next door cottage. It was laid out exactly like a mirror image of Petroc Tremayne's, except that here the living room was a shop, stuffed with a riot of colourful wool. Hand-knitted sweaters and shawls were on display; this was knitting, David realised, of a quite different kind from Elaine Chatham's long purple strip.

At the back of the shop was another door, leading to an inner lobby, and then into a small workroom. There was a desk with a laptop surrounded by what David supposed were wool samples, and on the wall above it was the spider. It was indeed a magnificent specimen; no wonder Annis had been driven into the street to look for help.

David picked up an empty coffee cup and trapped the beast, then wriggled an envelope underneath so that he could remove it and deposit it in the rough grass on the other side of the road. When he had seen it scuttle away, he returned to where Iris, Annis and Gawaine were standing outside the cottage.

"Annis, I can't thank you enough for looking after Great Uncle Petroc," Iris was saying as he approached.

Annis shook her head. "I didn't do much. And he was such a lovely man. I used to bring a DVD and a pizza, and my knitting, and we'd drink Petroc's whisky and watch the movie. Oh, I'm going to miss him so much!"

Gawaine turned to David as he joined the group. "And hast thou slain the Jabberwock?" he inquired.

"No, I've sent it to live its best life elsewhere," David replied. He presented Annis with the coffee cup and the envelope. "All done," he said.

"Thank you. I know it's stupid, but I really can't stand the creatures. And that's the third this week. One of them was lurking in a basket of cashmere laceweight." She shuddered. "I don't know where they're coming from."

Gawaine glanced at her, his head tilted rather like a curious cat. "Where was the third?"

Annis stared at him. "What?"

"You said there were three spiders. Where was the third?"

Annis hesitated, as if she couldn't quite believe the question. "In my bed," she replied at last. "I folded back my quilt, and there it was, waiting to pounce." She shuddered. "Let's not go there."

Gawaine shuddered in sympathy. "Let's not."

Both Annis and Iris were giving Gawaine a look that suggested they were contemplating something seriously weird. *They're not wrong*, David thought, amused.

Then Iris gave herself a shake. "The first thing I have to do," she said, "is go down to the supermarket. Are you okay to get on here?" she asked David.

"No problem," David replied.

"I'll come with you," Annis said. "I'm short of milk, and I can help you carry the bags."

She whisked away, back to her shop, stuck up a notice that read 'Back in 10 minutes', and rejoined Iris. Meanwhile Iris collected a couple of fabric market bags from a hook in the hall, and the two women headed off down the street towards the centre of the village.

Gawaine turned back into the cottage, and David followed. "What was all that about?" he asked.

His friend looked up at him, blue eyes wide and innocently inquiring.

"All that about the spiders?" David prompted.

Gawaine blinked. "Nothing. Just a thought."

David allowed himself a small sigh. Whatever idea Gawaine had got into his head, he wouldn't talk about it until he was ready. Meanwhile, there was this stack of junk to get through.

"You know," Gawaine went on, "before we tackle all this, I think we ought to check the rest of the cottage. There's no sense in wading through stacks of paper if Great Uncle Petroc left a note on his bedside table."

"True," David agreed. He led the way through the door at the far side of the sitting room, into a small lobby that matched the one in Annis's cottage. Gawaine opened the nearest door, which turned out to be the cupboard under the stairs. It housed a set of folding garden furniture, a pair of rubber boots, and a shabby raincoat hanging on the back of the door. Gawaine frisked the coat pockets, then closed the door again, shaking his head.

"Nothing in there."

"You don't think you should search right to the back?"

Gawaine gave him a disdainful look. "Certainly not, my dear David. I very much doubt that Great Uncle Petroc would leave any vital information in the depths of the glory hole. However, if you want to, feel free." He headed for the next door and pushed it open. "The kitchen," he added, disappearing inside.

David took the last of the doors, which led into the equivalent of Annis Radford's workroom. Here it was obviously where Petroc Tremayne had slept. The bed had been stripped, the bedding stored in a wooden chest underneath the window. A wardrobe with shelves attached held clothes; David searched through quickly but found nothing other than a wallet containing a few pounds, a couple of credit cards and a bus pass, and a few used ferry tickets in a jacket pocket. The drawer in the bedside table held a pair of glasses in their case and a book of crossword puzzles with a pen.

"Anything?" Gawaine asked, appearing in the doorway as David closed the drawer again.

David shook his head. "No, it's all very neat and tidy. Presumably Great Uncle Petroc kept his chaos in his sitting room."

"Or somebody tidied it for him," Gawaine mused.

"Tidied something away, you mean? I suppose that could have been Annis Radford. She seems to have had the run of the place."

"I assume she cleared out the kitchen," Gawaine

continued. "At least, there's no suppurating food in there. But that's just a kind thing that people do after someone dies. No, I think—"

He broke off suddenly, his attention arrested by several paintings on the wall opposite the bed. David hadn't paid them much attention, but now he saw that they were watercolours, and all of them looked as if they were of Morgarrow: the Abbey; the village; a boat with a white sail tacking into the harbour; a study of pink thrift growing between two rocks.

"I think they must be Iris's," Gawaine said, moving attentively from one to the next. "They're good – very good."

"Well, that's nice to know," David said briskly. "But they don't get us much further."

"Philistine," Gawaine murmured. With a last glance at the paintings, he drifted over to a door in the far wall, and opened it to reveal a small shower room. "This looks like an extension," he added. "Built when Great Uncle Petroc couldn't get upstairs any more."

The shower room also held nothing of interest. David felt a faint stirring of hope at the sight of a small wall cupboard. It was locked, though the key was hanging from a cup hook screwed into the side. When Gawaine opened it, there was nothing inside except for a few basic medications and a bottle of capsules which David assumed were Great Uncle Petroc's heart medicine.

"Nothing," Gawaine sighed, relocking the cupboard and returning the key to its hook. "I'm sorry, but there's no escape. We have to tackle the sitting room."

He was looking faintly exasperated as they returned. "I

have a terrible suspicion, my dear David," he said, seating himself at the desk, "that we're looking in the wrong place. Whatever was worrying Great Uncle Petroc, I don't think we're going to find it here."

"You're absolutely right," David agreed, glad of any excuse not to dive into the mounds of paper. "I think I'll ring Elaine Chatham, and see when I can go to look at the Abbey accounts."

Iris's return from the supermarket coincided with the appearance of Tom Turnbull, with his purposeful look and his slim document case. "I brought your will for you to sign," he announced as Iris showed him into the sitting room.

"That was quick," said Iris.

"No sense in letting the grass grow under our feet," Tom Turnbull responded. "It's pretty straightforward, and we discussed it all thoroughly yesterday. If someone here is prepared to witness it…" He glanced around.

"I will," Annis said; she had followed Iris in with one of the market bags, and now stood by the door clutching her carton of milk.

"No, you can't," Iris told her. "I'm leaving you this cottage – and the contents, for what they're worth."

David thought that Annis looked thoroughly taken aback. "Really?"

"Why not? You could use it to expand your business." Iris suddenly grinned, and added, "Mind you, I hope you'll have to wait about fifty years to take possession."

"I'm surprised there's enough business on Morgarrow to support a wool shop," Gawaine remarked to Annis, yielding the desk to Iris while she took the document Tom Turnbull produced for her, and sat to read it. "Or is the island full of knitters?"

"There are a few," Annis replied. "But you'd be surprised how many tourists, or pilgrims, think that a skein of yarn is a good holiday souvenir. I sell high quality, and a lot of my stock is produced locally – yarns that you can't buy anywhere else. I've customers who come back year after year, just for that."

"I suppose it beats a Cornish piskie key-ring," David murmured.

"Oh, I sell those as well," Annis said, looking amused. "Or rather, Cornish piskie stitch markers or French knitters."

Whatever those may be, David thought.

"I have one producer here on Morgarrow," Annis continued. "Over on the far side of the island. Her husband farms the sheep, she spins and dyes the wool, and I sell it. Real cottage industry. This is some of her wool."

She stepped forward to the wicker basket of knitting, handing her carton of milk to Gawaine, who stood holding it with a bemused expression. Annis picked up the knitting and held it out at arm's length; it looked to David like part of a shawl, in soft heathery shades, the whole thing dangling from some kind of cord, with pointy bits at each end.

"Iris, this is coming on really well," Annis said. "No one would ever think you're a beginner."

"Thank you," Iris said, glancing over her shoulder. "Annis started me knitting when I was here at Easter," she added. Turning back to the will, she reached for the pen that Tom Turnbull was holding out to her and scribbled her name on both copies. "There, that's done."

David moved up to sign as a witness, while Gawaine restored Annis's milk to its rightful owner.

"Thank you," she said. "It's for Merino. She would never forgive me if I ran out."

"Marina?" Gawaine asked, suddenly sounding interested.

"Not Marina, it's *Merino* – like the wool. She's my cat."

"You have a cat?"

Definitely interested. David suppressed a grin. *If Seff's into match-making, maybe she should have picked the knitting lady.*

"No knitting shop should be without a cat," Annis said, while David guided Gawaine over to the desk to witness the will. "Do you like cats, Gawaine?"

"Is the Pope Catholic?" David said.

"Well, you can come and meet Merino, if you like," Annis said. "I have to say, she's awfully cute."

Gawaine looked regretful. "Thank you, but David and I have promised to help Iris…"

"Why don't we all break for lunch?" Iris suggested. She handed one copy of the will back to Tom Turnbull, and slid the other into a pigeonhole of the desk. "We'll work better if we take a breather."

"Good idea," David said. He patted Gawaine on the shoulder. "So you can go and spend time with this desirable female. I mean the *cat*," he added, as Gawaine suddenly looked acutely embarrassed.

Annis stifled a spurt of laughter. She wasn't pretty, David thought, looking her over – her face was too thin, for one thing – but she had the most astonishing sea-green eyes he had ever seen.

"Why don't you all come?" she suggested. "I'm sure I can scratch up lunch."

"Thanks, but I have to go up to St Morwenna's," David said. "Elaine Chatham is going to show me the Abbey's books."

Chapter Six

...there's nothing so holy but money will corrupt and putrify it.
                             The White Devil, III.iii

Beyond the Abbey the road became an unpaved track, leading between steep banks covered in pretty, but as far as David was concerned, nameless wild flowers. Equally nameless birds were twittering in the bushes, and one – a lark, he assumed, because wasn't that what larks did? – was spilling song from high above his head.

To begin with, the track wound steeply upwards, then flattened out, while the banks gradually sank to become roadside verges with fencing on the landward side – presumably to restrain the sheep that nibbled the tough moorland grass. David wondered whether their wool was destined to be sold in Annis's shop.

Ahead of him a building loomed that had to be St Morwenna's Community. David guessed that the central part was original: a four-square house built of grey stone, which had been embellished at a much later date by two wings adorned by pilasters and finicky finials – the delusions of grandeur, David guessed, of some Victorian owner of Morgarrow.

Abandoning his architectural reflections, David

strode up to the front door and tugged at the doorbell. He heard the jangle of the bell and a moment later the door was opened. A young woman stood there; her long dark hair and ankle-length flowered frock made her look as if she too was left over from the Victorian era, except for the slice of pizza in the hand that wasn't holding the door.

"Hi," she said, holding the door wide. "Come in."

"Hi." David stepped into the panelled entrance hall. "I've come to see Mrs Chatham. She is expecting me."

The girl swivelled around. "Elaine!" The screech destroyed David's last impression of sweet Victorian maidenhood. "Someone to see you."

Elaine Chatham appeared from a door at the far end of the hall. "David!" she exclaimed, advancing with her hands held out, her shawl billowing around her. "Welcome! Are you going to have lunch with us?"

"No, thank you," David replied, though lunch time was approaching and he rather regretted not snatching a bite to eat at the hotel. "I'd rather get on with the job."

"Of course," Elaine said. "Come this way. I've got everything ready for you in my office."

She led David into a small room at the front of the house. The first thing David saw as he followed her in was a desk with a laptop, but when he headed towards it Elaine stopped him with a hand on his arm.

"I don't use computers, dear," she said, with a girlish giggle. "So confusing! That one is Roddy's. The documents you need are over here."

She indicated a stout kitchen table against the far wall. Neatly arranged on it were a hefty cash book of the type that Bob Cratchit might have found dangerously old-fashioned, a box file and a pad of paper, with a St Cadoc's mug filled with pens. *Ballpoints not quills,* David thought with relief.

"Those are the Abbey accounts?" he said.

Elaine nodded. "I'm sure you'll find everything in order. But if you need anything, just come and knock on the next door down. I'll be there."

"Thank you."

David took his seat at the table and began to examine his loot. He was surprised to find that the account book was filled in tidily and legibly, and the receipts in the box file were arranged in order. Thinking that whatever had bothered Great Uncle Petroc must have happened relatively recently, he turned back to the beginning of the previous tax year and set to work.

After about half an hour the unVictorian maiden reappeared with a tray that held a plate of hearty cheese and pickle sandwiches, a pot of coffee and a generous slice of fruit cake. David found himself thinking there was a great deal to be said for Elaine Chatham.

If there's something wrong here, it must be Roddy darling who's responsible.

As he worked through the accounts, David couldn't help his glance straying from time to time to the laptop.

Roddy must have one where he lives, on the mainland, he thought. *So why does he keep one here? Does he like to keep Abbey stuff separate from his work stuff? Or is it just for convenience?*

Everything was quiet outside. David supposed that the members of the Community would mostly be down at St Cadoc's, hassock-darning or brass polishing or whatever it was they did there. Elaine Chatham, he hoped, might be having a post-lunch snooze. In any case, he decided, he was going to have a look at that computer.

Leaving his table with the documents spread out, David slid into the chair in front of the desk and touched a key. The laptop immediately sprang into life, with a picture of the Abbey and a box for a password.

I wonder...

Secure passwords, David well knew, would be a mixture of upper and lower case letters, and numbers. Difficult to guess. Without much hope, he typed in 'Morgarrow', and wasn't surprised when the computer spat it back at him.

David stared at the uninformative screen. He knew he could only risk one more try. The computer would lock on a third failed attempt, and he dared not leave it like that; Roddy darling would know someone had been snooping, and it wouldn't be difficult to find out who.

Some people wrote their passwords down so they wouldn't forget them. Gawaine, for instance, had inscribed the beautifully secure password David had devised for him onto a post-it note and stuck it at the edge of his screen. But there was no sign that Roddy Chatham had done the same.

Seeking inspiration, David opened the single desk drawer to find post-it notes – sadly, blank – paper clips, sticky tape and rubber bands, and a scatter of business cards with Roddy's work address and his email address: RodChat91.

He wouldn't, would he? Is he really that stupid?

David could almost sense Gawaine looking over his shoulder and hear him murmuring close to his ear. "My dear David, what evidence of his intelligence have we seen so far?"

"Good point," David muttered. He typed 'RodChat91' into the password box.

Bingo!

The computer opened up onto Roddy's email page. Letting his gaze flick down the list, David saw that a good number of the emails came from Bernard White. Certain that he had cracked the problem, David opened one with 'Restoration Fund' in the subject line, only to find a list of sponsors for some future fundraiser that Bernard White wanted passed on to Elaine. It would obviously take more work to discover what, if any, nefarious designs the two of them had committed to email.

Later, David promised himself.

Investigating further, David bypassed with a shudder a website labelled 'HotSexyBabes', reflecting that he had found one reason why Roddy darling kept a second computer. Much more interesting was a PDF with the filename 'Morgarrow Moor'. David opened it, and sat staring in amazement as he scrolled through the pages.

Yes, I would call that something fishy...

Rapidly David opened his own email account, attached the PDF and emailed it to himself. Then he closed his email, closed the PDF and returned to his own seat at the table, waiting tensely until the laptop went back to sleep and no evidence of his snooping remained.

With a sigh of relief he returned to his examination of the accounts.

Much later in the afternoon, David returned to the hotel.

There was no sign of Gawaine, so David paused only to pick up his tablet, and headed for Iris's cottage. When he pressed the doorbell, Iris's voice called, "Come in!"

The sitting room looked even more chaotic than it had at first, but it was an organised chaos. Iris was sitting on a step stool, attacking the bookshelves with a duster. A nearby wastebasket was overflowing with the paper markers.

Gawaine was sitting at the desk. He had obviously not spent a great deal of time enjoying the delights of Annis's cat, because he had made progress, although David spotted cat hair on the sleeve of his otherwise immaculate suit. The documents that had been shoved randomly into the pigeonholes were now arranged in piles; the correspondence from the mantelpiece had vanished as well.

"These are mostly junk mail, and I think you can throw them away," he was telling Iris as David came in, pointing at one of the piles. "These are personal letters – I haven't read them – and these are bills. I can't tell if your great uncle paid them or not."

"Thank you, Gawaine," Iris said. "I'll have a look through them. I suppose there's nothing about this problem with St Cadoc's?"

"Not unless there's something in one of the letters. But there is one more thing…" Gawaine held out a crumpled yellow post-it note.

David crossed the room to look over his friend's shoulder. The post-it note read, 'Ring George. URGENT!' The URGENT was underlined three times.

"A three-line whip," Gawaine murmured. "Who is George?"

Iris came to take the scrap of paper, glanced at both sides, then shrugged. "I've no idea."

"It was on the top row," Gawaine said. "That suggests it was quite recent."

"Then just before he died." Iris sounded suddenly downcast. "I wonder if he ever made the call. I suppose we'll never know unless we can find out who George is."

"Look, never mind about George." David was impatient to reveal what he had discovered at St Morwenna's. "Shift over, Gawaine. There's something I want to show you."

"My dear David!" Gawaine murmured, yielding up the desk chair. "This sounds… significant."

"You bet it's significant." David sat down, propped up his tablet on the desk, and opened up the PDF that he had filched from Roddy Chatham's computer.

"Morgarrow Moor?" Iris leaned over David's shoulder to look more closely. "I've never heard of it."

The first page of the file showed an artist's impression of a row of dinky little chalets built around the curve of a beach with an idyllic seascape beyond. The next page showed one of the chalets in more detail, with views of the interior: a mock-rustic sitting room and a small but streamlined kitchen. That was followed by what looked like the centre of a village, with signs to a reception area, a leisure centre and a pub – The Merry Piskie.

"I don't understand," Iris said. "There's nowhere like that on Morgarrow."

"Then where is it?" Gawaine asked. "And what is it?"

"It's a brochure for a timeshare resort," David replied. "And I'm betting that it isn't anywhere, yet, except in Roddy darling's imagination."

"Timeshare..." Gawaine peered at the screen, looking puzzled. *If he asks what that is, I'll kill him,* David thought. "Is Roddy intending to invest in it?"

"If you ask me," David replied, "I think he's intending to build it."

"But that's ridiculous!" Iris exclaimed. "That would be a massive investment. Roddy simply hasn't got that kind of money. Unless..." Her voice trailed off.

David looked up, and met Gawaine's gaze. "Something fishy going on up at the Abbey..." he said.

Gawaine allowed himself a small feline smile. "Oh yes..." Sounding, for him, amazingly business-like, he continued, "Roddy Chatham – and, I don't doubt, Bernard White – believed that Petroc Tremayne would leave Morgarrow to St Cadoc's. Therefore they would control the island's income, from rents and so on. They could invest in this scheme, and make a... I believe you would say a killing, David?"

"A killing, yes," David responded. "Of course, they would give money to the Abbey," he added, "but don't tell me they wouldn't be skimming a good percentage off the top."

Iris was staring at them wide-eyed. "This is terrible! The extra traffic – they would need to build a better access road, and more facilities for the tourists. It would destroy the island!"

"But somehow," David went on as Iris sank into a distraught silence, "Great Uncle Petroc gets wind of this. Of course, he knew that they wanted to develop Morgarrow, but this would be the first time he'd found out that they'd actually made specific plans. He changes his will, which cuts off their source of funding. But sadly he dies before he can talk to you, Iris, and work out how to put a stop to it once and for all."

"But just a minute," Iris said. "This can't be right. They couldn't build anything without the agreement of the trustees. Father Magnus and Jenny Morland would vote against it, and so would Great Uncle, of course. Roddy might be able to persuade Elaine to vote for it, and naturally Bernard would, but that still leaves them without a majority."

"But then your great uncle dies," Gawaine said. "Leaving an opening for a new trustee."

"But that can't be Roddy," Iris pointed out. "The trustees have to live on the island – and good luck finding a place to rent. Great Uncle's tenants know they have a really good deal here, and they hang onto their property like grim death. I think Annis was the last person to move in, and she's been here more than five years."

"But… just a minute." Gawaine stood rigid, eyes half closed; David could almost see the little wheels going round. "None of this can happen until Great Uncle Petroc dies," he went on at last. "Because he owns the land, and he wouldn't give his permission. And although he is ninety-two, he shows no sign of dropping off the twig quite yet. Bernard White and Roddy Chatham must have thought they had a year or two to find accommodation for Roddy before they needed to elect a new trustee." He paused and took a long breath. "I had begun to wonder whether they might have… helped him on his way. But no. This shows that they had every reason for keeping him alive."

Iris was staring at him. David reflected that she wasn't the first person to realise that Gawaine's frivolous exterior concealed a mind that wouldn't hesitate to face up to unpleasant facts.

"That's... a relief, kind of," she said at last.

Gawaine nodded. "Venal, but not murderous."

"Okay, we can't get them for murder," David said, latching onto a problem that no one else seemed to have noticed yet. "But how about embezzlement?"

"The accounts!" Iris exclaimed. "Of course, we haven't asked you about the accounts. What did you find?"

"Not much," David replied. "I expected them to be in a total mess, but I couldn't have been more wrong. Elaine keeps her records pretty accurately. All the income by cheque or through a bank is accounted for, and there are receipts for all the outgoings. Where I think there might be a problem is with the cash donations – mostly the collections from the services."

"And there's a donations box in the Abbey," Iris added. "And cash from fundraisers."

"All the records are signed by two people," David continued. "And sometimes the two people are Bernard White and Roddy Chatham. There's nothing to stop them skimming a bit off – to pay for that, for example." He indicated the PDF of the timeshare brochure. "That's a professional job, and it wouldn't come cheap."

"They could even convince themselves they weren't doing anything wrong," Gawaine said, blinking unhappily. "After all, it's investment for the Abbey."

"If only we could find proof," Iris began. "But there's —"

The doorbell cut off what she had been about to say. Crossing to the window, she glanced out. "Oh, good grief, it's Bernard," she said. "I suppose he's come with the keys."

While Iris went to answer the door, David minimised the PDF on his tablet, and Gawaine arranged himself decoratively on the sofa, picking up one of the art magazines from the side table.

"Come in, Bernard," Iris said, showing the lawyer inside. "I was just about to make tea. Would you like some?"

"No, thank you." Bernard White's voice was thinly disapproving, as if Iris had offered him a shot of strychnine instead of a cup of the best Darjeeling. He was dressed just as severely as at the funeral, except for the incongruous rose, which at that time of day had started to wilt. "I'm not staying." He paused for a moment, as if he was considering what to say next.

"Have you come to drop off the Abbey keys?" Iris asked.

"I have not." The question seemed to galvanise Bernard White into action. "Nor will I. You are not a trustee, Ms Grant, nor are you likely to be, and therefore you have no right to the keys."

Iris's colour rose at the hostile tone. "But as owner of the island—"

"That is quite irrelevant," the lawyer said. "The articles of the Abbey trust state that each trustee must be permanently resident on Morgarrow."

"But I—" Iris glanced around the room as if to demonstrate that she was in possession.

"*Permanently* resident." Bernard White interrupted again. "But you have a job elsewhere, and presumably that is where you live. You can't be an Abbey trustee if all you do is drop in here for a few days whenever it suits you. Good afternoon, Ms Grant."

He went out, snapping the door shut behind him.

Iris stared after him, for a moment too furious to speak. "Now what am I going to do?" she said at last, sounding completely at a loss.

Gawaine gave her a puzzled look, as if her question wasn't quite what he had been expecting. "How long before they elect a new trustee?" he asked.

Iris seemed to give herself a mental shake. "As soon as possible," she replied. "But Bernard will delay as long as he can, in the hope that they can find some accommodation for Roddy." She let out a long sigh. "I wish I could live here all the time," she added. "But I need something to live *on*. I won't have the income from the island once I've given it to the Abbey."

"How about your art?" Gawaine suggested. "If those paintings in the bedroom are yours…"

"In the bedroom?" Iris sounded startled, then relaxed. "Yes, they're mine. I have sold a few. I wonder if it would work…" she continued. "I could teach here, on the mainland. Maybe run painting holidays… And I wouldn't have to worry about the rent on my flat." She gave a sudden, mischievous grin. "Oh, I'd love to see Bernard's face when I told him!"

"He and Roddy would be… somewhat disgruntled," Gawaine murmured.

"They'd be throwing fits. For one thing, they wouldn't be able to build *that*." Iris gestured towards David's tablet.

"They would need planning permission, though." David's thoughts had been running along another track. "Even if the Abbey owns the land, and the trustees approve the plans. Would they get it?"

"I'm pretty sure they would," Iris replied, sounding despondent again. "You only have to look at the mainland. Sometimes I think Cornwall is sliding down into one enormous theme park. And I'm sure Bernard knows plenty of people on the local council."

"And not only planning permission," David continued. "The land has to come from somewhere. What's there now? Is it a farm?"

Iris hesitated for a moment, considering. "I hadn't thought of that. David, let me look at that village centre again."

David went back to his tablet and called up the page Iris had asked for. She leant over his shoulder, studying it carefully.

"That building there," she said, pointing, "the one that's the pub. That looks older than the rest. It might be a real farmhouse. I'm sure I've seen it somewhere, but I can't think exactly where."

She riffled through the pile of junk mail on the desk until she found a blank sheet, and made a quick sketch of the building. "I'll go looking for it tomorrow," she said. "Today I have to see Father Magnus." There was an urgency in her tone that startled David; Gawaine had turned towards her, too, a puzzled look in his eyes. "Oh, just to give him the chess set that Great Uncle Petroc left him," Iris added. "I can show him the sketch, too. He might know where the farm is."

"Well, if not, I'll come with you and help search," Gawaine said.

David would never have thought that tramping over the wilds of Morgarrow looking for a farmhouse was remotely Gawaine's thing. But then, there was a mystery attached to it, and that was unquestionably his thing.

"Bring your sketch pad," Iris said, her expression bright with enthusiasm. "Seff says you draw."

Gawaine shrugged, faintly embarrassed. "I'm not in your league." Thoughtfully he picked up the post-it note that Iris had discarded, and stuck it back on the edge of the desk. His voice was meditative. "I wonder if the farmer's name is George."

Chapter Seven

Sure I did hear a woman shriek.
The Duchess of Malfi, II.iii

By that evening, clouds massed to cover the sky. The night was hot and oppressive. Not a breath of air came in through the open window of Gawaine's bedroom. Lightning was flickering over the hills on the mainland, but the storm did not break.

Gawaine was almost too tired to sleep, certainly too tired to cope with the book he had brought with him: Vasari's *Lives of the Painters* in the original Italian. He was driven to reading the folder of information provided in his hotel room; by the time dawn crept through his window he was fully conversant with the room service menu, the schedule of the ferry crossings and the times of the Abbey services.

Finally he gave up the attempt to sleep and headed for the shower. The gush of water refreshed him briefly, but by the time he was dressed the clammy feeling had returned. Glancing at his watch, he realised that he could be just in time for the early Eucharist at the Abbey.

Walking up the road, he felt the air like a damp blanket wrapping him round. Clouds covered the sky, the dark purple and yellow of a bruise. But it was not the suffocating weather that was making him feel uneasy.

From the beginning, Gawaine had felt surplus to requirements on Morgarrow. Whatever the machinations of Bernard White and Roddy Chatham, they belonged in David's area of expertise. And it looked as though David had found the answer to the puzzle that had brought them there in the first place.

Once we find the farmhouse, Gawaine thought, *it will be up to Iris what she does about it all. And we can both go home.*

The vast, gloomy interior of the Abbey seemed even vaster and more gloomy than Gawaine remembered from Petroc Tremayne's funeral. The eight o'clock congregation was small, and mostly young: he guessed they were students from St Morwenna's Community.

The service was short, without hymns or sermon. The celebrant was Jenny Morland, the young priest in charge; Gawaine noticed that she was wearing a long green stole, and recognised the knitting skills of Elaine Chatham.

When the service was over, the priest waited by the door to say goodbye to everyone as they filed out.

"Mr St Clair," she said, smiling as Gawaine approached. "It's good to see you. Would you mind waiting a moment? There's something I'd like to ask you."

"Of course." Gawaine stood back, examining the leaflets on a table by the back wall while the last of the congregation disappeared. He picked up a single sheet, a potted history of the Abbey, and read a more detailed version of what Iris had told them: how it had been built in the Middle Ages, refurbished by the Victorians, then abandoned between the two World Wars. It had been opened up again as a Millennium project, with Father Magnus as the first priest in charge.

Turning over these facts in his mind, Gawaine was startled to realise that Jenny Morland had come to join him.

"Let's sit here," she said, pointing the way towards the nearest pew.

As she took her seat, composedly arranging the folds of her chasuble around her, Gawaine found that he was revising his opinion of her. At the funeral she had seemed shy, diffident, quenched by the stronger personality of Father Magnus. But she had led the service with authority, and she was calmly self-assured now.

"I know you're one of Iris Grant's friends," she began.

"Not exactly," Gawaine said. "We – David and I – we've only known her for a few days. Another friend of ours asked us to come and help her with something that had been worrying her great uncle."

Jenny nodded. "Petroc Tremayne. We all miss him."

"Is that what you wanted to talk to me about?" Gawaine asked.

"No – or not exactly." Jenny paused, frowning thoughtfully. "I just wondered... I know she must be grieving for Petroc. But do you think she's all right otherwise?"

Gawaine found it was difficult to answer that. He couldn't help remembering how Seff had said that Iris had been edgy, and he had seen some of that for himself, in the way she had reacted to Bernard White when he refused to give her the Abbey keys.

"I'm not sure..." he replied at last.

"I'll tell you why I ask," Jenny continued. "I live here at St Cadoc's – I have a flat above the cloister – and I stayed up last night, watching the late night movie." She smiled faintly. "Not the brightest thing to do, with an early service this morning. Anyway, when I was ready to go to bed, I glanced out of the window and I saw someone crossing the cloister, with a torch."

"And that was Iris?"

"Yes – the thing is, I'm the only person who should be on the site after we close the gates, which is either at sunset or after the last service of the day, whichever is later. The precinct gates stay open, but if the main Abbey doors and the cloister gate are locked, then no one should be able to get into the building. So I went down."

Gawaine was impressed. He doubted that Jenny Morland would have known beforehand that the intruder was Iris. She could have found herself facing some variety of nasty thug.

"Oh, come on!" Jenny had obviously read his thoughts. "What is there worth stealing round here? So, I went down – by then it was after midnight – and found it was Iris, about to go into the Abbey by the side door. She jumped about a foot when she saw me."

"What did she say?" Gawaine asked.

"She told me she wanted to take some photographs of the Abbey after dark, so she could make a painting."

"And you didn't believe her?"

Jenny shook her head emphatically. "Not a word. For one thing, the sky was so cloudy you could hardly see a thing. Besides, Iris sounded really embarrassed – guilty – and I could tell she was making it up as she went along. But I just accepted it, and asked her how she got in. She told me that the cloister gate was unlocked, and that was a flat lie, because I'd locked it myself earlier that night."

"That is… extremely peculiar," Gawaine murmured. *She must have had a key to let herself in. Did Bernard White change his mind?* Given the lawyer's hostility to Iris, he couldn't imagine it.

"You're telling me," Jenny said. "So I showed her out, told her if she wanted to take photographs she should let me know and I'd happily fix up a time. Then she left. And what I wanted to ask you, is, does that fit in with what you know about Iris? I'm worried about her."

"It is worrying," Gawaine agreed. "And I'm sorry that I can't imagine what she really wanted. I'll try to find out, but we're not on such terms that I can ask her outright."

"Of course not. I wouldn't want you to," Jenny assured him. "It's just that I feel something is troubling her." She sighed and rose to her feet. "I'll add her to my prayers."

Gawaine rose too. "We may not be here for much longer, but if there's any more I can do, please let me know."

Jenny thanked him and retreated to the vestry, leaving Gawaine to mull over what she had just told him. Wandering about the Abbey at night, lying about her reason for being there: that was, as he had said, extremely peculiar behaviour, and if anyone but a clerk in Holy Orders had told him about it, he might have hesitated to believe it. Yet somehow it seemed to be a relevant piece in the jigsaw that was Iris.

There's something going on here quite separate from what we've been told up to now.

When Gawaine emerged into the open, the Abbey precincts were deserted. The rest of the congregation, he assumed, had headed up to St Morwenna's for breakfast. The air was even more humid, and the clouds seemed low enough to touch the Abbey's weathercock.

As he reached the road leading to the hotel, Gawaine thought that he heard a cry, coming from behind the Abbey, between the building and the cliffs. He halted, listening, but the sound was not repeated.

Uneasy, even while telling himself it was probably nothing, Gawaine trekked around the bulk of the Abbey until he reached the wide stretch of rough grass that separated it from the cliff edge. A path crossed the grass, leading up from the village, past the Abbey and along in the direction of the house where the Community lived.

In every direction nothing moved; the view of the village was cut off by a massive outcrop of rocks stretching from the edge of the cliff almost as far as the drystone wall that enclosed the Abbey precinct, and straight ahead all Gawaine could see was the ferry churning its way towards the harbour on the mainland.

Just to make sure, he ventured up to the edge of the cliff and peered over. He caught no more than a glimpse of waves creaming around spiky rocks before a sudden gust of wind struck him and almost lifted him off his feet.

Gawaine staggered back, a nasty picture forming in his mind of himself impaled on the rocks. While he struggled to recover his balance in the blustering wind, a seagull was swept over his head, letting out a harsh and, he was sure, a mocking cry.

"Seagulls!" he exclaimed.

As he fought his way, head down, back to the road, thunder crashed out and the clouds opened up, releasing a torrent of rain. Within minutes he was soaked through; raindrops bounced up all around him, turning the road down to the village into a fast-flowing stream. Muttering under his breath an imprecation in Ancient Greek, Gawaine fled for the hotel.

Crossing the lobby, he stood in the doorway of the lounge and spotted David comfortably ensconced in an armchair, watching the storm through the picture window with the help of a pot of coffee. The morning paper lay disregarded on his lap.

He looked up, obviously having heard Gawaine's approach, or the small waterfall he brought with him. "Where have you been?" he asked. "I thought you must be still in bed."

Drenched and shivering and thoroughly disconsolate, Gawaine clung to the last shreds of dignity. "I couldn't sleep because of the heat," he explained, watching the puddle that was gradually spreading at his feet. "So I went to the eight o'clock service at the Abbey – and got caught in this. Perfectly frightful – I thought I would have been blown off the cliffs."

David looked faintly surprised. "I didn't think you'd ever heard of eight am," he remarked. "Or just that it's a story made up to frighten children."

Gawaine gave him what he hoped was an icy glare. "Very amusing."

"You won't be going out with Iris," David said. "Not in this."

Gawaine had already realised that; even once the storm was over, the roads and farm tracks would be a sea of mud. "No," he sighed. "I suppose I'd better phone her."

He retired to the hotel lobby, where he could drip in peace, fishing out his mobile phone as he went. He could hear the ringing for some time, and began to think that Iris must be out – maybe sharing a cup of tea with Annis and the cat Merino. Then he heard Iris's voice against a background of blustering wind and pouring rain.

"What?"

Gawaine blinked at the sharp tone. "It's Gawaine here," he said. "I thought I'd better ring. We can't go looking for the farm in this."

"No, of course we can't." Guiltily Gawaine realised that he must have called at a really inconvenient time. "Maybe tomorrow. I'll talk to you later." She rang off.

Gawaine stared at the silent phone for a moment, then looked in on David again, back in the lounge. "Put off until tomorrow," he said. Still feeling anxious, he added, "She sounded annoyed. I hope she wasn't annoyed with me."

"Why would she be?" David asked. "This weather is enough to annoy anyone. Now go and get changed before you flood the place."

"I suppose…" Gawaine headed for his bedroom, still wondering why Iris had been so extremely out of temper.

When he returned, dried and restored, he saw with thankfulness that David had managed to extract more coffee from the maw of the hotel kitchen. He poured a cup while Gawaine took the seat next to him.

Rain was still drumming on the roof; water was streaming down the window, and splashing into the puddles already forming in the hotel garden. Shrubs bent under the force of the wind; a roof tile sailed gracefully through the air and smashed to bits on the garden path. The mainland was invisible, and the narrow channel between it and the island was filled with surging waves. Lightning forked down and thunder rolled out again.

"I hope no boats are out in that," David remarked.

"I hope no one is out in that," Gawaine responded, clasping his hands around the coffee mug. "I saw the ferry, heading for the mainland harbour, just before the storm struck. I can't imagine it would go out again."

He took a deep gulp of coffee. "You know," he continued, "after the service, Jenny Morland told me something very strange – about Iris."

He repeated the priest's story about surprising Iris in the Abbey cloisters at midnight, and the lie she had told about finding the cloister gate unlocked. "It's very odd," he finished.

"Maybe not," David objected. "She might have really wanted to paint the Abbey at night. It might make a good picture – all moonlit and sinister."

"Yes, very *Castle of Otranto*," Gawaine murmured. "But then, why sound guilty – and why lie about the gate? And how did she get in, when she didn't have keys?"

David gave an exaggerated sigh. "You're detecting again, aren't you? Only this time there's really nothing to detect. She sounded guilty because she hadn't expected anyone to see her, and maybe Jenny Morland had forgotten to lock the gate, or maybe the lock hadn't caught when she turned the key. It's not important."

"Perhaps you're right," Gawaine admitted, wishing he could feel as convinced as David sounded.

"And in any case," his friend added, "it's got nothing to do with why we're here. It's really none of our business."

At least Gawaine could agree with that. "You know, my dear David," he remarked, "I think we're done here. We – or rather, you – have certainly found out what was worrying Great Uncle Petroc."

David nodded. "I ought to go back to St Morwenna's and finish looking at the Abbey accounts – though I don't expect to find anything more than I've seen already. And you seem to want to go traipsing over the moors looking for farmhouses."

Gawaine cast an uneasy look at the weather outside. "Wading, rather," he murmured. "I just thought if we do find the farmhouse – and therefore the farmer – he may be quite happy to give up his land to build that resort. Maybe he has been offered a hefty bribe, and maybe he would be somewhat… displeased, when he finds out that it isn't going to happen. I just don't think that Iris should be walking into that alone."

"Ah, chivalry!" David grinned affectionately at his friend. "I hope you've loaded up your gat."

"Gat?" Alarmed, Gawaine almost spilt his coffee. "Surely not. 'A soft answer turneth away wrath', and all that."

David shrugged. "Well, if you want to confront a pissed-off farmer with a rook rifle and a couple of overambitious dogs," he said, "it's your funeral."

Soon the worst of the storm began to ebb. The thunder and lightning grumbled off across the mainland, though the rain still fell, dashed against the hotel window by the wind. But it was not until early afternoon before the storm blew itself out and the rain finally stopped. The sea still looked choppy, with white tops to the waves, but the worst of the surge had died down. The ferry reappeared, ploughing its way across the channel towards the island.

"I left my tablet at Iris's yesterday," David said, as he

and Gawaine got up from their lunch table in the hotel dining room. "I think I'll go down there and pick it up. And then I'll head back to St Morwenna's and deal with the last of those accounts."

"I'll walk down with you," Gawaine responded, hoping to make sure Iris was still talking to him, after she had bitten his head off earlier. "I want to fix up a time for tomorrow, and find out if Iris has found out any more about the mysterious George."

Water was still sluicing down the road into the village and dripping from the trees. A stiff breeze was tearing the clouds into rags. Hardly anyone was stirring towards the village centre or around the harbour, except for a small knot of people waiting for the ferry. It seemed as if it was too soon to venture out after the storm.

Approaching Iris's cottage, Gawaine noticed that the curtains at the sitting room window had not been drawn back. An uneasy feeling stirred inside him.

"I don't like the look of that," he murmured, stepping up to ring the doorbell. "I hope Iris is all right."

"She was fine when you rang," David pointed out. "Annoyed, but fine."

"That was hours ago."

There was no response to the doorbell, and none when Gawaine rang for the second time.

"Let's try round the back," David suggested.

A footpath led around the back of the cottage and continued past Annis's house and down into the village. On one side was fenced-off moorland, on the other the cottage gardens enclosed by white palings. Gawaine opened the first gate and headed towards the back door of the cottage.

Reaching for the door handle, he suddenly halted. His uneasiness on seeing the curtains hardened into something more urgent. The upper half of the door was divided into small panes of glass; the pane nearest the handle had been broken. Gawaine could see shards of glass glinting on the doormat inside.

David came up behind him. "What are you—" he began, then broke off as he saw the damage.

Thoroughly frightened now, Gawaine had to force himself to push the door open and let himself into the kitchen.

"Wait—" David said.

Gawaine paid no attention. He crossed the kitchen and hurried through the lobby as far as the door of the sitting room, which was standing open. Here he stopped, letting out a soft choking noise from his throat. His vision blurred; he had the horrible feeling that he was going to faint, until he felt David's hands gripping hard on his shoulders from behind.

Iris was lying on the sofa, still wearing pyjamas and a dressing gown. Her eyes were wide, staring, her tongue protruding from her gaping mouth. Her face was empurpled; Gawaine would hardly have recognised her.

It was clear that someone had strangled her.

Chapter Eight

Strangling is a very quiet death.
The Duchess of Malfi, V.iv

David came up behind Gawaine and gazed over his shoulder at Iris's body. He stood paralysed by horror for only a few seconds. Then he gripped Gawaine by the shoulders, spun him around and thrust him out through the lobby and the kitchen, into the garden. Gawaine sank onto a garden bench under the kitchen window, while David took out his mobile phone to call the police.

"They're coming over from the mainland," he said, when the call was over. "I suppose it'll be a while."

Gawaine looked up at him; he was chalk white, his eyes looking unnaturally large, and he was shivering. "We were supposed to be helping her," he whispered. "We should have been here."

David knew that was nonsense, but he also knew that nothing would stop Gawaine from feeling guilty. "We couldn't have known," he said. "No one could."

Gawaine simply shook his head.

The time dragged by; David wondered if the police had their own transport from the mainland, or if they would have to wait for the next ferry.

"Someone must have broken in to see what they could

steal," he said after a while. "The storm would be a good cover."

"Yes, I suppose…" There was a faint note of interest in Gawaine's voice, as if he was beginning to recover from the shock as his mind got to grips with the problem. "Iris only moved in yesterday," he continued. "Whoever did it could have thought the cottage was still empty. Then when Iris surprised him…" He shuddered and fell silent again.

By this time the sky had cleared. Sunlight dazzled on the puddles along the garden path, and on raindrops hanging from bushes and clumps of flowers. Great Uncle Petroc had made an old-fashioned cottage garden, with yellow roses massed along the fence, pinks and lupins in the beds and little creeping things David couldn't identify growing between the flagstones of the path. Everything was neat and tidy; David detected the hand of Annis, particularly as her garden next door shared many of the same plants.

As if the thought had called her up, Annis opened her kitchen door and poked her head out. "Is everything all right?" she asked.

David swallowed; it was hard to find words to explain that everything was not all right, and for Iris nothing would ever be all right again. He could obviously expect no help from Gawaine, who was still huddled on the bench, his gaze fixed on his clasped hands.

"David?" Annis prompted, emerging into her garden.

"I'm sorry," David said. After all, there was no way to hide what had happened. "Iris is dead."

To her credit, Annis didn't collapse into hysterics, as he had been afraid she might. Her eyes widened, and she took a deep breath. "Is she—" she began, and then broke off. "Are you sure?"

"Oh yes," David said grimly. "Quite sure. We're waiting for the police."

"The police?" For the first time Annis looked thoroughly shaken. "You mean it was…"

David nodded. "It looks as if she was strangled."

Annis pressed a hand to her mouth, obviously struggling for self-control. After a moment she said, "Do you want to come over here? I could make some tea."

"Thank you."

David touched Gawaine on the shoulder; his friend looked up, then made a massive effort to emerge from his stunned state, and followed David out into the lane, through Annis's garden and into the house.

Annis led the way into the shop. "Sit over there," she said, waving them towards a cushioned settle in one corner behind a low table strewn with knitting patterns. She locked the shop door and turned the sign to CLOSED, then headed back to the kitchen. "I'll just put the kettle on."

While they waited, a small, delicate tabby and white cat rose from a basket under the table, stretched, then sprang up onto Gawaine's lap. Automatically Gawaine began to stroke her; in the midst of the stress David felt a flicker of amusement to see that Gawaine had not wasted his time in ingratiating himself with the cat Merino.

"Tea won't be long," Annis said, reappearing with a tray of mugs, milk jug and sugar bowl. Her voice was tight; it was obviously an effort for her to stay calm. "Do you know what happened?"

"It's hard to say," David replied. "One of the panes on the back door is broken. We think someone might have got in, thinking the place was still empty. Did you hear anything?"

Annis shook her head.

"A very quiet death..." Gawaine murmured, looking up from the cat. "Besides, the storm would be a cover for it. You haven't had any trouble here?" he added to Annis.

"No. I did have a window broken a couple of weeks ago, but I think that was just mindless vandalism. Or kids too scared to own up. Certainly nothing was stolen." She shivered, and added, "There's next to no crime on Morgarrow. It's horrible to think—"

She broke off at the sound of her kettle shrieking in the kitchen and hurried out.

David noticed that the worst of Gawaine's shock had ebbed, and not only because of the soothing purr of the cat Merino on his lap. He was looking thoughtful; a slight frown had gathered between his brows.

"Have you something on your mind?" he asked.

Gawaine's frown deepened. "There's something... something odd, about that room where Iris..." His voice shook; he took a deep breath and started again. "But I can't quite call to mind what it is."

"Just don't start," David said, beginning to feel alarmed.

"I'm not sure I have a choice." Gawaine managed a faint, melancholy smile. "If only it was a simple burglary..."

It never is, David thought, with a queer sense of foreboding. If Gawaine thought he had had seen something, then he probably had. All David could hope for was that the police would see it, too, and leave Gawaine out of it.

Wondering what it might have been, David tried to remember exactly what he had seen in the few frozen seconds when they had discovered Iris's body. But the memory of her face was too vivid; the rest of the room was no more than a blur.

He was still trying to picture it when Annis came back and dumped a fat brown teapot on the table. "The police have arrived," she said. "I told them you were here. They said they would come over to take your statements once they'd got themselves organised."

"I suppose they have…" Gawaine waved a hand vaguely. "Fingerprint people and so on."

Annis nodded. "All the bells and whistles, as far as I could see. Poor Iris… she would have hated her home being invaded. She was so excited about moving down here permanently."

"She told you about that?" David was slightly surprised. It was only the day before, after Bernard White's visit, that Iris had come up with the idea, and she hadn't sounded as if she had made up her mind.

"Yes, I invited her to supper last night," Annis replied. "We discussed it. We were thinking of ways that we might work together. Of course, that won't happen now." Her voice choked as she added, "It would have been such fun."

She poured tea, her hands shaking a little so that she splashed some on the tray. David would have preferred something stronger, and guessed that Gawaine would too; however, the tea was very welcome.

But he had hardly had time to take a mouthful when there was a ring at the door of the shop. Two figures stood outside, dark silhouettes against the sunlight that had followed the storm.

"Here they are," David muttered as Annis went to let them in.

The man in the lead was tall, cadaverous, with thinning dark hair and a pinched expression. The woman who followed him was small and unobtrusive – mousy, even – and kept well in the background as her boss strode across the shop and confronted Gawaine and David.

"Detective Inspector Bradshaw, Detective Sergeant Godwin," he snapped, flipping out his ID and pocketing it again all in one swift movement. "And you are?"

David introduced himself and Gawaine.

Inspector Bradshaw's gaze suddenly hardened, cold as a breeze off the Arctic. "I've heard of you before," he told Gawaine. "Thinking you can do better than the police. Well, I'm telling you here and now that I'll have no interference in my investigation. Keep your nose out."

"I assure you, Chief Inspector," Gawaine responded, at his most affected, "I have absolutely no intention of interfering."

The Inspector made the noise usually spelt 'Hmph!' "So what happened?" he asked.

David described how they had arrived at Iris's cottage, noticed that the curtains were still drawn, then saw the broken window pane in the back door and entered to find Iris lying dead on the sofa. Sergeant Godwin made notes, while Gawaine listened in silence, stroking the cat Merino. Annis took her own mug of tea behind her shop counter and began fiddling about with her till; she still looked not far away from tears.

"You didn't enter the sitting room?" Inspector Bradshaw asked when David had finished.

"No."

"And that's all you have to tell me?"

"No, Inspector." Gawaine spoke for the first time. "I telephoned Iris at about nine o'clock this morning. So she was alive then."

"Useful," Bradshaw commented, sounding reluctant to admit that Gawaine might say anything relevant. "What was the nature of your call?"

"Iris and I were supposed to be going for a walk," Gawaine explained. "But that was obviously impossible, because of the storm. So I called her, and we put it off until tomorrow." His mouth tightened, as though he had realised afresh that their walk, and their search for the farmhouse, was never going to happen.

"The storm hit at about quarter to nine," Inspector Bradshaw said thoughtfully. "You phoned the victim at about nine. And that was the last contact you had?"

Gawaine nodded.

"And did you—?"

Whatever Bradshaw was about to say was lost as the shop doorbell rang again. Annis went to answer it and admitted a uniformed police officer.

"We've found the victim's bag, sir," he said to Bradshaw. "Stuffed under the rose bushes beside the garden gate."

He flourished the object he was carrying; David recognised the bag, made of paisley patterned tapestry, with a leather shoulder strap. Iris had been carrying it the day before when she moved down to the cottage. Now it was dark with rainwater; Annis darted forward to rescue her knitting patterns as the officer deposited it on the table.

"Let's see what we have here," Bradshaw said. "Open it up."

The officer, who was wearing gloves, unfastened the zip and began to draw out the items inside. David watched: a packet of tissues, a cheque book and ballpoint pen, sunglasses in a case, a crumpled supermarket receipt and a half-finished roll of mints. And a large handful of keys.

"No purse or phone," the Inspector said when his subordinate had rooted around in the bag and found nothing else. "He obviously took what was valuable and dumped the bag on his way out."

With a glance at the Inspector, Gawaine reached forward, then stopped himself and drew back to let the officer begin to separate the keys. "Can you tell me anything about those?" Bradshaw asked.

There were three separate sets. The first David recognised as the one Iris had used to let herself into the cottage on the day before. The second was a single security key; David guessed it was the key to Iris's flat. So far, so unremarkable, but David felt a spark of interest as he looked at the third: a large number of keys of different sizes, each one with its own tag. The key fob was a chunky black circle with a Celtic cross incised in silver.

"Main door... cloister gate... chapter house..." Gawaine leant forward to read out the tags, disturbing the cat Merino, who poured herself off his lap and sat disdainfully washing herself in the middle of the shop floor. "Priest's vestry... vestry safe..." He sat back. "These are the Abbey keys."

He glanced at David, who read a warning in his eyes to say nothing. *So Iris acquired the Abbey keys after all. I wonder how.* But none of that was relevant now, and there was no point in going into it with the Inspector.

Bradshaw certainly wasn't taking much interest in the keys, turning to ask his officer what else had been found in the cottage.

"There's a box upstairs with a few bits of jewellery, and some paintings," the officer replied. "It doesn't look as if he went up there at all. Probably couldn't get out of there fast enough, once he'd killed her."

"The paintings are probably ones that Iris did herself," Gawaine said. "She was an artist."

Bradshaw grunted. "Not worth much then."

"Wait a minute," David said. "I left my tablet there last night; are you saying it's gone?"

"Sorry, sir." The officer shrugged apologetically. "We didn't find anything like that."

Faced with the tragedy of Iris's death. David felt no more than a mild flash of annoyance. Everything significant on the tablet was secure, unless the thief was also an IT expert. *Except Roddy's brochure,* he told himself, then dismissed the thought. That didn't matter now.

"There is this, too, sir," the officer said. He delved deep into a pocket and brought out a clear plastic bag with something coiled up inside it. David got a good look at it as he handed it to the Inspector. It was a plastic cable with a pointy bit at each end, very like the one that held Iris's knitting.

"Is that—" he began.

"The ligature, yes, sir," the officer said.

Bradshaw stared at it, turning the bag from side to side. "Peculiar looking object."

"It's a circular knitting needle," Annis pointed out.

The Inspector seemed to realise for the first time where he was. Glancing around, he saw a display of various knitting needles, hanging from a spinner near the shop counter. "He got it here?" he asked, fixing Annis with a hard stare.

"No, it—"

"There's a basket of knitting in the cottage, sir," the officer interrupted. "I assume he just grabbed the first thing he could lay hands on."

Bradshaw gave a brisk nod. "That makes sense." Annis opened her mouth to say something else, but the Inspector was already forging on. "So it's pretty obvious what we've got here. The thief burgled the cottage thinking it would be empty, taking advantage of the storm when no one would be about. The victim disturbed him, and…" He spread his hands. "There you have it."

"No!" Gawaine suddenly sat erect, blue eyes blazing. "I've remembered… I knew from the first there was something wrong about that room."

"Other than a dead body?" Bradshaw said, heavily sarcastic.

"Yes, other than that." Gawaine was obviously making a massive effort to keep his voice steady. "There was no water on the floor."

Chapter Nine

> For I am going into a wilderness
> Where I shall find no path nor friendly clew
> To be my guide.
>
> *The Duchess of Malfi*, I.i

Inspector Bradshaw paused for a moment before dismissing his uniformed officer back to the crime scene next door. Once the man had returned Iris's items to her bag and departed with it and the knitting needle, the inspector turned back to Gawaine. "What do you mean, no water on the floor?" he asked.

"When I looked into the sitting room, and saw Iris lying on the sofa," Gawaine began, his voice tightly controlled, "the floor was completely dry. But you saw the roads out there. When David and I came in, we tracked mud through the kitchen. No one could have come in during the storm without leaving wet footprints. Even if he wiped his shoes on the mat, his clothes would have been dripping."

The inspector listened in silence. David thought that he looked disturbed, but at the same time as if he didn't want to believe what he was hearing.

"Are you telling me you noticed all that?" he asked when Gawaine had finished. "You came across a dead body and you still looked at what was on the floor?"

"He does that," David put in.

Gawaine winced at the Inspector's plain speaking. "I don't ask to do it," he murmured.

"But that would mean..." Bradshaw let his voice trail off. He was frowning as if he couldn't quite process everything it would mean.

"He came before the storm began," Gawaine continued, at his most pedantic. "Iris knew him – I think we can safely assume 'him' – and let him in. She didn't think she had any reason to be afraid of him. She—"

"He must have been there when you phoned her," David interrupted, suddenly understanding. "She was annoyed with him, not with you."

Gawaine nodded. "Exactly. That's another reason I say she wasn't afraid of him. If she had been, she could have asked for help. Or made up an excuse to get me – or both of us – down here as soon as possible." He blinked thoughtfully. "Iris and her visitor were having an argument. She thought she could handle it, and then... then it all went wrong." His voice shook on the last few words.

"But what about the broken window in the back door?" Sergeant Godwin asked.

Bradshaw gave her an irritated look; David guessed it was her job to take notes and keep her mouth shut. "Done to make it seem like a robbery," he said.

"I think so," Gawaine agreed. "He took Iris's bag – and your tablet, David – removed her phone and her purse and dumped the bag in the bushes on his way out through the back garden. After which he vanishes from human ken."

Bradshaw thought about that for a moment, then

straightened up, radiating brisk efficiency. "Right," he said. "Sergeant, organise a house to house; find out if anyone saw him, coming or going. DNA and fingerprints should give us something." His glance flicked from Gawaine to Annis and then back again. "So Ms Grant sounded annoyed on the phone," he continued. "Have you any idea why, or who might have annoyed her?"

"I know she had a problem with Bernard White, one of the Abbey trustees," Gawaine replied, sounding reluctant to throw even a potential murderer to the wolves. "And Roddy Chatham, who wanted the vacant place on the board of trustees, after Petroc Tremayne died."

David wasn't sure how much Inspector Bradshaw knew about the politics of Morgarrow, but Sergeant Godwin seemed to grasp something, at least, as she busily made notes.

"And what was all that about?" the Inspector asked.

"Something to do with the development of the island," Gawaine told him; David noticed with relief that he was keeping very quiet about the plans for Morgarrow Moor. *I don't want to get done for snooping on Roddy's computer.* "Bernard White and Roddy Chatham wanted to develop, to raise money for the Abbey, but Iris was against it, and as Petroc Tremayne had left the island to her…"

The inspector let out a grunt. "I see. We'll need to look at her will. Do any of you know who was her solicitor?"

It was Annis who replied. "Tom Turnbull, of Turnbull and Madden."

Inspector Bradshaw swivelled around and spoke to Sergeant Godwin. "Make a note. You can go to see Turnbull later." With a nod to Gawaine, he added, "Thank you for your help, but we can take it from here. You had both better come across to the station tomorrow; we'll write up your statements and you can sign them." He sounded more conciliatory than when he had first arrived, but David still wouldn't have called him friendly.

"Should I come too?" Annis asked.

"Not at present, miss," the Inspector said. "Not unless you have anything to add."

"Well, the knitting needle—" Annis began, only to break off as the Inspector shrugged.

"It just happened to be at hand," he said. "It could just as well have been a belt or her dressing gown cord."

With a brief farewell he went out. Sergeant Godwin gave the display of knitting needles a brief spin, eyeing the various packets, before she followed him. Annis gazed after them with a disgruntled expression.

Gawaine leaned back on the cushions of the settle, looking particularly languid and fragile in contrast with Bradshaw's brusque competence. But his next words were swift and to the point. "What about the knitting needle?"

"I think Sergeant Godwin might have an inkling," Annis said. "But she's obviously not paid to think."

"So what does she think?" David asked.

"She thinks it came from here."

"And did it?"

Annis shook her head emphatically. "No. I could tell just by looking at it that it's a cheap brand. I told you before, I sell quality. I wouldn't have a thing like that in my shop." She sounded disgusted, as if someone had accused her of selling rotten fish. After a moment's pause, she continued, "I don't think it belonged to Iris, either. She only started knitting when she came down here at Easter, and I gave her the correct needle to make her shawl. Why would she buy another when she hadn't started another project?"

Gawaine sat up with a sudden intake of breath. "But that would mean—"

"That the murderer brought it with him. Yes," said Annis.

"Who else do we know who knits?" David asked.

He and Gawaine had taken leave of Annis and were walking back to the hotel. Police were still moving in and around Iris's cottage; Gawaine paused, gazing down at their launch, which was drawn up at the jetty. He had reverted to his usual slightly affected demeanour; David knew it was his way of distancing what they had seen.

"Elaine Chatham," he murmured thoughtfully. "She's a much bigger woman than Iris; she might have the strength to strangle her."

"Elaine Chatham is a dotty old dear who wouldn't hurt a fly," David said. "I won't hear a word against her."

Gawaine's mouth quirked in a smile. "She's corrupted you with her fruit cake, my dear David. But she knits, and I would guess that she can't afford to go and buy spiffy top of the range needles from Annis."

"True. But it's not only Elaine who could get hold of her needles."

"You mean Roddy Chatham?" Gawaine, David realised, was way ahead of him. "Yes, he would certainly have access to his mother's knitting basket. And he has an excellent motive for killing Iris. Now that she's dead, St Cadoc's gets the island, and there's a vacant cottage just waiting for Roddy to move in. He wouldn't know that Iris left it to Annis."

"Then would he know that she left the island to St Cadoc's?" David asked. "Or about the letter that Great Uncle Petroc left for her?"

"Probably not. But consider: Iris has no close family, so who else should she leave it to? There's only one thing that bothers me."

"And that is?" David asked.

He moved off, and the two of them strolled on together towards the hotel. It was a few moments before Gawaine replied.

"Why a knitting needle?" Clearly it was a rhetorical question, because he didn't wait for David to answer. "There are far more convenient ways to strangle your victim. And it's something that might occur to a woman more easily than a man. If Roddy used it, didn't he realise he would be throwing suspicion on his mother?"

"Or on Annis," David said. "And she is someone we ought to take a look at."

Gawaine turned to look at him, blue eyes wide with shock. "Annis wouldn't—"

"Oh, yes, I know she has a cute cat. But look..." David ignored Gawaine's murmur of protest. "The murderer vanishes after he – or she – breaks the window in the door and stashes the bag under the bush. Where better to vanish to than the house next door?"

"You're right, of course..." Gawaine shook his head, a pained expression on his face. "And she has motive. She knew that Iris was leaving her the cottage – but would that be enough to kill for?" He shrugged uneasily. "And then there's Bernard White," he continued, clearly desperate to change the subject. "Is there a Mrs White who knits? Does she make jumpers for all the little Whites?"

"Bernard White is rather old to have little Whites," David pointed out.

"Grandchildren, then," Gawaine said with an airy wave of one hand. "Of course, Annis would know about all the knitters on the island, though it might be less than tactful to ask her."

"It would be a very bad idea to ask her," David told him. "You know that Bradshaw will be gunning for you if you start invading his patch."

Another shrug. "That, my dear David, is his problem."

David suppressed a sigh. Even though he joined in with Gawaine's speculation, he couldn't approve of it. He always tried to persuade Gawaine not to involve himself in these affairs; he always failed. It would be even harder this time, when he had known Iris and liked her. But there would be tough times ahead; there always were.

"You know," Gawaine said as they approached the hotel, "there's something we've completely forgotten about."

"There is?"

Gawaine did not reply immediately. Entering the hotel, he headed straight for reception. David meanwhile, feeling the need for something stronger than tea, made for the bar. By the time Gawaine joined him he had acquired two glasses of brandy and a table in the far corner.

"So what did we forget?" he asked, pushing one of the glasses over to Gawaine.

Gawaine picked up the glass, sniffed, and sipped. A

fugitive frown crossed his face, as if the brandy failed to measure up to his standards. But he made no comment, instead unfolding a leaflet that he must have picked up at reception. Reading it upside down, David saw that it was a list of the ferry times.

"My dear David," Gawaine began, "it may have escaped your notice, but we are on an island. We have been looking at means and motive, but we also need to consider who could have been on Morgarrow at the time Iris was killed."

"Which was…what time did you make that phone call?"

"Round about nine o'clock. And we found her body… when?"

"Around two. So, five hours," David said. "Of course, the police can narrow it down, but they're hardly likely to tell us."

"We can narrow it down, too," Gawaine pointed out. "If we're right that the murderer was in the cottage when I phoned – and he must have been, or why was the floor dry – they surely couldn't have gone on arguing for hours." His voice grew tight as he added, "I would guess she must have been dead by ten, and probably earlier."

He let out a sigh and leaned back, his eyes closed. David thought he looked exhausted. But the pause was only brief; a moment later he leaned forward again, consulting the ferry timetable.

"The first ferry of the day leaves the mainland at eight," he said, "and leaves here at eight thirty. Iris was still alive then. So our murderer either lives here on Morgarrow, or he came across on that eight o'clock ferry."

"Bernard White, Elaine Chatham, Annis Radford,"

David said. "But it seems as if we can discount Roddy Chatham."

Gawaine frowned thoughtfully. "He could have got here. He could have been on the ferry. He might even have spent the night before at St Morwenna's with his mum."

"But he couldn't have got away again." David reached over and spun the leaflet around so that he could consult the timetable. "If he commits a murder after nine, the earliest ferry he could catch is the nine thirty. He would never have planned it like that, because he'd be very late for work. Unless he phoned in, and told them he'd missed the eight thirty."

"That would apply to Bernard White, too," Gawaine murmured.

David shook his head. "When you're a partner, you can rock up to the office whenever you feel like it."

"If you say so, my dear David. Anyway, as it happened, there was no nine thirty ferry, because of the storm. So if Roddy, or anyone else, came across from the mainland, they were stuck on Morgarrow until the afternoon." He gave a faint, cat-like smile. "I wonder where he would go?"

"You don't need to know," David pointed out, feeling that he had to have one last try at steering Gawaine away from the dangerous shoals of investigation. "Once we've seen Bradshaw tomorrow and signed our statements, we can go home. Forget all about this."

The last few words were a mistake; he knew that as soon as they were out of his mouth.

Gawaine shivered. "I can't forget it. I feel..." He looked for a word.

"You're *not* responsible!"

"No, just… involved. We came here to help Iris."

"Which we did. Except for exactly where they meant to build the timeshare. Our bit was done. We didn't sign up for murder."

"Of course, my dear David, you're exactly right," Gawaine sighed. "And I know you'll need to go back to work next week. But I can't leave, not if there's anything I can do. I just can't."

Chapter Ten

> ...to aspire some mountain's top
> The way ascends not straight, but imitates
> The subtle foldings of a winter's snake.
> *The White Devil*, I.ii

"I phoned my boss first thing this morning," David remarked. "I've arranged to work remotely for the time being."

He and Gawaine were standing by the rail of the ferry as it chugged its way across the strait separating Morgarrow from the mainland. After the storm of the day before the sky was a serene blue, with a stiff breeze fluttering the surface of the sea.

Gawaine cast him a glance, half guilty, half massively relieved, then returned to his contemplation of the ship's wake creaming out behind. "I'm sorry..." he began.

"No need," David interrupted. "It's perfectly fine. Don't you think I'd rather be here than stuck in an office in London? I have a conference coming up soon, but we can worry about that later."

Gawaine gazed at him anxiously. "Do I have permission to worry about it now?"

"No way!" David declared. "You don't have permission to worry about anything – though I suppose nothing will stop you worrying about Iris's murder."

"Alas, no," Gawaine said with a sigh.

"The only thing is," David went on, "I shall have to buy another tablet, or hire a computer, or something, since the murderer nicked mine. I can do it once we've been to the police station and signed our statements.

"I also phoned Seff," he continued, when Gawaine did not respond.

The memory of that phone call was still vivid in his mind. Seff had let out a sharp exclamation when he told her that Iris was dead, and as he explained to her what they knew he could hear sounds from the other end which he realised at last were Seff's struggles to stifle her sobs. When she finally spoke again, her voice had a hard, bright edge that told of anger mixed with her grief.

I've never seen Seff cry before. They must have been really close.

"Iris was her friend, of course, and she's getting herself assigned to the story," he told Gawaine. "She's coming down; she said she expects to be here tonight, or if not, tomorrow, as early as she can make it."

Gawaine blinked, looking vague and a little lost. "I should have thought about her," he murmured. "We'll need to book her a room."

"Already done," David said, feeling complacent. "And let's hope by the time she arrives we'll have something to tell her."

David used his smartphone to locate the police station near the end of one of the steep cobbled streets of the little mainland town, situated between an ice cream shop and an antique market with separate stalls crammed together under the one roof. Gawaine lingered wistfully in front of the antique market window, but David hustled him along into the much less appealing establishment next door and introduced them both to the desk sergeant.

For a few moments they were kept waiting, while Gawaine paced about nervously, clearly worried at the thought of encountering Inspector Bradshaw again. David didn't blame him; however, the first person to appear was the uniformed officer they had seen in Annis's shop the day before.

"If you'll come this way, sirs…"

He led them into a small room which seemed to be a mixture of lab, store-room and office, where he efficiently scanned their fingerprints and took DNA samples.

"Just for the purpose of elimination," he assured them.

Gawaine endured the process with apparent fascination, but David could tell that he was still edgy. He didn't begin to relax until the officer had finished and showed them into an office where Sergeant Godwin was waiting for them.

"Good morning," she said, indicating two chairs that faced the desk where she was sitting. "Have a seat. This shouldn't take long."

She opened a file, took out two sheets of paper and slid one across the desk to each of them. As David had expected, it was the typed version of the statement he had given Inspector Bradshaw the day before; he read it through, signed it with the pen the sergeant held out to him, and slid it back towards her.

He expected, once Gawaine had signed his version, that they would be dismissed. Instead, Sergeant Godwin sat back in her chair, her hands clasped at her waist, fingers interlaced, and let her gaze flick between them. David noticed that she had lost her subdued mousiness, or at least she was now an alert, bright-eyed mouse, with every whisker twitching.

"Mr St Clair," she began at last, letting her beady gaze rest on Gawaine, "I know you've done useful work of this kind in the past…"

Gawaine let a murmur of protest escape him; David knew he would never have called what he did 'work', even if sometimes it had been useful: more a kind of convoluted drifting among disparate elements, until suddenly they came together with a satisfying – and sometimes terrifying – click.

"I ought to tell you that Inspector Bradshaw meant everything he said to you yesterday," Sergeant Godwin went on, ignoring the murmur. "He can't stand interference, and he's in a specially bad mood at the moment, because on top of everything else, we've got a missing person. So if you cross him, he *will* deal with you."

"Then I shall endeavour not to… er… cross him."

"Good." The sergeant smiled. "Then talk to me about knitting needles."

Gawaine exchanged a glance with David, as if he wasn't at all sure what Sergeant Godwin wanted. David didn't feel particularly enlightened, either.

"Ms Radford at the knitting shop didn't think the needle belonged to Iris," Gawaine said at last. "And it didn't belong to her, either."

"But she has a shop full," said the sergeant.

"But not that kind. She says it's a brand she doesn't stock."

Sergeant Godwin gave a disbelieving sniff. "Even if that's true, just because she doesn't stock it, doesn't mean she doesn't *have* it," she pointed out. "My granny used to knit. She had boxes of wool, and more knitting needles than you could shake a stick at. All different kinds. I can see I'm going to have to have a chat with Ms Radford."

She rose to her feet, bringing the interview to an end. But as she was about to open the door for them to leave, she stopped. "Mr St Clair, I meant what I said earlier, about Inspector Bradshaw. But if you do happen to have any… ideas, that you feel like sharing, share them with me, would you?" She took out a business card and handed it to Gawaine. "That gets you straight to me. Have a nice day, now."

Gawaine tucked the card away in an inside pocket and stood in the street outside the police station, looking confused. "Is she really going behind Inspector Bradshaw's back?" he asked.

David felt equally taken aback. "It looks as if she is."

"I think I agree with you, my dear David," Gawaine said. "Machiavelli is alive and well and working for the police. All the same," he added more seriously, "there may come a time when I have reason to phone her."

"Let's go and get lunch," David suggested as they moved away from the police station. "I'm getting fed up with hotel food. And we passed a promising Italian place along here."

Gawaine agreed; neither of them said anything more about the murder until they were sitting in a booth with bowls of steaming pasta in front of them and *Santa Lucia* playing over the sound system.

David poured glasses of what looked like a fairly decent Chianti. "So where are we?" he said.

"Not very far," Gawaine said with a sigh.

"Then let's take stock. Suspects. Motive, means and opportunity."

Gawaine took a sip of wine, frowning slightly as he began to focus his attention on what they already knew, and what they still needed to discover. "Means, we know," he began, clearly trying to sound efficient. "The knitting needle. Which suggests a knitter, or someone with access to knitting… stuff, or…" He let his voice trail off, as if a disturbing possibility had nudged its way into his mind.

"Or someone who deliberately acquired the thing because it had some significance. Or he wanted to throw suspicion on a knitter." David, guessing what he meant, was rather less squeamish about putting words to the thought.

"But no one has anything against Annis…"

"That we know of," David reminded him. "And surely Roddy Chatham wouldn't want to incriminate his dear old mum."

Gawaine took a couple of bites of *penne al pollo*. "Obsessing over the knitting needle is getting us nowhere," he said with a frustrated sigh. "As for motive, we know about Roddy Chatham, Bernard White and the timeshare scheme."

"And Annis and the cottage."

Gawaine didn't look grateful for the reminder. He wouldn't like to think about Annis, her cheerful shop and her friendly cat, and then imagine her tightening that cable around Iris's neck. He shuddered and took another mouthful of wine.

"There might be someone else – someone not connected with Morgarrow – who has reason to want Iris dead," he pointed out.

"There might," David agreed. "There's Iris's ex, for one."

"Her ex… oh, that actor Seff told us about."

"Yeah, Jake Fletcher. Jake the werewolf. Suppose he's one of those nasty stalker types. 'If I can't have her, no one else can.' She dumped him, remember."

"But surely he's now disporting himself among his amorous female fans," Gawaine said. "Would he be so obsessed with Iris?"

"He might. Remember that Iris dumped him *after* he had his big break. That must have been a real blow to his masculine pride."

"You mean, *How dare she?*" Gawaine asked.

"Exactly."

Gawaine let that suggestion lie for a moment, and David didn't press him. "If Jake Fletcher did strangle her," he continued, "or if it was anyone else who doesn't live on Morgarrow, then he had to get there. Either on the eight o'clock ferry, or the day before, in which case—"

"Where did he spend the night?" Gawaine finished for him.

"Maybe Jake talked Iris into letting him spend it with her."

Gawaine shook his head. "If they were on those terms, why kill her?" he asked. "Unless… maybe his role in that film was taking him over. I have read *Dracula*, you know."

David rolled his eyes. "*Dracula* was vampires. Jake was a werewolf."

Gawaine waved an airy hand. "Werewolves… vampires… You see one of the undead, you've seen them all."

David almost spat out a mouthful of Chianti. A moment later he forced himself to be serious. If Gawaine was retreating like this into farce, it only meant that he was finding the unpleasant possibilities of Jake Fletcher's stalker tendencies and sexual compulsion too much to cope with.

"Okay," David said. "Let's leave Jake Fletcher on the back burner. He could have found his way to Morgarrow, but there are people with much stronger motives who are already here. Bernard White, Roddy Chatham, Elaine Chatham—"

"I thought you said she wouldn't hurt a fly," Gawaine interrupted.

"I don't think she would, but we can't discount her. If Roddy made lots of money from the timeshare, he would surely toss a bit to his mum. We don't know that she likes living in that great barn of a house, baby-sitting a load of students." He hesitated, then added, "I'll let you put her on the list if you let me put Annis."

Gawaine sighed, looking dejected. "Very well. And there's one more person we need to add."

"There is?"

Gawaine nodded. "George."

"George? As in 'Ring George. Urgent'?"

"The very same," Gawaine said. "If I'm right, and George is the farmer whose land was destined to become the timeshare resort."

"You mean he might have expected a massive pay-out if the island belonged to St Cadoc's?" David asked, sharing out the last of the carafe of wine between their glasses.

"Exactly. He could have come to discuss the matter with Iris, and it all got out of hand."

"Having brought a knitting needle with him, just on the off-chance that he needed to strangle her?"

Gawaine put down his fork and ran his hands through his hair. "We always come back to that." He pushed his bowl away and picked up his wine glass, turning it between his fingers. "You know, my dear David, I have the feeling that if we knew why he chose the knitting needle, we'd be well on the way to solving this."

Chapter Eleven

Misfortune comes like the coroner's business,
Huddle upon huddle.
The White Devil, III.iii

Leaving David to sort out a new computer, Gawaine took the shuttle bus from the town centre to the ferry terminal, which consisted of a kiosk for ticket sales, a coffee stall and a chain stretched between two bollards barring access to the slipway. Two or three cars were waiting, while the ferry manoeuvred into position.

Several other people had boarded the bus, and when they reached the terminal Gawaine hung back until they had bought their tickets, before he approached the kiosk.

"That was quite a storm yesterday," he remarked as the ticket-seller fossicked around in the till for his change, peering short-sightedly at the coins before he handed them over.

"It was that." The seller was an old man, white-haired, with a beard birds could nest in. His voice had a warm Cornish burr. "I had my doubts that the eight o'clock ferry would get back here safe."

"Eight o'clock is very early," Gawaine continued, hoping that he sounded like someone putting on time until the ferry arrived, rather than trying to discover if a potential murderer had been on board. "You can't get many passengers at that time."

"No, but that's when we send the post and the papers over," the old man said, sounding quite happy to pass the time with a bit of chat. "You're right there aren't many passengers – just a young lad and his girlfriend yesterday."

"Students from St Morwenna's Community?" Gawaine suggested.

"Wouldn't be surprised."

By this time the ferry had docked, and one of the crew appeared to unhook the chain and wave the cars forward. Gawaine nodded farewell to the ticket-seller and joined the other foot passengers as they boarded.

He didn't feel that he had learnt very much. The two students the old man had described were unlikely murderers, and it didn't sound as if the 'young lad' could be Roddy Chatham. *Although,* Gawaine thought, remembering the ticket-seller's white hair and wrinkled face, *maybe anyone under forty looks like a 'young lad' to him.* He decided that he couldn't quite discount Roddy darling.

When the ferry docked at Morgarrow Gawaine didn't want to go back to the hotel, where there would be nothing to do but sit and brood. Instead, he wandered off in the other direction, into the village.

The centre was a cobbled square – or more like a triangle – with a market cross in the middle. Around it were various shops: a post office and newsagent; a small supermarket; a bakery, a pub and a couple of cafés. The rest were selling souvenirs of various levels of desirability, from plastic piskies to local pottery and paintings.

Gawaine reached for his sketchbook, intending to draw the market cross, only to check himself when he remembered that today he should have been sketching with Iris, on their quest to find the farm displayed in Roddy Chatham's timeshare brochure. Thoroughly dispirited, he turned back towards the hotel, then thought that he might drop in on Annis for some quality time with the cat Merino.

As he approached the wool shop, Annis appeared in the doorway, with the little tabby wreathing around her ankles. "Gawaine!" she called. "I need to tell you something."

Gawaine headed towards her, noticing as he did so that Iris's cottage next door had police tape across the doorway and a uniformed constable on duty outside.

"When I had supper with Iris the night before she died," Annis said, when Gawaine had paid the cat Merino her tribute of strokes, "she told me about the timeshare brochure that David found on Roddy Chatham's computer. She wasn't pleased."

"I can imagine," Gawaine responded. "It would change the character of the island."

"The thing is," Annis went on, "Iris showed me the sketch she made of the pub in the new development, and I'm pretty sure I recognised it. I mean, the farmhouse that it is now."

Gawaine's interest quickened. "Really?"

"Yes. You remember I told you about my producer – the spinner and dyer that I buy wool from? Her husband farms that land."

"Her husband's name wouldn't be George, by any chance?"

Annis stared at him. "Yes – George Pengelly. Do you know him?"

"I know of him." Gawaine frowned, thinking rapidly. "I need to talk to him."

He realised that Annis was giving him what he might have described as an old-fashioned look. "I wouldn't recommend it," she said. "George Pengelly isn't what I might call friendly."

"How perfectly frightful," Gawaine murmured, remembering David's description of a farmer with a rook rifle and a pair of ambitious dogs. He took a deep breath. "I still have to talk to him."

"You don't think he might have something to do with…" Annis gestured towards the next door cottage, her voice dying away.

Gawaine wasn't sure how much he wanted to tell her. He didn't know her very well; for all he knew, her shop could be the hub of village gossip. "No," he replied, though he wasn't sure if that was true. "But I'd like to know how it happened that his farmhouse was to be transformed into… what was it? The Merry Piskie?" He braced himself, trying to look – and indeed feel – full of drive and resolution. "Can you tell me how to get there?"

"I can do better than that," Annis responded. "I have to go there tomorrow to collect some wool from Kate – that's George's wife. You can come with me, if you like."

"Thank you." Gawaine tried to hide how massively relieved he felt. "What time shall I come?"

"I won't open until mid-day," Annis said. "I thought I would leave here about ten, if that's okay." As Gawaine agreed, the telephone in the shop started ringing. "I'd better get that," she added with a quick smile. "See you then."

With a last farewell to the cat Merino, Gawaine turned away, only to hear his name being called from further down the street. He halted and looked behind him to see Elaine Chatham, carrying a loaded market basket. Giving him a wave, she surged up to him, shawls flapping.

"Mr St Clair! So nice to see you. What have you done with your friend?"

"David?" Gawaine smiled and reached out to take the basket. "He's on the mainland, buying a computer. His tablet was stolen when—"

"Oh, yes, dear Iris," Elaine interrupted. "Terrible. So terrible. And now Bethany…"

Gawaine had noticed from the first that behind the cheery façade she was looking strained. He had assumed it was the stress of learning that murder had been committed on the island, but now he wondered if there was some other reason. "Bethany?" he asked.

"One of my students. She's been away; she wanted to visit her parents. She was supposed to come back yesterday. But there hasn't been any sign of her, and she isn't answering her phone. We're all dreadfully worried."

Gawaine remembered Sergeant Godwin mentioning a missing person when he and David had visited the police station that morning. *Could that be Bethany? If so, she hasn't been missing all that long.*

"Have you called the police?" he asked.

Elaine nodded. "I phoned her parents at first, of course. They told me she left in time to catch the night coach, and we expected her back on one of the early ferries. Then of course, the storm... But she didn't appear when the ferries started up again in the afternoon... I'm sure I don't know what to do!"

She and Gawaine set out side by side up the road that led to the Abbey and, eventually, to St Morwenna's. Elaine shuddered and turned her face away from Iris's cottage with its police presence. "What is happening to Morgarrow?" she asked. "What if something awful has happened to Bethany?"

"There's no need to worry yet," Gawaine said, trying to reassure himself as much as Elaine. "She might have gone to visit friends for a day or two."

"But that's not like her!" Elaine's voice rose almost to a wail. "Not without telling someone. And she's so young... She's just left school and she's spending her gap year here at St Morwenna's. And now this! I'm awfully afraid she's had some sort of accident."

"The police will find her." Gawaine felt it was a feeble comment, but there was not much else to say.

Elaine just sighed, as if she didn't believe him. Gawaine wasn't sure that he believed it himself.

He felt an urgent need to question Elaine about her son: whether Roddy Chatham had spent the night before the murder on the island. But, he reflected, it would be the height of tactlessness to ask a mother whether her son was in a position to commit a murder. *There must be another way of settling that.*

He walked with Elaine as far as St Morwenna's, refused her offer of tea, then turned back towards the hotel. As he approached the Abbey, he spotted Father Magnus leaving by the main door. The old priest raised his hand to wave, then beckoned him over. Gawaine met him in the shade of one of the Celtic crosses that sprinkled the surroundings of St Cadoc's.

"I hear you found Iris Grant's body," the old priest began. "A terrible experience."

Gawaine murmured agreement.

"If you feel you'd like to talk to someone," Father Magnus went on, with what Gawaine could only describe as a grim twinkle, "you had better ask Jenny. She's much better at that sort of thing."

"I think I shall be fine, Father," Gawaine responded. "But thank you."

"I wanted to ask you if by any chance you know what happened to my keys," Father Magnus said. "I lent them to Iris, the day before she died, and of course she never had the chance to return them."

Gawaine remembered the set of Abbey keys with the chunky Celtic key fob that the police had found in Iris's bag. *So they belong to Father Magnus!* He remembered too how agitated Iris had been after Bernard White refused to give her a set. Almost at once she had decided to visit Father Magnus, to hand over the chess set Great Uncle Petroc had left him.

But what if that was just an excuse? What if her real reason for seeing him was to ask to borrow the keys?

"I think the police have them, Father," he replied to the old priest's question. "You may have heard, her murderer took her phone and her purse, and stashed her bag in the bushes by the garden gate. There was a set of Abbey keys in the bag."

Father Magnus snorted. "I suppose I'd better get in touch with the police."

"Iris didn't say why she wanted the keys?" Gawaine asked, hoping to solve the mystery of why she had been wandering around the Abbey cloisters at midnight.

But Father Magnus seemed not to have heard the question. He was already off, striding down the road that led to the village, his black cloak belling out around him in the stiff breeze. He raised one hand in farewell as he went.

For a few moments Gawaine stayed where he was. The mystery of Iris's midnight visit to the Abbey – small in comparison with the vast mystery of her death – was niggling at him, far more, he suspected, than he could justify.

It could hardly be something nefarious, not if Father Magnus was prepared to lend her the keys. Always supposing she told him why she wanted them... but surely he wouldn't have lent them without a good reason?

Movement on the road distracted Gawaine from his thoughts: a group of students heading back to St Morwenna's from the village. Unwilling to meet them, imagining being questioned about his discovery of Iris, Gawaine headed around the back of the Abbey and joined the cliff path.

The wind – though nowhere near as strong as the day before – still discouraged him from going too near the cliff. There was no fence, though for most of its length the path kept well away from the edge. Gawaine skirted the outcrop of rocks in the narrow gap between it and the drystone wall; beyond it the hotel and the village came into view. The cliff here wasn't quite so sheer; the ground fell away in a tumble of broken rocks, with grass and clumps of pink-flowering thrift and the occasional thorny bush rooted in the cracks.

As he left the Abbey behind him, Gawaine spotted a splash of blue among the branches of one of the shrubs. At first he dismissed it as some item of rubbish thrown up by the storm. But when he looked more closely he realised that it was a bag, with a long shoulder strap tangled among the branches.

"Oh, good grief..." he murmured to himself.

Venturing closer to the edge, he looked down to see a steep slope of rocks and scree with a scatter of boulders at the bottom, and even a foot or so of pebbly beach between that and the sea. If he fell, he told himself, he might break a limb or two, but he was reasonably likely to survive.

That is so comforting.

Gawaine tried to convince himself that the errant bag was no concern of his, and in any case was probably trivial. But what it contained might not be trivial to its owner, and much as he might like to, he couldn't just go away and leave it there.

Besides, he thought, remembering the other abandoned bag, under the bush in Iris's garden, *it might have something to tell us.*

Nervously he began to edge his way down towards the bag. The slope looked a lot more precipitous now that he was actually committed. He had only covered a yard or so when the scree shifted under his feet and he began skidding downwards. He had a split second's vision of himself lying broken on the rocks below when he was brought up short by the bush he was aiming for.

An inch long thorn had driven itself into his palm. For a moment Gawaine watched the blood drip, then decided that stuck in this precarious position this was no time to start binding the wound up with a handkerchief. Besides, he collected an impressive array of scratches as he untangled the bag strap from branches that seemed determined not to let it go.

Finally he was able to sling the strap over one shoulder and address himself to the climb back to level ground. It looked a long way away; the slope loomed threateningly above his head. The whole island seemed to be rocking gently.

What was I thinking? I do not do heroics.

Eventually he braced himself and achieved safety in a single mad scramble. He had a nasty moment when the cliff edge began to crumble away under his weight, but eventually he pulled himself up, then stood on the path for several moments and tried to stop shaking.

The hotel was not very far ahead; the path led alongside a neat box hedge, and there was a gate which gave into the hotel garden. Gawaine collapsed onto a nearby bench and began to examine his loot.

The bag was made from blue denim, the fabric still pulpy from the previous day's rain. A flower had been pushed through the buckle of the strap; it had once been a rose, Gawaine thought. One flaccid yellow petal still clung on: heartbreaking to think that it had survived the tumult of the storm when so much else – including, Gawaine suspected, the bag's owner – had been destroyed.

Inside the bag were the usual items any woman would carry: a purse, a phone, keys, sunglasses in a case, a plastic pouch with a few bits of make-up. And a diary. Water had saturated it, the pages gummed together, but when Gawaine carefully folded back the cover he could still read the name inscribed on the first page.

Bethany Fox.

Feeling sick, Gawaine fumbled in his pocket for his phone and the card which Detective Sergeant Godwin had given him, and began to dial her number.

Chapter Twelve

I knew last night, by a sad dream I had,
Some mischief would ensue.
The White Devil, V.iii

"What have you been doing to yourself?"

David tracked Gawaine down in the hotel bar, sipping at a glass of Prosecco. He was looking white and strained, and his hands, always exquisitely kept, were badly scratched, with a couple of broken fingernails.

"Having an adventure," Gawaine replied, his voice flat and colourless. "I don't recommend it."

Once David had acquired himself a Scotch and soda, his friend embarked on the story of his afternoon, from his conversation with the ticket-seller at the ferry terminal, with Annis about the farmhouse and with Elaine Chatham about her missing student. He finished with his retrieval of the bag.

David had to hide amusement at the thought of Gawaine scrambling about on the cliff, at the same time as he was appalled by what might have happened. "You must be out of your tree," he commented.

Gawaine gave a tiny shrug. "Maybe, but seeing that the bag belonged to Bethany Fox, it's not hard to guess what happened to her."

"It sounds like an accident." David felt sick at the thought of it. "Maybe she went too close to the cliff edge, and the wind caught her."

Gawaine's eyes were dark and distressed, as if he was imagining the scene. "Sergeant Godwin said she would alert the coastguard. And there's something else," he added. "Finding Bethany's bag there means she must have been the girl on the eight o'clock ferry."

"Yes, but didn't you say she was with her boyfriend?" David objected. "What happened to him?"

"Who is the boyfriend, what is he?" Gawaine murmured. "And more to the point, where is he?"

"Unless they both went over."

Gawaine shuddered. "Don't."

"Then maybe he wasn't her boyfriend," David said. "Unless they were glued together, all your ticket-seller saw was two young people being friendly. Maybe she knew him, but once they got to Morgarrow, they parted and went their separate ways. She took the cliff path up to St Morwenna's and he went... well, wherever."

"Maybe he went to visit Iris," Gawaine said sombrely.

"What?"

"Think about it." Gawaine paused, taking another sip of Prosecco, then continued, "Unless Iris's murderer was already on the island, then he was the man on the ferry. Maybe he was Roddy Chatham."

David looked at the idea and liked it. "Bethany would know him; he's supposed to be up at St Morwenna's all the time, getting under his mum's feet. They could easily have had a little chat, to pass the time on the crossing. Or maybe Jake the werewolf was there," he added after a moment. "Your ticket guy didn't say if she had a big dog with her?"

He was rewarded by seeing a spark of amusement in Gawaine's eyes. "My dear David, in case you hadn't noticed, it's not full moon." He sighed, looking thoughtful. "I think we've done all we can about Bethany," he said. "It's Iris who's our real problem."

"So what do you propose doing about it?" David asked.

Gawaine seemed to brace himself, draining the last of his Prosecco. "Tomorrow," he said, "I'm going to look for George."

On the following morning David headed into the hotel restaurant for breakfast to find Seff Brown there, neatly spooning up a bowl of fruit and yogurt. He thought she looked unusually subdued, though she brightened when she glanced up and saw him.

"Hi," he said, heading over to her table. "You made it, then."

"Only just," Seff replied. "I had to go to court yesterday for a case I've been following, and then my train was late, and I almost missed the last ferry. So," she added. "what's been happening since we spoke yesterday?"

"Give me a couple of minutes, and I'll tell you."

David went to load a plate at the buffet and acquire a cup of coffee from a machine that gave off alarming gurgling and spitting noises. Returning to Seff's table, he launched into a recital of the previous day's events, interspersed with bites of breakfast.

"Then this girl on the ferry must have been Bethany Fox," Seff murmured. "Seeing that Gawaine found her bag half way down the cliff." She grinned suddenly. "I'd have given something to have seen that."

"It's the man we're most interested in," David said, refusing to speculate on the entertainment value of Gawaine almost breaking his neck. "We don't know who he was or where he went. And if—"

He broke off at the sight of Gawaine wandering into the restaurant, with a vague, ruffled air, as if he was half asleep. Spotting David and Seff, he tacked across to their table, and sank into the chair David pulled out for him. Close up, David could see how white and strained he looked; haunted, even.

"My dear Persephone!" He was obviously making a massive effort to assume his best social manner. "How delightful!"

David didn't wait to hear Seff's response, heading instead for the coffee machine and returning with a cup which he set down in front of Gawaine. "Bad night?" he asked.

Gawaine shuddered. "I spent hours falling off that cliff."

"Maybe your subconscious is trying to tell you something," Seff suggested.

"Then I wish it would be rather more explicit," Gawaine murmured with a pained look. He fell silent, sipping his coffee.

"David, you were telling me about the man on the ferry," Seff said.

"Yes, we think he might have been the murderer," David told her. "In which case, he was Roddy Chatham. He has the best motive of anyone who doesn't live on the island."

"The only motive, I should think," Seff said.

"Well, there's always Jake the werewolf," Gawaine put in from his semi-conscious state.

Seff stared at him. "Jake the—" She broke off, laughing. "You mean Jake Fletcher? Why on earth would he want to kill Iris?"

"He might have been stalking her..." David suggested, knowing how weak that sounded. "Or even trying to get back together with her."

Seff shook her head emphatically. "Not a chance. The only person Jake Fletcher loves is Jake Fletcher. Trust me, I know him. Anyway, he's somewhere way up north, shooting 'Son of the Werewolf' or 'Werewolf II' or whatever. And the gossip mags say that he's going around with his co-star."

Gawaine blinked, vaguely puzzled. "Gossip mags?"

Seff reached out and patted his hand. "You don't want to know. But Roddy Chatham is a definite possibility," she added more briskly, turning back to David. "Has he an alibi?"

"No idea," David replied. "And Inspector Bradshaw isn't going to like it if we start asking questions at his place of work."

Seff tsked. "What an unenterprising pair you are," she said. "Do we know where Roddy works? Have you their phone number?"

David had to reply no to both of those questions, wincing as Seff rolled her eyes. "They might know at reception," he said, rising and heading in that direction.

The hotel manager was on duty at the desk, and pointed David to a rack where local businesses displayed their flyers and cards. "Winton and Briggs," she told him, when he asked her where Roddy Chatham worked. "If you're looking for a holiday property, they're the best people to see."

David passed that nugget of information to Seff as he handed her the business card.

"Ideal," she said, and added, glancing at her watch, "It's gone nine. They should be open."

She took out her phone and dialled.

David exchanged a glance with Gawaine while they waited; under the influence of the coffee his friend seemed to be reviving, at least enough to go and fetch a second cup under his own steam.

"Good morning," Seff began. "My name is Ms Brown, and I'm terribly sorry, but I've made the most awful mistake."

David stared at her. Within a few seconds Seff had transformed into something... well... girly. Her voice had gone up a tone, and he thought he could detect a faint American twang.

"It was the other day, the morning of the storm," Seff continued. "I had an appointment with your Mr Chatham, to go and view the *cutest* little cottage, and when the storm hit, I didn't come in. But I *completely* forgot to call you."

She fell silent, listening, flashing a grin at David as she did so.

"Oh, then it really didn't matter, did it?" Seff continued down the phone. "That's *so* kind of you."

"Is this the Seff we know and love?" David murmured to Gawaine.

Gawaine's brows twitched. "Love? My dear David, is there something you're not telling me?"

"Oh, no, that's not necessary," Seff said, before David could think of a suitable response. "Thank you *so* much." She ended the call.

"Never did I think—" David began.

"David, just don't go there," Seff interrupted. "It worked. Roddy Chatham called in sick the morning of the storm. The manager said that they phoned to put off all his appointments, but somehow they missed mine."

"Which didn't exist," David said. "What if his boss starts asking Roddy darling about this mysterious Ms Brown?"

Seff shrugged. "Then they'll probably think that this ditsy woman had got it all wrong. Anyway, that's not our problem. We know now that Roddy Chatham wasn't at work on the morning of the murder."

"So where was he?" Gawaine asked.

"Here on Morgarrow, murdering Iris," David said.

"I wonder…" Gawaine let his voice trail off, and said no more, but David couldn't help thinking that he wasn't entirely convinced.

Chapter Thirteen

Dost think to root thyself in dead men's graves
And yet to prosper?
The White Devil, IV.iii

When Gawaine set out for the village to keep his appointment with Annis, the sky was a clear blue, with a few white puffs of cloud floating high above. The lark was on the wing, the snail on the thorn, and a murderer on the loose. Gawaine couldn't pretend that he was looking forward to meeting Annis's producer, Kate Pengelly, not if it meant an encounter with her hostile husband George.

David was not with him. "I'm supposed to be working remotely," his friend had reminded him. "So I'd better, you know, *work*."

Seff had taken herself off on the nine thirty ferry, meaning to interview the police. "I'll try to have a word with the ferry crew as well," she said. "They might know something about the man who was on the ferry with Bethany Fox. If it was Roddy Chatham, they might even have recognised him."

Annis appeared as soon as Gawaine rang the shop doorbell and let him in. "Good grief, you look awful," she said. "Are you sure you're up for this?"

Gawaine waved a hand, trying – and failing, he was certain – for an air of studied nonchalance. "I'm perfectly fine, thank you," he told her, then added, "I found Bethany Fox's bag half way down the cliffs yesterday."

"That looks bad." Annis bit her lip. "She hasn't turned up, then?"

"If she has, I haven't heard," Gawaine replied. "Did you know her?"

Annis shook her head. "I don't have much to do with St Morwenna's, and I gather Bethany hadn't been here long." She paused, sighing. "We'd better get on," she said at last.

She collected two large plastic tote bags, rolled them up and tucked them under her arm. Then she led Gawaine out through the kitchen and into the back lane.

"This is the quickest way," she explained. "We could go through the village and round by the road, but it's much further, and I don't have a car."

A couple of hundred yards further along the lane a steep flight of steps led up between grassy banks and onto the moor. Sheep were cropping the grass on either side, and raised their heads to give Gawaine and Annis an incurious look as they passed by.

"There's something I want to ask you," Gawaine said after they had been walking for a while.

Annis gave him an enquiring look, but didn't speak.

"You said Iris had supper with you, the night before she died," Gawaine continued. "And she decided that she was going to give up her job and come to live here permanently. Do you know if she told anyone else?"

"Oh, yes." Annis smiled faintly, as if she was

remembering. "She rang Bernard White, while we were having our coffee. It was quite late, and I don't think he was best pleased."

"I don't suppose he was best pleased by what she had to tell him, either," Gawaine murmured.

"Well, of course I didn't hear," Annis said. "But that's what I gathered. Iris had a good laugh when she put the phone down. She was on a bit of a high, and I don't think it was all because of the wine we'd been drinking." Her expression grew shadowed. "And then the next morning…"

Gawaine nodded understanding.

So Bernard White knew that Iris could become a trustee, he thought. *And if he knew, then Roddy Chatham probably did, too.*

"Did you tell the police about that?" he asked.

"I did. Sergeant Godwin came to talk to me yesterday." Annis sighed. "She's still fussing on about that knitting needle. I don't think I convinced her that it wasn't one of mine."

Gawaine felt vaguely uneasy about that. If the police believed that the needle had come from Annis's shop, they would ignore any other possibilities. *But at least they know now that Bernard White and his cohort had a good motive for killing Iris.*

Annis left him to his own thoughts until they reached the top of a small rise, where she halted. "There you are," she said, with an expansive gesture towards the landscape ahead of them.

The track sloped gently downwards; in the valley bottom Gawaine saw a cluster of farm buildings. The main house was stone-built, with a wide porch projecting from the middle of the façade. One or two gaps showed in the roof where slates were missing, and the whole place had a neglected air.

Beyond the farm gate the track continued across the moorland where more sheep were doing whatever sheep did while they grew the wool that kept Annis and Kate Pengelly in business. Further still, hazy with distance, Gawaine could make out the glimmer of the sea.

He let his gaze travel back to the farmhouse. Scruffy as it looked, he could still recognise the outlines that lay beneath its tarted up reincarnation as the Merry Piskie pub, the jewel in the crown of Roddy Chatham's timeshare village.

"Yes, this is the place," he said.

"Then let's go."

Annis led the way down the track to the farm gate. Everything was still and quiet; Gawaine could easily have believed that the whole place was empty, abandoned.

"At least George is out," Annis said. "If he was here, the dogs would be making a racket. George doesn't like visitors."

"And the dogs even less, I suppose," Gawaine murmured.

Annis nodded. "He tolerates me, because I bring money for Kate – that translates into beer money for George." She gave a quick grin. "At least, some of it does. We fiddle the books, Kate and I."

She let herself into the farmyard through a kissing gate beside the main five-barred affair that was tied up with a piece of hairy twine. "Kate knows I'm coming," she said. "I expect we'll find her round the back, in the old dairy."

Gawaine followed Annis as she skirted the main farm building and knocked on a half open door. A tuneful but random humming was coming through the gap, to break off at the sound of Annis's knock.

"Come in!" a voice called.

Gawaine entered in Annis's footsteps, and then stopped in surprise. Where the outside of the farm had been neglected, here everything was clean and orderly. The quarry-tiled floor was gleaming; down one side of the room were sinks and wooden drainers, while opposite was an old-fashioned kitchen range. Here two large pots were simmering, and a woman stood in front of them, stirring one of them with a wooden rod.

"Good morning, Kate," Annis said.

The woman – Kate Pengelly – turned. She was tall, and Gawaine guessed she was about fifty. Her greying hair was drawn back into a knot at her neck, and she was flushed from the heat of the range. She wore jeans and an intricately hand-knitted jumper.

Where there are hand knits there are needles, Gawaine thought.

"Hi, Annis," Kate said, and turned a curious look on Gawaine.

Annis introduced him. "Gawaine is interested in the Morgarrow development," she said. "He would like to ask you about it."

Kate's eyes narrowed into an unfriendly stare. "Development? I don't know anything about any development. But if you're another of these people trying to bribe George to give the farm up, I've nothing to say to you."

"No – quite the opposite," Gawaine assured her,

appalled that she should think that. "I was a friend of Iris Grant. There is a plan to develop this part of the island, and Iris was going to put a stop to it, before she died."

Kate shook her head. "That was a terrible thing."

"It was. And I'd like to find out who killed her. I think you might be able to help me."

To his surprise, Kate let out a crack of laughter. "And you think it might have been my George? Not a chance. He wouldn't have the guts."

Gawaine glanced at Annis, shocked that a woman would say that about her husband. But Annis was listening with a closed expression that gave nothing away.

"No, I don't think that," Gawaine told Kate. "But it would help if you told me what you know. You said that someone was trying to bribe your husband to give up the farm?"

Kate turned away and gave her pots a stir. When she turned back, she seemed to have made up her mind. "It was that lawyer – Bernard White, they call him. He came over here one day not long after Easter. He and George had a long talk."

"What was it about?"

"You don't think George would tell me?" Kate's tone was sneering. "No, but he was very pleased with himself. He told me he was giving up the farm because Bernard White had promised him money. So I asked him where we were going to live, and what would happen when the money ran out. George said he'd been promised a job and somewhere to live – but of course it would mean I had to give up all this." She waved a hand to indicate her bright little oasis in the midst of dilapidation.

"That's terrible," said Annis.

Kate shrugged. "That wouldn't matter to George, provided he got what he wanted."

"So what did you do?" Gawaine asked, though he was fairly sure what the answer would be.

"I spoke to Petroc Tremayne. After all, he owned the island, and at first I thought he must have been the person who sent Bernard White. But he didn't know anything about it."

"He wouldn't have been happy," Annis said.

"He wasn't. He said he would investigate, and also that he would talk to George. But I think he must have died before he could do anything. George still believes that the deal – whatever it is – is going ahead."

"And it might," Gawaine said. "But it's possible that the person who killed Iris did it to stop her interfering. And any little scrap of information I can find—"

"Well, I've told you all I know," Kate said. "Annis, can we get on? George should be back soon."

"Of course." Annis glanced at Gawaine. "George likes to spend his mornings 'working', by which he means wandering over the moor with his dogs, and he'd just as soon I was gone before he gets back. So would I, for that matter."

"He's… violent?" Gawaine asked, trying not to show how nervous Annis had made him.

"Oh, I'm not scared of him," Annis said, with a quirky smile that showed Gawaine she had guessed how he was feeling. "I'd just rather avoid any unpleasantness."

Meanwhile, Kate had pulled out one of the plastic bins that lined the far wall. "This is what I have: fingering weight, hundred gram skeins, about four hundred metres."

"Oh, brilliant!" Annis exclaimed, plunging her hands

into the bin and drawing out the wool: skeins in muted colours, mostly blue, grey and green. "These will walk out of the shop. I'll take them all, unless you want to keep some back to sell yourself."

"No, it's all yours," Kate said. "Oh, and there's this." She delved into another bin and brought out a bag of soft, creamy wool. "It's what Claudia White ordered. I've added an extra skein to be on the safe side."

"Claudia is Bernard White's wife," Annis told Gawaine, holding up the bag of wool admiringly. "She has another grandchild on the way – I think this is number six. And she knits them all the most beautiful baby shawls."

So Bernard White does have access to knitting needles, Gawaine thought. *Interesting.* He wondered why, if Petroc Tremayne had known that Bernard White was involved, he hadn't tackled him directly, instead of sending for Iris. Then he answered his own question. *He wouldn't trust anything Bernard White might have told him.*

"And there's this," Kate continued. From yet another bin she drew out a shawl, what looked like yards and yards of exquisite lace in tones from the palest lilac to deep purple. Crystal beads glimmered among the lace.

"Kate, that's fabulous!" Annis exclaimed.

"Do you want it?" Kate asked.

"Do I want it? Stand still while I bite your hand off. I'll display it in the shop. Unless you would like to buy it?" she said to Gawaine. "Is there a Mrs St Clair?"

"Alas, no," Gawaine said. "It is beautiful work."

"I assume George doesn't know about this?" Annis asked.

Kate shook her head. "I knitted it while he was down in the pub."

"Then I'll write you a cheque for the wool, and when you're next in the village I'll pay you for the shawl in cash."

Gawaine assumed that was what she had meant by 'fiddling the books'. He felt a pang of sympathy for Kate, with a husband who had so little respect for the beautiful things she made that he was prepared to take it all away from her.

Somehow there has to be a way to get this development stopped.

Annis wrote out her cheque and packed the wool and the shawl into her plastic tote bags. While she was doing that, Gawaine could hear the distant barking of a dog.

"Okay, we're out of here," Annis said. "Goodbye, Kate. Let me know when you have another consignment."

As they skirted the house to reach the gate, a man was approaching from the moorland track. He was short, with broad shoulders, his dark hair and beard badger-striped with silver. He carried a shotgun in the crook of one arm. To Gawaine's surprise he looked fairly civilised, not the *Wuthering Heights* inhabitant he had been expecting.

The dogs were another matter. One was a black and white border collie. The other was a breed that Gawaine could not categorise, except that it had far too many teeth.

"Good morning, George," Annis said as they approached the gate.

"Morning." George Pengelly sounded distinctly unenthusiastic. "You've been visiting Kate. I hope you paid her."

"Of course."

Turning his gaze on Gawaine, who managed not to

flinch at the hostility in his cold grey eyes, George Pengelly added, "Who's this?"

"Just a friend," Annis replied calmly. "He came to help me carry the bags."

"Good morning, Mr Pengelly," Gawaine said.

George Pengelly grunted. "You'd better make the most of that wool," he said to Annis. "There might not be much more."

"That would be a pity," Annis responded. "Well, we must be getting on. I have to open the shop. Come on, Gawaine."

She passed through the kissing gate, and Gawaine followed, doing his best to hide his trepidation at being on the same side of the barrier as the dogs.

But they stayed close by their owner, and George Pengelly said nothing more – only, as he and Annis headed up the track, Gawaine was aware of the farmer's gaze boring into his back until to his relief a fold of the moorland hid him and Annis from sight.

Saying goodbye to Annis, Gawaine was heading back to the hotel when he noticed the ferry manoeuvring into its place at the end of the slipway. Seff was on board, standing by the rail, easily recognisable by her bright chestnut hair and her even brighter scarlet jacket. She waved to him, and he waved back, turning down towards the harbour to meet her.

By the time Gawaine joined her, Seff had disembarked and walked up to the road, where she was talking to a man Gawaine assumed was one of the ferry crew. He was young, tall, with tangled dark hair, and neglecting his duties to have a chat with Seff was obviously giving him no trouble at all.

A couple of cars and a number of foot passengers were making their way off the ferry, while more were waiting to board. No one was paying much attention to Seff and her companion.

"So did you notice the two passengers on the eight o'clock ferry?" Seff was asking as Gawaine strolled up. She glanced at him. "Hi, Gawaine," she said, then turned her attention back to the crewman. "Would you know them again?"

"I'd know her," the crewman replied. "She was a looker, y'know?" His hands sketched a shape in the air. "Tall, blonde hair... The police reckon she might have been that girl who disappeared. They showed me a photo, but it wasn't that clear... It could have been her, I suppose."

"And the man with her?"

The crewman shrugged. "He was just a bloke. Youngish... could have been a student."

"But you didn't recognise him? He wasn't one of your regulars?"

Come on, Gawaine thought. *Tell us he was Roddy Chatham. Then we could be home and dry.*

To his disappointment, the crewman shook his head. "*I'm* not a regular," he explained. "This is just a vacation gig for me."

"Were they together?" Gawaine asked.

The crewman turned to him, his forehead creasing with his effort to remember. "Not sure," he said at last. "She was making up to him. You could see she fancied him. The bloke, yeah, he wasn't feeling any pain. He was happy enough to let her take a selfie with him."

"Selfie?" Gawaine murmured.

Seff gave him a prod in the side. "You might wind

David up like that," she said, "but it doesn't work with me. All the world and their dog knows what a selfie is. So they took a selfie together?" she asked the crewman, her gaze suddenly intensifying.

"Yeah," he replied. "Next to the rail, with the Abbey in the background."

"Interesting," Seff said. "And when the ferry docked… did they go off together?"

"Reckon not," the crewman told her. "The bloke went that way." His wide gesture could have incorporated the hotel or the Abbey – or Iris's cottage. "The girl—"

"Oi!" The shout came from the ferry. Another crewman – an older man – was standing on the ferry steps, waving. He did not look pleased. All the passengers who had been waiting had now boarded and the ferry was getting ready to leave.

"Sorry, gotta go," the crewman said. As he ran down the slipway, he glanced over his shoulder and added, "I was busy. I didn't see."

Gawaine and Seff stood side by side in silence as the ferry's car doors closed and it began to move slowly into the channel.

"Bethany's phone was terribly wet," Gawaine remarked after a moment. He was trying not to give way to the excitement that was starting to build inside him.

"These things can be fixed," Seff responded. "Gawaine, I think you had better ring the police. We might just have tracked down a photo of our murderer."

Chapter Fourteen

The oftener that we cast our reckonings up,
Our sleeps will be the sounder.
The White Devil, II.i

"So." David picked up the bottle of Chardonnay and filled three glasses. "Tell me what you got up to this morning."

Gawaine and Seff exchanged a glance. "You go first," Seff said.

David had met the others when they returned to the hotel, and all three of them were seated around a table in the restaurant. Gawaine, he was glad to see, looked livelier than he had first thing that morning, though he was in one of his thoughtful spasms, on a completely different plane of existence from mere mortals.

"Come on," David prompted, when Gawaine did not respond at once. "Give. Do we have a murderer?"

"Undoubtedly we do, my dear David," Gawaine replied. "Identifying him, however, is another matter. But we have made some progress."

He went on to describe his visit with Annis to the Pengelly farm, the extra information he had gleaned from Annis, and all that Kate Pengelly had confided about her husband George. "It seems as if Bernard White had offered him a massive bribe – Kate didn't know how much, or quite what it was for. George wasn't telling. But we can guess that George had been persuaded to surrender his lease so that St Cadoc's could take over the land. George wouldn't have to look after all those tiresome sheep any more, and when his farmhouse had been transmogrified into a pub, he would be able to continue pickling his liver at his convenience."

"The Pengellys would stay on at the farm, then?" David asked.

"There, or somewhere nearby. According to Kate, Bernard White had promised George a job and accommodation. She didn't know what sort."

"And Great Uncle Petroc got wind of this?"

Gawaine nodded. "Yes, it was Kate who told him. She was horrified, because George had made it clear that she would lose her business. Great Uncle Petroc promised to fix it, but before he could do anything, he died."

"How convenient for George," Seff commented.

"I know," Gawaine admitted, turning to her. "And if Petroc Tremayne had been walloped with the traditional blunt instrument, I might be suspicious. But he was ninety two years old, and his heart gave out."

"Unless George threatened him with the blunt instrument, and he died of fright," David suggested.

Gawaine took a meditative sip of his Chardonnay. "Possible, but really, my dear David, I think we're straying from the point."

"Which is?"

"That we need to look hard at George Pengelly for the murder of Iris Grant."

"Do you know—" David began, then broke off as the waitress appeared with three ploughman's lunches.

Once she had gone, and everything was shuffled around on the rather too small table, it was Seff who broke the silence.

"That's all very interesting," she said, cutting a wedge of cheddar, "but let's put George on hold for the moment, while I tell you what I found out this morning."

"Okay," David responded. "Go ahead."

"I went to the police station and spoke to Inspector Bradshaw," Seff began, "but he was playing his cards very close to his chest. He's sticking to the story that Iris's murder was the result of a robbery gone wrong, and I didn't tell him that I know different. He gave me the usual guff about hoping to make an early arrest, but that was all. Either he has no idea what he's doing, or he's keeping very quiet about it."

"You might have got further with Sergeant Godwin," David said.

"Oh? I didn't see him."

"Her," Gawaine said. "Inspector Bradshaw warned me off, but Sergeant Godwin seemed very happy to listen to anything I might want to tell her. I don't know what's going on between those two, but I think Sergeant Godwin is angling to make an arrest behind her superior's back."

"Can she even do that?" Seff asked, then shrugged. "Not our problem, but I'll make a point of talking to her. I did find out a bit of information," she continued. "The police have released Iris's body, and her funeral is scheduled for next Tuesday. I believe the Abbey people are arranging it."

"That might turn up something," David commented.

Gawaine looked doubtful, but said nothing.

"Anyway, never mind all that." Seff flipped a hand impatiently at David. "You want to hear what the ferry crewman just told us."

David listened with growing amazement as Seff recounted the conversation about the two passengers, and especially about the selfie the girl had taken. "Have the police managed to access the photo?" he asked.

"I phoned Sergeant Godwin," Gawaine told him. "She said that they are already working on Bethany's phone, but they haven't recovered anything yet, because of the water damage. She said she would let me know if they do." He paused, then added, "Of course, it could all be nothing. The murderer is just as likely to have been on Morgarrow all the time."

"I'm confused," David said.

Gawaine glanced at him. "My dear David, that must be so distressing for you. So unusual."

"I'll do my best to bear it."

"Moving on," Seff said repressively. "There's something else we haven't thought of. We've been fixated on the ferry, but is that the only way someone could get to the island? They might have hired a boat."

David shook his head. "I doubt it. Wouldn't that mean providing ID to the hiring place, and maybe leaving credit card details? If the murderer did come from the mainland, he wouldn't want to leave traces."

"A very good point, my dear David," Gawaine said, gazing at his glass of wine as if he might see a solution reflected in it. "But it's worth checking."

"Leave that to me," Seff said confidently. "I can go and talk to the boat hire places – though I'll be surprised if the police haven't already done that."

Gawaine sounded doubtful. "Inspector Bradshaw warned us off…"

"Of course he did." Seff gave Gawaine a pitying look. "You're an aristocratic amateur sleuth. You shouldn't exist. You don't belong in the twenty-first century. Can you wonder that you get up a hard-working copper's nose?"

Gawaine shook his head helplessly. "I am as the Good Lord made me, my dear Persephone."

If the Good Lord exists, what was he thinking? David wondered. "I'm sure he didn't intend you to get arrested," he said aloud.

"Anyway, Bradshaw hasn't warned me off," Seff asserted. "I'm just an industrious hack trying to make a living… It'll be fine."

"Meanwhile, why don't we take stock?" David suggested. "Run through all our suspects, and work out what we know."

"Good idea," Seff said. She bent to retrieve her bag, and slid out a notebook and pen. "Okay, fire ahead. I'll scribe for you."

"This is off the record," David warned her.

Seff rolled her eyes. "Thank you for that insight, David. How would I cope without you to remind me of the law of libel?"

David ignored that; he was so used to Seff Brown being annoying that there was no point in protesting. "Who do you want at the top of the list?" he asked Gawaine.

Gawaine sighed. "It has to be Roddy Chatham," he

said, though he didn't sound entirely happy about it. "He has plenty of motive: to stop Iris becoming a trustee, and possibly to acquire the cottage for his own use."

"And means," David added, while Seff scribbled diligently. "He could have filched that knitting needle from his mum."

"And he could have been the guy on the ferry," Seff finished. "As far as we know, he doesn't have an alibi for that morning. What do you think, Gawaine?"

Gawaine frowned slightly. "Of course, my dear Persephone, I have very little experience in these matters, but do you think that any woman of taste and intelligence would find Roddy Chatham sufficiently... alluring to want a selfie with him?"

"We don't know that Bethany was a woman of taste and intelligence," Seff retorted. "If you ask me, she was a ditsy teenager ready to flutter her eyelashes at any man who wasn't obviously repellent." She grinned suddenly. "We do have a man that she certainly *would* find alluring. Jake the werewolf."

David could see that Seff was joking, but Gawaine fixed an intense blue gaze on her, clearly taking her seriously. "That's very true. Perhaps you should put him on the list."

Seff let out a long sigh. "Come on, Gawaine. Jake Fletcher has no motive. I don't buy this stalker theory. That's not him at all. And if it was Jake, why a knitting needle, for goodness sake?"

"That does pose a difficulty," Gawaine admitted. "And I suppose if he had been on the island, he's famous enough for someone to have recognised him."

"Not necessarily," Seff said, frowning thoughtfully.

"He hasn't really got going on the celebrity circuit yet. His movie is only just out and his character – the were as opposed to the wolf – has a shaggy black wig."

"What about his alibi?" David asked. "Isn't he filming somewhere?"

"Yes, in the Lake District," Seff replied. "Lots of rocks and mountains…"

"And lakes," Gawaine put in.

"And lakes. And the odd castle. Real werewolf country. If Jake had disappeared off the set for a couple of days, he would certainly have been missed."

"Let's get on," David interrupted, afraid the conference was going to dissolve into pointless speculation. "You know, that guy on the ferry could have nothing to do with this at all. There are far more likely suspects. What about Bernard White?"

Gawaine nodded to him, acknowledging the change of subject. "The same motive as Roddy Chatham. And his wife knits; Annis collected some wool she ordered from Kate Pengelly."

"Then should she go on the list?" Seff asked swiftly.

"Maybe, but it's doubtful. She has grandchildren; would she have the strength?" Gawaine took another sip of his wine. "Besides, we don't know whether she had any idea about what her husband was plotting, or whether she would have approved of it if she had."

"And we've no idea what either of them was doing on the morning Iris was killed," David pointed out.

"True. Although Annis told me that Iris phoned Bernard White the night before, to tell him she was going to live on the island." Gawaine allowed himself a faintly feline smile. "It wouldn't be beyond the bounds of possibility that he visited her the next morning to have it out with her."

"I like Bernard White," Seff said, ending her notes with a flourish. "He was an utter snake that day when the will was read. But I like George Pengelly, too. What about him?"

"A man without the guts to commit a murder," Gawaine replied, "at least, according to his wife, and who would know if she didn't? He might be capable of the kind of behaviour that makes an affray outside the pub, but Iris's death strikes me as a bit too subtle."

"You said he spends the morning wandering around with his dogs," Seff reminded him. "That means he has no alibi, and he could easily have wandered over in this direction."

"But would Iris have let him in?" Gawaine asked. "And what did he do with his dogs?"

"He had motive," David pointed out. "The development wouldn't happen while Iris owned the island. He didn't know – none of them knew – that she was only a caretaker until she could hand it over to the Abbey. And he had access to a knitting needle."

Gawaine murmured agreement, though he didn't look too sure. "There are two other people we should add to the list," he said, sounding reluctant. "Elaine Chatham… and Annis Radford."

"He likes Annis," David told Seff. "And her cat."

Gawaine gave him what was surely intended to be a filthy look, though it failed miserably.

"Surely we can discount Elaine Chatham," Seff said. "We wouldn't think twice about her, if it wasn't for the knitting."

"And the possibility that she would benefit from the development," Gawaine reminded her. "But I agree she's unlikely. And I should be extremely surprised if she wasn't up at St Morwenna's at that time in the morning, making breakfast for her brood of students."

"We can easily check that," David said, then added, "Annis is a different matter. She has motive: the cottage. Her place is awash with knitting needles. And she has the best opportunity of anyone, being Iris's friend and living next door."

He felt a pang of guilt to see how unhappy Gawaine was looking, but he knew it had to be said.

"And there we are." Seff finished writing, flicked through her notes, then tore the pages out of her notebook and presented them to Gawaine. "There's a murderer on that list."

"Thank you, my dear Persephone." Gawaine was looking abstracted again. "I'm sure we've done what Sergeant Godwin would call 'useful work'. But there are some points we haven't considered."

"Oh – what are they?" David asked. "I think we've been pretty thorough."

"Indeed we have," Gawaine agreed, "when you consider our suspects. But we haven't given a thought to Iris herself."

"What do you mean?"

"Well, Seff, you said she'd been particularly edgy since her great uncle died. We have no idea why. And we don't know what drove her to let herself into the Abbey grounds at midnight. What was she doing there?"

"But surely that can't have anything to do with who killed her," Seff objected.

Gawaine blinked unhappily. "Perhaps not, and yet... And there's something else," he added.

"What now?" David asked.

"The spiders, my dear David. We really ought not to forget about the spiders."

Chapter Fifteen

Oh, I am in a mist!

The White Devil, V.vi

David Powers sat on the low wall that surrounded the Abbey precinct, enjoying the sunshine and listening to a rousing hymn coming from the building. Gawaine, he assumed, was in there somewhere, it being Sunday morning. Certainly he was nowhere to be found at the hotel.

Their discussion with Seff the day before had seemed to clear the decks, but David didn't feel that they had made much progress in finding out who had strangled Iris Grant. The whole affair of Bethany Fox, he felt, was a massive red herring.

We don't even know she's dead. Maybe she went off with the chap on the ferry. And why was Gawaine wittering on about spiders? David added to himself. *Spiders have nothing to do with this.*

And yet, he had to admit, there had been other times when Gawaine had latched on to some apparently irrelevant detail which later proved to be the pivot of the case.

The singing had stopped. The main doors of the Abbey swung open and the congregation began to emerge. There was quite a crowd, more than David had expected, and at first he couldn't see Gawaine.

He spotted Bernard White, conspicuous because of his height. A woman was with him; David assumed she was his wife. She was so small and looked so frail that David immediately crossed her off the list of suspects.

Elaine Chatham followed them out, surrounded by a gaggle of young people David supposed were her students at St Morwenna's. She exchanged a cheery greeting with the Whites, then headed for the gate. Spotting David, she veered across to him.

"David! How lovely to see you! Did you enjoy the service?"

"I wasn't actually in church," David responded.

"Oh, you missed a treat." Elaine seemed quite unfazed by having inadvertently confronted an atheist. "Jenny preaches so well. Anyway, you must come to lunch. Come along – I'm not going to take no for an answer."

"Thank you, but I'm waiting for Gawaine."

"Then you must bring him as well. Such a nice young man! Come up as soon as you're ready."

"Thank you," David repeated, as Elaine retreated, shawls a-flutter, surrounded by her entourage.

Scanning the crowd again, David noticed Seff, emerging from the Abbey in deep conversation with an older man and woman he had never set eyes on before. She saw David and waved to him, but stayed with her companions, heading out through the gate and down towards the village.

I wonder what all that is about, David thought.

Finally Gawaine appeared as the last of the crowd

began to disperse, and strolled across with a more relaxed air than David had seen for several days.

"I'm sorry for keeping you waiting," he said. "I wanted to speak to Father Magnus, but he seemed to be too busy. I get the feeling that he's trying to avoid me."

"Maybe he thinks you're going to bug him about Iris and the keys."

"In that case, my dear David, he would be entirely correct. I do want to er... bug him." Gawaine gave an elegant shrug. "Still, he will keep."

"By the way," David said, detaching himself from the wall, "you have a fan."

"A fan?" Gawaine made a slight waving motion with one hand.

"No, a *fan*. An admirer."

Gawaine's brows went up. "Really? Who?"

"Elaine Chatham," David replied. "She thinks you're – and I quote – such a nice young man."

Gawaine looked briefly embarrassed, then allowed himself a smug smile. "She is evidently a woman of impeccable taste."

"Hmm. I'll stick with 'dotty old dear', myself. Anyway, she's invited us both to lunch up at St Morwenna's."

One of the students was hovering by the door when Gawaine and David arrived at St Morwenna's. "Hi," she said. "I'm Sophie. Chattie – Mrs Chatham – told me to look out for you. It's this way."

Gawaine and David followed her down a long passage and into the dining room. It was long and narrow, wood panelled half way up the walls, with dim portraits of

Victorian grandees hanging above. The dining table and chairs looked as if they might have been filched from some long-ago committee room.

In the midst of all this stifling formality, the room was filled with lively activity. Students were fetching plates of food from a kitchen hatch at the far end, while others were finding themselves seats around the table.

Elaine Chatham bore down on them as soon as they set foot inside the door. "There you are! It's lovely to see you. Sophie, dear, find them seats and introduce them."

David had expected that Gawaine would slip into his usual affected social manner as Sophie guided them to a couple of seats. Unexpectedly he seemed relaxed, even looking forward to the encounter.

"That's Tom," Sophie said, indicating a chunky redhead sitting opposite, with a face covered in freckles and a friendly grin. "And that's Nathan." He was tall and lanky, with dreadlocks stretching almost to his waist. "And next to Nathan is Grace."

In contrast to Sophie, who was small and fair, Grace was taller and looked athletic; her dark hair was cut in a thick fringe across her forehead. David thought she would have looked magnificent on a horse.

Sophie took a seat beside David, while servers appeared and plonked down plates of roast beef and Yorkshire pudding. David was mildly surprised; he had been expecting something much more abstemious than these heaping plates.

"Chattie's cooking," Tom said. "We all do our stint in the kitchen, of course, but she's in charge."

Meanwhile most people had found their seats, and

Elaine Chatham, at the head of the table, achieved silence by tinkling her fork against a glass. "Jenny, dear, would you say Grace?"

Jenny Morland, opposite her at the foot of the table, rose and obliged, and added a prayer for Bethany. "Dear Lord, take care of her," she finished, "and bring her safe home."

"There's not much hope of that," Sophie said with a sigh.

"I half expected that Bethany wouldn't come back," Tom said. "We heard that you found her bag on the cliff, and if it wasn't for that, I'd have thought she'd just decided to give up on us."

"She obviously wasn't happy here," Nathan agreed. "I don't think she would have seen the year out."

"She meant to stay for a year?" Gawaine asked.

Tom, ingesting a large segment of Yorkshire pudding, merely nodded.

"She was doing her gap year," Sophie explained. "At least, that was the idea. Quite a few people do that. Others come in their long vac – this is my third time."

"So why was Bethany unhappy?" David thought that the students seemed to be a cheerful and welcoming bunch. "Nobody was unkind to her, surely?"

"No, we're all lovely," Nathan replied with a grin. "I just think Bethany had got the wrong idea about what we do here."

"In what way?" David prompted.

"She thought it was all going to be worship songs and falling in love with Jesus," Sophie said, a sarcastic edge to her voice. "She couldn't get her head around Abbey life."

"Yeah, it was Father Magnus who set things up," Tom put in. "And he's more Catholic than the Pope."

Gawaine seemed uninterested in this nugget of information, his gaze still turned on Sophie. "You didn't like Bethany?"

"I didn't *dislike* her," Sophie told him. "And I was certainly never nasty to her. But she was very young. I mean, she was only eighteen, but she was younger than that in how she behaved. And I suspect she'd been Daddy's little princess. She didn't want to work. She couldn't see the point of stitching kneelers when she wanted a big emotional experience."

"Who sweeps a room as for thy laws makes that and the action fine," Gawaine murmured.

Nathan gave Gawaine an approving nod, though David suspected that the sentiment was not original. "She really didn't like the prayer rota," Nathan continued. "Especially if she had an early shift. She was always trying to swap, or get someone else to do it for her."

"Prayer rota?" Gawaine asked.

"Oh, we have two people praying in the Lady Chapel from after the first service of the day until the beginning of the last one. We all do an hour. There are enough of us that we only have to do it once a day, and maybe not as often as that."

"And Bethany didn't want to?" David asked.

Sophie shook her head, then said, "Oh, here we all are badmouthing Bethany, and it's really not fair. She was sweet. It's just that this was the wrong place for her."

"So why was she here?"

Grace, who had been working her way steadily

through her plate of roast beef, raised her head. "I think she had a crush on Iris."

"On *Iris*?" Gawaine repeated, while David said, "Did she know Iris?"

"Oh, yes," Tom replied. "Did no one tell you? Bethany used to be one of Iris's students. She'd just finished her art A Levels."

"She came here over the Easter weekend," Grace continued. "Just to have a look at us, and see if she liked us. Iris was here, and she ran an art workshop in the Abbey. We made banners for the Easter Sunday service."

"Yeah, it was *brilliant*." Nathan's eyes lit with enthusiasm. "They were mostly old sheets and broom handles and poster paints, and they turned out *awesome*."

"We stored them in the crypt afterwards," Sophie said. "You should go and have a look."

"Trouble was," said Tom, "Bethany must have got the idea that it was like that all the time, and it's just not."

Nathan nodded agreement. "She hadn't been here long when she went off to visit her parents. As Tom said, we were surprised that she came back."

"Better if she hadn't," Sophie said, her eyes dark and sombre. "She must have been caught in the storm and swept off the cliff into the sea."

"We don't know that," Grace said. "She could still turn up."

Tom shook his head, though he didn't object out loud.

"Maybe you could find out what happened to her," Sophie suggested to Gawaine. "We know you're looking into Iris's murder. Chattie told us all about you."

"Yeah, that would be great," Nathan said, his eyes lighting with enthusiasm. "Do the Poirot thing."

Gawaine murmured something inaudible, embarrassed as always when anyone mentioned his reputation. Besides, as David well knew, his role model was Sherlock Holmes.

"Shut up, Nathan, you idiot," Sophie said, and added to Gawaine, "We don't want to bug you. But if there's anything we can do to help, you only have to ask. We all liked Iris. It's terrible, what happened to her."

Gawaine nodded, briefly thoughtful. "There may be something," he said eventually. "Could you just talk about the Abbey? Tell me what goes on here – specifically on the day of the storm?"

"Sure, no problem," Tom said. "Jenny opened up that day at about seven thirty, like every morning. She usually takes the early service, which starts at eight. It finishes at around eight thirty, and then the first pair on the prayer rota would take themselves off into the Lady Chapel, and the rest of us who were at the service would come back here for breakfast."

Nathan let out a long, replete sigh. "Chattie's breakfasts," he murmured. "You haven't lived…"

"That wasn't all of you at the service?" Gawaine asked, looking up and down the table. "I was there, and I didn't think there were so many."

"No, not everybody," Sophie said. "We're all supposed to attend one service every day, but it doesn't matter which one we pick. Except for Sunday morning. There's no eight o'clock that day, but the ten o'clock is High Mass, with all the bells and whistles."

"Bells and smells," Nathan corrected her. "I swing a mean thurible."

"Yes, we're all trained servers," Sophie said. "And then on Sunday afternoon there's a kids' service. Grace usually helps with that. She's good with the little moppets."

Grace looked up from her plate and showed teeth. "They fear me."

"Anyway, to get back to the day of the storm," Tom continued, "I didn't go to the service, but I got there just after. I was in the vestry, photocopying flyers for our next fundraiser, and Grace was on greeting duty, welcoming any pilgrims and telling them about the Abbey. And there were a few more of us, doing cleaning and what have you."

"And then the wind got up, there was a massive clap of thunder, and the rain came drumming down," Grace said. "I was out in the cloister, explaining the carvings on the pillars to some academic guy from Cambridge, and I could hardly hear myself speak. And then we started to get people coming in to shelter."

"Were there many?" David asked. He had no idea where Gawaine was going with this, but he felt he ought to do his bit and keep the conversation rolling along.

Grace shook her head. "It was a bit early. Hardly anyone comes across on the eight o'clock ferry, and of course we know now that there were no others until the afternoon."

"So anyone in the Abbey that day must have been staying on the island?" Gawaine said.

"Right. There's the hotel, and lots of the villagers do B and B," Tom told him.

"I saw a guy in the cloister," Grace continued. "He'd managed to get there in the dry, at least. I told him he was welcome to come into the church." She paused, rolling her eyes. "Then I saw him a bit later, with his feet up on a pew, smoking a spliff."

Gawaine looked confused. "Spliff?"

"Weed," David explained with a sigh of exasperation. "Marijuana. Illegal substances."

"Yeah, some people have no idea what a church is for," Tom put in. "Grace, do you remember the birdwatcher? Came in absolutely soaked, moaning about his camera."

"Yes, and why wasn't there a cup of tea," Grace said. "At least, when I tackled spliff guy, he put it out and put his feet down. Called me 'girlie' and told me I was cute." She snorted. "I don't do cute."

"But we love you anyway," said Nathan.

Gawaine was looking thoughtful as he and David left the Community and headed down the track towards the hotel. "If Bethany was the girl on the ferry…" he began.

David, replete and looking forward to an afternoon with his feet up, found it a struggle to focus his thoughts on the missing girl.

"…and she must have been, because otherwise how did her bag end up half way down the cliff," Gawaine continued, "then she disappeared somewhere between the harbour and St Morwenna's. That doesn't give her – or us – much scope."

"Sophie said she must have walked up the cliff path and got swept into the sea when the storm hit."

Gawaine winced, clearly not liking that picture. Then

as he went on David realised that he wasn't just being squeamish.

"The timing is all wrong. Think of it. The ferry would dock at about eight fifteen. Say eight twenty by the time she says goodbye to her *inamorato*. The wind got up at about a quarter to nine. Twenty-five minutes. If she walked up the cliff path she should have been safe in St Morwenna's by then."

David saw his point. "We could walk it. Time it."

"We could."

By this time they had almost reached the Abbey. Gawaine turned as if to go back, then halted, rigid. "I'd forgotten..." he whispered. All colour had drained from his face; his eyes were wide and haunted.

"What's the matter?" David asked.

"I think I heard her die." Gawaine's voice was hoarse; he swallowed and tried again. "The morning of the storm, I was coming out of the Abbey when I heard a cry coming from the cliffs. I went over there and looked, but I couldn't see anything, and I thought it must have been a seagull. Then the storm started, and I headed back." His hands clenched. "If only I'd had a better look..."

"That's nonsense," David said, deliberately harsh. "Once she went over, there wouldn't be anything you could do. Besides, it might have really been a seagull. Didn't you say that you found Bethany's bag much further down, nearer the village?"

Gawaine shrugged uneasily. "That doesn't mean anything. Given the wind and the rough sea..." He stood still, irresolute, looking utterly miserable.

"Let's think about this," David said. "This has to be the

guy on the ferry, right? And he'd have a reason to kill Bethany, because she's seen him, and she'd suspect he'd killed Iris."

"But Iris isn't dead yet," Gawaine objected; he looked slightly more animated, as David had known he would once presented with a puzzle.

"No, of course not. But once word got out... The ferry guy has only one chance to deal with Bethany, before she gets back to St Morwenna's. So he follows her up the cliff path and shoves her over. *Then* he goes back to the village and kills Iris."

"A busy morning..." Gawaine blinked thoughtfully. "Could he have done it in the time?"

"That's what we're going to find out. Come on, show me where you heard this cry."

David followed Gawaine as he trekked around the outside of the Abbey precinct until they reached the cliff path. Glancing around, he spotted the sharp rocks below and the massive outcrop of boulders that cut off the view of the village and the harbour.

"A nice sheltered spot," he remarked. "Ideal for a quick murder."

Gawaine shivered. "Don't."

David slid out his mobile phone. "Okay, I'm going to call you," he said. "You go back to where you were when you heard the cry, and let me know when you're ready. I'll head for Iris's cottage, and you need to tell me when you think the rain would have started. We'll see if I manage to get there in time."

Gawaine nodded. "That should work. I'll walk through what I did that morning," he said. "It will help me with the timing."

He headed off, back to the far side of the Abbey, while David called him on his phone. A moment later he heard Gawaine say, "Right. Now."

David set off, walking briskly, resisting the impulse to run. *He wouldn't run. Nothing draws the attention like someone running. Besides, we know that he had to get to the cottage before the rain started, but he didn't.*

Gawaine's voice came again over the phone as David was heading past the hotel garden. "It's raining now."

David halted. He wasn't sure whether he was glad or sorry that their theory had been disproved. "Nowhere near," he told Gawaine. "I'm just passing the hotel."

"So the murderer couldn't have killed both women. That wasn't the cry I heard." Even over the phone David could hear the relief in Gawaine's voice. "Except that Bethany might have died by accident," he added a moment later, worried again. "That cliff edge isn't stable."

"It still leaves us with the problem of timing, though," David reminded him. "If Bethany walked up from the ferry, she should have been long past the point where you heard the cry." When Gawaine did not respond, he added, "Sometimes a seagull is only a seagull."

"Hmm…" There was scepticism in Gawaine's voice as he rang off.

Chapter Sixteen

For women's resolutions, in such deeds,
Like bees, light oft on flowers, and oft on weeds.
The Devil's Law Case, I.i

After breakfast on the following morning, David retreated to the hotel lounge with an extra cup of coffee, hoping for half an hour to relax before he went back to his room to work. Seff was sitting near the window, doing something journalistic on her tablet; she looked up as David took the seat beside her.

"What happened to you yesterday?" he asked. "I saw you leaving the church with some random couple."

"They weren't a random couple," Seff replied. "They were a source of information."

Before David had the chance to respond to that, Gawaine appeared from the stairs that led to the bedrooms, drifted into the dining room, then drifted out a moment later with a mug of coffee. He sank into the armchair next to David and let out a long sigh.

"Seff is going to tell us about her latest conquest," David told him. "If you're awake enough."

Gawaine waved a hand. "Please proceed, my dear Persephone."

"I want to tell you about the boat hire people first," Seff

said, closing up her tablet. "Not that there's much to tell. I tracked down four different firms, and none of them hired out any boats on the morning Iris was killed. They could see there was a massive storm coming. They hired some out in the afternoon, once it was all over, but that's far too late to be any use to us."

"But it's useful to know that," Gawaine murmured. "It closes off one possibility. That means that the murderer was already on the island, or he came over on the eight o'clock ferry."

"Good," David said. "That settles that. So, Seff," he continued, "who were those people you met at church?"

"Their names are Geoff Carter and his wife Megan," Seff began. "Yesterday I shared a pew with them. They run the local supermarket, and they invited me to Sunday lunch."

Gawaine was perking up with the aid of the cup of coffee. "That sounds promising. Can I assume that they're plugged in to all the local gossip?"

"They are indeed," Seff replied. "And more than that, they know Bethany. Megan said she used to come to the supermarket almost every day to buy chocolate. Comfort food, Megan said. She thought she was unhappy up at St Morwenna's."

David exchanged a glance with Gawaine. That confirmed what the students had told them at lunch the day before; they hadn't thought that Bethany would stick it out for the full year.

"I don't think the Carters approve of St Morwenna's," Seff went on. "Geoff said that the students hang out behind the supermarket for half the night, messing around and leaving litter."

Gawaine blinked, confused. "I thought the Community lot would have better things to do with their time," he said. "You would hardly come to work in the Abbey for a year, or even for your long vacation, if you were looking for ways to make a nuisance of yourself."

David nodded agreement. "Maybe it's the local kids, but Geoff prefers to think it's the incomers."

"Whatever," Seff said. "They rattled his cage the other night, when someone kicked over their bin and set their dog off. And listen – this is where it gets really interesting – Bethany was in the shop the morning of the storm. Megan must have been the last person to see her before she disappeared."

Gawaine sat erect, narrowly managing not to spill his coffee. "She's sure?"

"Quite sure. Bethany came in just after they opened, and said she'd come off the ferry. She bought a chocolate bar, and Megan told her to hurry back to St Morwenna's, because she thought it was going to rain."

"But to get from the supermarket to St Morwenna's, she would have to pass Iris's cottage," David said.

He glanced at Gawaine, to see his friend's gaze fixed and brilliant. "She knew Iris…" Gawaine breathed out.

"She did?" Seff put in sharply.

"Bethany was one of Iris's students," David explained quickly, reluctant to break Gawaine's concentration. "That's how she came to join the Community."

"She knew Iris," Gawaine repeated, "the storm was coming, and she had to pass the cottage."

"You think she went in?" Seff said.

"She might have."

"That makes sense. She was certainly in the right place at the right time," David responded.

"Or the wrong time." Gawaine relaxed, frowning. "Wait a minute. Let's work it out. The ferry would dock at about eight fifteen, Bethany goes to the supermarket, buys her chocolate, then heads up the road... She would reach the cottage at – oh, about eight twenty-five. Long before Iris was killed. She rings the bell, Iris answers, lets her in—"

"Hang on, that doesn't work," David interrupted. "That means Bethany would have been there when the murderer arrived."

"If the guy on the ferry was the murderer," Seff added, "then he would have been already there. And he would hardly have killed Iris in front of Bethany."

"Then maybe Iris didn't let Bethany in." Gawaine was looking more confused than ever. "If Bernard White, say, was tackling her about the Abbey Trust, she wouldn't have felt like exchanging small talk with Bethany. So Bethany went on, up to St Morwenna's... And her delay in the supermarket would put her on the cliff path at about the time I heard that cry."

"So maybe it was an accident." Seff had begun to sound irritated. "*Something* must have happened, but how can we find out what? It's like a knot where you can't find the ends."

"A Gordian knot," Gawaine murmured. "Yes, my dear Persephone, you're right. Something happened. Did Bethany meet the murderer, or... There is another possibility." His voice shook on the last couple of words.

"You mean, do we put her on our list?" David said.

"Oh, that's—" Seff had obviously been about to say 'nonsense', then thought better of it. "Then where is she now?" she asked.

"I have absolutely no idea," Gawaine replied.

David had just drained the last of his coffee and decided reluctantly that he had frittered away enough of the morning when he saw the outer doors of the hotel swing open; a man entered and approached the reception desk.

"Good grief!" Seff exclaimed, half rising from her seat and then sinking back again.

"Is that someone you know?" Gawaine asked.

"Unfortunately, I do," Seff replied. "That's Jake Fletcher. Jake the werewolf, Iris's ex. Has he actually bothered to turn up for Iris's funeral?"

"Goodness!" Gawaine leaned forward, fixing Jake with a curious stare. "I hope we all have our crosses and garlic ready."

"Garlic is *vampires*," David pointed out. "For werewolves you need a silver bullet."

"And an ancient blunderbuss," Gawaine said, rapt. "Or would a catapult work?"

"Hmm..." David was sceptical. "It depends if you have to penetrate the skin—"

"Or fur."

"As you say, or fur. I think—"

"Can't you two shut up?" Seff said, exasperated. "I want to listen."

The wall separating the lounge from the reception area was made of glass panels, and the doors stood open, giving a good view of what was going on. David took a closer look at the newcomer; Jake Fletcher was tall, fair and very sleek. His designer suit had a black armband tacked to the sleeve of his jacket. His shirt was open at the neck, and David caught a glimpse of a gold chain.

"I'm sorry, sir," the receptionist – who happened to be the hotel manager – was saying. "We're fully booked."

"Oh, come on!" Jake exclaimed. "Don't you know who I am?"

The manager was unimpressed. "Yes, sir," she said. "You're someone who didn't make a reservation. If you like to take a seat in the lounge, I'll send you some tea and ring round to see if I can find you a B and B."

Jake Fletcher's remark about tea made Gawaine wince. "Make it a Scotch," he said, and stalked through into the lounge, leaving his wheeled suitcase for some minion to deal with.

"Hi, Jake," Seff said.

Jake halted, staring. "I might have known I'd find you here." His tone was truculent, but when Seff refused to rise to the bait he threw himself into an empty chair. Seff introduced David and Gawaine, but Jake didn't seem to be paying much attention.

"Can you believe this dump?" he demanded. "I could *buy* this crummy hotel, and they can't even find me a room!"

Gawaine leaned across and murmured into David's ear. "I hadn't realised that that the pay for impersonating werewolves was quite that high."

David shrugged. "Who can say?" At a rough guess, he thought, Jake was flinging himself into the role of movie star; his performance might have been effective on the boulevards of Hollywood or the beaches of Barbados, but it cut very little ice on Morgarrow. The local demand for teen werewolf movies was probably not that high.

Meanwhile, one of the hotel waiters had appeared with Jake Fletcher's Scotch; he tossed it off and slammed the glass back on the tray. "Get me another."

"So what are you doing here, Jake?" Seff asked when the waiter had gone. "I thought you were filming."

"I am," Jake replied. "But they gave me a couple of days off for Iris's funeral. Why else would I be here?"

"Well, since you and Iris weren't together…"

Jake waved a hand dismissively. "Oh, that would have all blown over," he said. "I know what you chicks are like. You never say what you mean. I know if Iris hadn't died, she would have been begging me to take her back."

Seff's eyes narrowed. David guessed that she was trying very hard not to explode. Her voice was even when she spoke at last. "I don't think that you knew Iris at all."

"Hey, I lived with Iris!" Jake protested. "We were going to get married. We—" He broke off. "I just thought of something," he went on after a moment. "I could stay in Iris's cottage. It's not like she needs it any more."

Seff cast an exasperated look at David and Gawaine. *Can you believe this guy?* "I don't think the police have finished," she said. "It's a crime scene."

"Oh, I'm sure we can sort something out," Jake said. "After all, the cottage is mine now."

David shot an astonished glance at Gawaine; his friend was gazing at Jake with an expression of intense interest.

"What do you mean, it's yours now?" Seff asked.

"Iris left it to me," Jake replied, in a tone that suggested

Seff should have expected nothing else. "When we got engaged, we both made wills, leaving what we had to each other. Iris would have done very well if I'd been the one to die," he added complacently.

"How nice for her," Seff said waspishly. "In any case," she continued, "all that is irrelevant. Iris made a new will, the day before she died."

"We witnessed it," David said.

"But she – why would she do that to me?" Jake sounded honestly bewildered.

"Because it was over, Jake." Seff's tone suggested that she was talking to a mentally challenged three year old. "You weren't together any more. Iris had moved on."

"Moved on?" Jake's eyes narrowed as his gaze flicked from David to Gawaine and back again. "You mean she was with one of you guys?"

Seff gave an exaggerated sigh. "Believe it or not, Jake, there are ways of moving on that don't involve a man. Iris intended to move down here, and make a living from her art. She left the island to St Cadoc's and the cottage to Annis Radford. I'm sure you could come to hear the will read tomorrow after the funeral, if you don't believe me."

"Annis..." Jake still sounded confused. "Oh, yeah, the chick with the wool shop. But she has a cottage. Why does she want another one?"

"You would have to ask her that."

"I feel—" Jake broke off as the waiter appeared with his second Scotch; he took the glass and stared moodily into its depths. "I feel sick. Just sick," he went on. "I thought we had something, Iris and me. And we had great times in that little cottage. Memories, y'know?"

"My heart bleeds," Seff said.

Jake looked up, injured. "There's no need to be like that. Hey, Seff," he went on a moment later, sounding suddenly enthusiastic, "why don't I give you an interview? All the stuff about Iris and me. How I'm down here trying to recapture the great times we had together – the movie star and the unknown little artist. It would be a great career move for both of us."

"Sorry," Seff snapped. "I don't do the wildlife column."

Before Jake could respond, the hotel manager came through from reception, to stand beside his chair and hold out a sheet of paper. "Your B and B, sir," she said. "That's the address. Go straight down the main street, across the square, and it's the first house on the right."

Jake took the paper with a muttered, "Thanks."

"There you are, all sorted," Seff said brightly. "Off you go, Jake. We'll see you at the funeral tomorrow."

Chapter Seventeen

> I do love these ancient ruins.
> We never tread upon them but we set
> Our foot upon some reverend history.
> *The Duchess of Malfi*, V.iii

Once Jake Fletcher had grumbled off towards his Bed and Breakfast, David and Seff departed to their separate work. Left at a loose end, Gawaine wandered up to St Cadoc's. He wasn't sure what to do next, or how to make sense of his tangle of suspects, as unyielding as the Gordian knot, or a skein of yarn that had received the attentions of the cat Merino.

With no service taking place, the building seemed vaster and bleaker than ever, the few people in there ant-like in proportion. The two students on the prayer rota were on their knees in the Lady Chapel; a few other people, unknown to Gawaine, were wandering about, some of them with one of the leaflets relating the history of the Abbey. At the far end of the nave were set trestles and tall wooden candle stands, in readiness for Iris's coffin.

There was one spot of colour in the whole of the Abbey, in front of the pulpit, where a woman was arranging flowers: a mass of roses and lilies and trailing sprays of greenery. As he approached, Gawaine recognised the small, fragile woman he had seen in church on the previous day, alongside Bernard White; he assumed she was his wife.

She must have heard his footsteps, for as he drew closer she turned to him and smiled. "Good morning. You're one of Iris's friends, aren't you?"

Gawaine introduced himself.

"I'm Claudia White," the woman said, holding out a hand. "Bernard White's wife." She paused, setting another lily into her arrangement, then added, "It's terrible, about poor Iris. They tell me it was you who found her. That must have been such a shock."

"It was," Gawaine agreed.

"She had so much to offer the island," Mrs White went on. "And she was so young. Bernard is particularly upset, because – you might not know this, but they didn't part friends."

"I realised that," Gawaine responded. He also realised that Mrs White wanted to talk, and all she needed from him was a slight nudge. "Most regrettable."

"I'm sure they could have sorted out their differences," Mrs White said. "Bernard only wanted to develop Morgarrow for the sake of the Abbey, and the people. I don't think Iris would have objected if she'd really understood what he was proposing. It would all be most tasteful, and in character with the island."

Mrs White clearly hasn't seen the Morgarrow Moor brochure, Gawaine thought, while murmuring sympathetically.

"I know Bernard can be a bit short," Claudia White continued. "He was so exasperated with Iris, especially that night when she rang up and said that she was going to make her home here. He was so furious he rang Roddy Chatham and George Pengelly right away, and arranged a meeting for the following morning. So unnecessary, I thought. All he needed to do was wait a while for tempers to cool, and then talk it out with Iris over a cup of tea. But there—" She sighed. "That's Bernard all over."

"That would have been the morning of the storm?" Gawaine asked, all his senses twitching. "The meeting?"

"Yes, and they both arrived soaking wet," Mrs White said. "Trailing mud and water all over my carpets and furniture. And Bernard was just as bad," she added. "He was pottering about in the garden after breakfast, and he came in drenched."

Very interesting, Gawaine thought. *So Roddy Chatham was on the island that morning. I wonder if he spent the night here, or came across on the ferry. George Pengelly was in the village, too, and if they were both wet they arrived after the storm started. Either of them could have been in Iris's cottage committing murder.*

While he was cogitating, Mrs White had continued setting flowers in her arrangement, picking them out of a large cardboard box that lay open beside the flower stand.

"Gawaine, dear, I wonder if you could do me a favour," she said at last. "I need two more vases, but they're down in the crypt, and I'm really nervous about tackling the stairs. I'd be so grateful if you could fetch them for me."

"Of course," Gawaine said, slightly disconcerted to be addressed as 'Gawaine dear'. "Where do I go?"

"The stairs are over there," Mrs White said, pointing. "When you get down, you'll see an enormous wooden cupboard. The vases are in there – I need the two big brass ones. Oh, that's so good of you!"

Gawaine headed in the direction she had indicated, and came to a flight of steps leading down into darkness. A sign saying 'Do Not Enter' was attached to a rope stretched across the opening. Gawaine unhooked the rope and pressed a light switch at the top of the stairs; to his relief a sickly yellow light shone out below, enough for him to see where he was going.

The steps were stone, worn away in the middle and slippery from centuries of feet. Gawaine wasn't surprised that Mrs White hadn't wanted to make the descent. He wasn't too keen on it himself, clinging to the rope fixed to iron rings along the wall as he edged his way downwards.

As soon as he reached the crypt he saw the cupboard, stretching almost all the way across the far wall. It was made of dark wood, crumbling away in places, obviously a massive refuge for woodworm, spiders and mice.

More ecclesiastical paraphernalia was ranged around the walls: flower stands, candle holders, a massive wooden cross that probably belonged in a Good Friday procession, and a number of banners. Some of those, Gawaine realised, must be the ones that the students had made with Iris; a couple of plastic crates of art materials were stacked beside them.

Even in the dim light the banners glowed with colour: sunbursts, peacocks, butterflies and every kind of flower, a whole world singing the joy of the Resurrection. Gawaine bowed his head for a moment and murmured a prayer for Iris, that she had at last found that joy.

Then he turned his attention to the cupboard.

Swinging open the first set of doors he was confronted with a collection of mouldering sheet music, piles of tatty hymnbooks, something that might once have been an altarcloth before several generations of mice had brought up their young among its folds. No brass vases.

Gawaine moved on to the next set of doors. This part of the cupboard was obviously vase storage; one shelf was filled with smaller ones, while in the larger space at the bottom were the two brass vases that Claudia White needed. He pulled them out, resolutely ignoring something that scuttled away at the movement.

He was closing the doors again when his attention was caught by the items on the shelves above the vases: a pair of tarnished brass candlesticks; more candle holders of various sizes and shapes; numerous small boxes of wood or metal; a couple of incense boats; statuettes of angels or the Virgin Mary; several crosses on stands. Each of them bore a small paper disc, inscribed with a number in spidery Victorian script.

Odd, Gawaine thought, looking more closely. In the space at the bottom where he had found the vases, there were two pictures, each with its own paper disc. His interest quickened, only to wither again when he saw what the pictures were: one a valiant attempt to render *The Light of the World* in crewel wool, patchy now from the attentions of the mice, one an early photograph so stained and faded that it was impossible to tell what the subject had been.

Closing the doors, he turned away, then still pricked by curiosity turned back and opened up the third and last section of the cupboard. Here the shelves were crammed with an array of similar objects, also labelled with paper discs. He wondered why they were stored here; none of them seemed to have any particular value.

Realising that he had poked around for too long, Gawaine closed the cupboard up again and transported the two vases back up the stairs to where Mrs White was finishing off her first arrangement. He breathed a sigh of relief that he had managed to carry out his task without breaking his neck.

"Tell me, Mrs White," he began, when her effusive thanks were over, "what are all the things stored in that cupboard, the ones with little paper discs attached?"

Claudia White smiled. "Oh, those are such a trial to Bernard!" she exclaimed. "They're votive offerings, mostly Victorian. He would like to make a bonfire of the lot, but of course, you can't do that, can you, not when they were given to St Cadoc's?"

"I suppose not," Gawaine murmured.

"Mind you, don't go thinking there's anything valuable. We have been through them. There was a nice Communion set, silver, and of course we use that, but the rest…"

An idea was beginning to grow in Gawaine's mind. "And the discs?" he asked.

"Oh, those are catalogue numbers," Mrs White told him, "although I think the catalogue must have disappeared years ago. If you're interested, Father Magnus might know something about it. He's writing a history of St Cadoc's, so he has all the documents."

Saying goodbye to Mrs White, Gawaine went out and sat on the Abbey precinct wall in the sunlight, thinking.

Iris was down in the crypt, storing her banners and her art materials. Might she have seen something in that cupboard...

He felt as if he was just on the point of teasing free one end of his knot. Iris had been caught in the cloister after dark, lied about it, and seemed obviously guilty. Maybe she had been on her way to the crypt, intending to remove – to steal – something from that cupboard.

No! Everything in Gawaine recoiled from accepting that. *I'd believe it of Roddy darling, but not Iris.*

All the same, he couldn't shake the conviction that he had just learned something important. He only wished that he knew what it was.

Chapter Eighteen

Cover her face; mine eyes dazzle; she died young.
The Duchess of Malfi, IV.ii

Exactly a week after her great uncle had been buried in the Abbey precinct, Iris Grant was laid to rest beside him. David felt a weird sense of *déjà vu*, with much the same group of mourners in attendance at the graveside. The two additions were Annis Radford, white-faced and clearly grieving, and Jake Fletcher, whose sombre, quiet demeanour was quite different from his bombast of the day before.

Maybe he really does miss her, David thought.

He noticed that Inspector Bradshaw and Sergeant Godwin had also appeared, though they kept their distance and did not approach anyone else. "Homing in on their prey?" David muttered to Gawaine.

"I wish they were," Gawaine sighed.

Then you don't have to. David understood the words his friend had not said.

The ceremony over, the two police officers departed, not joining the group who gathered in the Chapter House afterwards to hear the reading of the will.

Elaine Chatham plopped herself down comfortably with her knitting bag; this time the long strip was scarlet. Beside her, Roddy was fidgeting; he had a truculent look.

"What the hell is holding him up?" he muttered, glaring at Tom Turnbull who was neatly laying out his papers.

"Patience, Roddy darling," his mother responded. "You can't rush these things."

Roddy merely grunted.

Gawaine had once again settled himself on the seat with the carved feline on the arm; he was caressing it nervously as he waited. He had a wary look; David guessed he was hoping to learn something from the reactions to Iris's will.

In the end, there were no reactions of any significance. Jake Fletcher, who was not mentioned at all, had the good sense not to protest, merely casting a brief smile at Annis when Tom Turnbull read out the clause leaving her the cottage. Among the smaller bequests were Iris's art books left to the school where she had taught, and an amber pendant, left to Seff. Everything else – including the island – went to the Abbey.

"About time," Roddy Chatham commented loudly.

Bernard White shot him an annoyed glance; now that the island belonged to the Abbey Trust, David assumed, he would want to proceed discreetly.

"Tom, you and I will have to get together," he said.

Tom Turnbull, collecting up his papers, nodded assent. "Sure, Bernard. Get your secretary to ring me tomorrow."

Meanwhile Roddy Chatham, who seemed not to know 'discreetly' got up and marched across the room to stand in front of Annis. "You'll rent me the cottage, right?" he said.

Annis rose to face him. "I'm sorry, Roddy," she responded, her voice pleasant. "I have plans for it."

"What plans?" Roddy's face was slowly becoming suffused

with anger. "You want money, don't you? I've got money." He held out a hand, rubbing his thumb and fingertips together.

Gawaine gave a tiny shudder, evidently overcome by the evidence of such vulgarity. "Maybe an intervention…?" he murmured to David.

"I think she has it well in hand," David murmured in reply.

"I'm going to expand my business," Annis explained. "I could offer classes. Knitting holidays. Maybe Kate Pengelly would come and teach spinning." Ideas were obviously starting to bubble out of her. "I'm sorry," she repeated, "but I'm not looking for a tenant."

Roddy glared at her for a moment, then spun around and stamped away. At the door he halted, looking back. "You'll be sorry. This isn't over," he spat, and added, "Bitch."

"Roddy!" Elaine Chatham exclaimed, eyes wide with shock.

"No 'darling' there," Seff whispered.

Roddy vanished through the door, ignoring his mother, and the sound of his footsteps died away.

"I'm so sorry," Elaine continued. "Annis dear, please forgive him."

"It's fine, Elaine," Annis responded, though she looked pale and distressed.

That seemed to be the signal for everyone to rise, ready to leave, as if they could abandon the memory of the ugly little scene behind them.

Elaine Chatham, stuffing her knitting into her patchwork bag, raised her voice to be heard over the general movement. "Please come up to St Morwenna's, all of you. I've prepared a little send-off for Iris."

"We should go," David said. "Elaine will—" He broke off as he realised that Gawaine was not listening. Instead, he stepped forward to intercept Father Magnus as he headed for the door. "May we have a word, Father?"

The old priest sighed, looking down at Gawaine from a craggy face set in an expression of exaggerated patience. "If you must."

"You know that I'm trying to make sense of what happened to Iris," Gawaine continued. "I think it might help if I knew why she was so desperate to have the Abbey keys. Is there anything you can tell me?"

Father Magnus went on looking down at him in silence for a moment; Gawaine held his ground, but David could see that he was struggling not to be intimidated.

"No," Father Magnus replied after the pause had dragged on for what felt like hours. "There's nothing at all that I can tell you."

He stalked off, the picture of devout cussedness.

Gawaine stood looking after him in silence, puzzled at first, until to David's amazement a look of enlightenment spread slowly over his face.

"What?" David said.

Gawaine did not reply, as if he was transfixed by some vision that only he could see. The rest of the group filed out past him, like a river parting around some particularly recalcitrant rock.

"What?" David repeated as the last of them departed.

Gawaine started, blinking, as if dragged back from somewhere else altogether. "I can't… no, I have to think this out," he said.

Frustrated, David realised there would be no getting

sense out of him in this mood. Taking him by the elbow, he steered him out of the chapter house and down the Abbey's side aisle towards the main doors and the open air.

"Let's go and eat Elaine's sausage rolls," he said. "Maybe those will stimulate the little grey cells."

Seff was waiting for them by the Abbey doors. "What's bugging him?" she asked David, nodding towards Gawaine, who still seemed to be far off in a world of his own making.

"He's thinking."

Immediately Seff looked interested. "Really? What happened?"

"Nothing, as far as I could see," David replied with a shrug. "He tried to get some information from Father Magnus, but Father Magnus wasn't talking. Hey," he continued with a sudden thought. "You don't suppose Father Magnus was involved somehow?"

"With Iris's death? Come on, David, not even you could take that seriously! Iris was on Father Magnus's side – or he was on hers."

"Maybe," David responded. "But maybe we've just taken that for granted. He's been avoiding Gawaine for days. That's pretty suspicious, if you ask me."

He led the way down the path to the precinct gate, only to halt a moment later as he spotted Annis Radford and Jake Fletcher standing close together beside one of the Celtic crosses that dotted the ground.

"Good grief," Seff said, blank astonishment in her tone.

Jake was twiddling the end of the silk scarf that Annis used to tie up her hair. His head was bent, and he was whispering something into her ear. Annis's face might have been hacked out of flint.

"That looks somewhat... inappropriate," Gawaine murmured, returning abruptly to the land of the living. "Do you think we ought to rescue her?"

Before anyone could reply, Annis took a step backwards. She said something too low to be heard; Jake's lecherous expression changed to one of chagrin. He stared at Annis in silence for a moment, then flounced off through the gate and down the road towards the village. Annis watched him go, a furious look on her face, until David and the others caught up with her.

"Are you okay?" Seff asked her.

Annis turned, startled. "Oh – yes, I'm fine. It's only Jake, though why I'm suddenly his flavour of the month, I've no idea. He asked me to dinner. If I didn't know he was pond scum, I might have accepted."

"Pond scum?" Gawaine inquired. "Not that I would presume to disagree with you..."

Annis let out a gusty sigh. "It was when he was down here with Iris at Easter. Iris had gone off somewhere with her painting stuff, and Jake came into the shop. He suggested I should close up and take him upstairs for – in his own words – 'a quickie.'"

"That's disgusting," Seff said, looking as if there was a bad smell under her nose. "But I'm not surprised. What did you do?"

Annis hesitated. "Er... I convinced him it was a bad idea to annoy a woman with access to lots of sharp pointy things. He wasn't pleased. Which makes me ask myself why he's all over me now."

"Did you tell Iris?" David asked, wondering if that was why Iris had dumped him.

"No." Annis sounded troubled. "I knew how much she loved Jake, and how hurt she would be. I was trying to decide what to say, and then the next day they left before I managed to catch her alone. I was so relieved when I found out they weren't together any more."

"So was everyone who knew her," Seff said.

"You know, it's just occurred to me," David said. "Until yesterday, Jake Fletcher thought he was going to inherit Iris's cottage. You don't suppose he would have murdered her for that?"

Gawaine gave him a speculative look, as if he was actually considering the possibility. But before he could speak, Seff broke in.

"Surely not. He could buy any number of scruffy little seaside cottages, if he wanted to. But it hardly fits with the celebrity lifestyle. A beach house in Florida, now…"

Gawaine nodded slowly. "I'm afraid you may be right…"

"Yeah, it's a lovely thought," Seff agreed. "Sorry, David. Well, enough of Jake the werewolf," she continued briskly. "Annis, are you coming up to St Morwenna's?"

Annis fell in beside them as they left the Abbey precinct. The weather had turned sultry again, and David wondered whether they were in for another storm. Clouds were massing above the mainland, and hot wind was blowing in from the sea, flattening the grass on either side of the road.

"Gawaine," he began after a moment, "do you see any chance of wrapping things up any time soon? That conference I told you about is coming up. I would get out of it if I could, but..." He hated the idea of leaving Gawaine here to cope on his own; it would be better if he could persuade Gawaine to leave too, but he knew how little chance there was of that.

"I have the same problem," Seff admitted reluctantly. "I can't justify staying here much longer if nothing is happening."

David caught a glance of alarm from Gawaine, instantly suppressed. "I have... a kind of idea." A slight frown gathered between his brows. "There's a lot of dead wood to be cleared away, and a few indications that are starting to fit together."

"And what are they?" Seff asked, instantly alert. "Come on, Gawaine. Give."

Good luck with that, David thought. *Gawaine never 'gives' until he's ready.*

Once he had thought that Gawaine's habit of delay until he could expound his whole case was intolerably theatrical; now he knew that expounding took so much out of his friend that he couldn't be expected to do it more than once.

"Soon, I hope," Gawaine responded. "It would really help if I could see that selfie on Bethany's phone."

"Sergeant Godwin hasn't been in touch?" David asked.

Gawaine shook his head. "Maybe I'll try to see her tomorrow. Though in a way..." he added meditatively, "it might help even more, if there was no selfie at all."

"What do you mean by that?" Seff asked sharply. "We know there was a selfie."

"We know there *was*." He relapsed into his earlier thoughtful state.

"Maybe this evening we could go over what we know," David suggested, trying to fill the silence. "I'd like to pinpoint where everyone was at the time Iris died. That might throw up something."

"Is there anything I can do to help?" Annis asked.

"There might be," Gawaine said, coming back to life and turning to her. "How many people on Morgarrow know that you're frightened of spiders?"

"Pretty well the whole island," Annis replied with a rueful laugh. "There was a monster among some fruit at last year's Harvest Festival in the Abbey, and I almost shrieked the place down."

"Good," said Gawaine. "That's very good."

And he refused to say any more.

Chapter Nineteen

Death and diseases through the whole land spread.
The Duchess of Malfi, I.i

Rain had fallen in the night, clearing the air, and a fresh breeze was ruffling the surface of the sea as Gawaine headed down into the village. But the bright day did not match his mood. He was resolutely trying to ignore the cold feeling in the pit of his stomach when he thought that within a few days David, and Seff too, would have to leave. He imagined himself as some abandoned ghost, wafting his way around the island, unable to depart but of no practical use if he stayed.

Something has to happen. Soon.

His discussion with David and Seff on the previous evening had not been useful. Of the people with a motive to kill Iris, Elaine Chatham could be placed up at St Morwenna's, and Bernard White in his own garden. Annis was presumably at home, too, though there was no proof of that. Roddy Chatham and George Pengelly had arrived for their meeting with Bernard White after the storm had started, which would mean that in theory at least they had the time to kill Iris.

Roddy Chatham has to be top of that list. But somehow I'm not happy...

It was hard for Gawaine to imagine that Roddy had crossed to Morgarrow on the ferry and on his way to Bernard White's meeting had just popped into Iris's cottage to strangle her. But for lack of anything else to do, he was on his way to time how long it would have taken him to reach the Whites' house afterwards.

Iris's cottage was still fenced off with police tape, with a uniformed constable on duty. staring stolidly ahead of him with the expression of the terminally bored. Gawaine nodded and wished him good morning.

"Morning, sir."

"Everything quiet?" Gawaine asked.

"Yessir." As Gawaine was turning to leave, he suddenly added, "There was one thing. The chap I relieved this morning said there was somebody lurking around the back in the early hours."

"Really?" Gawaine's senses had begun to tingle. "Did he say who?"

"No, he told me he went round and shone his torch, but he didn't see nothing. He reckoned it was kids."

A convenient conclusion.

Gawaine murmured a farewell and went on, glancing at his watch to fix the time. Heading towards the centre of the village, his mind picked away at this extra nugget of information, but he couldn't make it tell him anything useful. Why would Iris's murderer want to return to the scene of his crime? Perhaps after all it really had been children, scaring themselves and maybe making up ghoulish tales of Iris's ghost. Though the early hours of the morning was a strange time for children to be out.

What were their parents thinking?

Bernard White's house stood at the far end of the village, a little way away from the end of the village street. It was, appropriately enough, white, situated at the top of a gentle rise and surrounded by a picket fence.

As Gawaine approached, he glanced at his watch again. Seven minutes. But if Roddy Chatham had been running – as he would be, through the torrential rain, with the memory of his crime pursuing him like the vengeful Erinyes – he could probably do it in five. Gawaine wasn't sure what that told him, but he tucked the fact away with all the others that didn't seem to fit anywhere.

It's like a jigsaw, with masses of pieces, and no picture on the box.

As soon as the thought came to him, Gawaine drew to a sudden halt. *What if it isn't one jigsaw? What if it's two – or even three?*

Before he could work out what that might mean, a cheerful voice hailed him. "Hello, Gawaine!"

Claudia White had just emerged from behind a splendid display of roses, that stretched all along the front fence. She had a pair of secateurs in her hand; pink, yellow and white petals drifted around her as she dead-headed vigorously. "Did you want to see Bernard?" she asked. "I'm afraid he's in the office."

"No, thank you, I'm just out for a walk."

Claudia smiled. "I'd invite you in for coffee, but I'm expecting my U3A group in ten minutes. We're teaching ourselves Italian."

Gawaine nodded farewell. "*Spero che vada bene,*" he said. "*Arrivederci.*"

He went on his way to the accompaniment of delighted giggles.

It occurred to Gawaine, as he made his way back to the village, that the murderer had left Iris's cottage by the back door, and if he was heading towards the Whites' house he would have used the back lane.

So where is this end of it? Gawaine wondered, wishing he had a better sense of direction.

At this end of the village several lanes led off the main street, some straggling down towards the sea, while others opposite led up the hillside. Gawaine's explorations led him past the village hall and a building inside a fenced yard that announced itself as St Cadoc's Primary School. Altogether the village was bigger than he had imagined at first.

These reflections occupied him until he found the place where the back lane emerged parallel with the main street, then branched off across the nearest hill. Glancing at his watch again, Gawaine followed it.

The lane led at first beside pretty gardens, and then behind the shops that clustered around the main square. Gawaine identified the back of the supermarket, a covered storage area, where according to Geoff Carter the youth of Morgarrow gathered. A group of recycling bins stood to one side; presumably it was one of them that had been tipped over and set off the Carters' dog.

Is that significant? Probably not, Gawaine decided, reflecting that he was getting into such a state that he would start to see clues everywhere.

Continuing on, he had almost reached Annis's cottage when her back door opened and she emerged, a cat carrier in one hand. To Gawaine's dismay, he saw that she was crying.

"Annis, what's the matter?" he asked, halting by the gate.

Annis looked up, clearly startled to see him. "It's Merino," she replied. "Look."

Nervously – because he had little experience of weeping women – Gawaine let himself into the garden and joined her where she had crouched on the path near the back door. The cat Merino was lying on her side, her breath coming fast and shallow. Her paws were swollen and there was a bluish tinge on her lips.

"She's eaten something," Annis said. "Some rotting meat, or…" She stifled another sob.

"Is there anything I can do?" Gawaine asked.

Annis shook her head, making a massive effort to pull herself together. "I've phoned the vet. I'm to take her in; there's a ferry in ten minutes."

Gently she began to move Merino into the cat carrier. Merino let out a plaintive meow, then lay limply in Annis's hands.

Gawaine began to look around for whatever might have made Merino ill, thinking that if he came across a half-consumed bit of wildlife he would be able to bury it. But he found nothing until something gleamed out from among a clump of lupins through the fence in Iris's garden.

When he went around to examine it, he found a tin of sardines. The lid had been rolled back and the sardines mashed up. Specks of white sprinkled the surface, and at one end was a deep depression where the cat Merino had made inroads on what must have seemed an unexpected treat.

Not much doubt where that came from, Gawaine thought, repressing a pulse of fury. *Roddy darling must have been the person the police officer heard lurking about in the early hours.*

Picking up the tin gingerly, by the very edges, he took it back to show Annis, who was heading for her gate with the cat carrier.

She stared at the tin, drawing in a shocked breath. "What's that white stuff?"

"I'd guess aspirin, or something like it," Gawaine replied. "It's toxic to cats – oh, but not necessarily lethal," he continued hastily.

"And we know who put it there!" Annis said through angry tears. "Roddy Chatham – after that scene at the will reading. He said it wasn't over. But he's bound to deny it, and we'll never prove anything."

"Oh, I think we can," Gawaine assured her. "I don't suppose he was all that careful about fingerprints and DNA when he set his trap. I'll come over on the ferry with you, and take this to the police. Have you got a bag?"

Annis hurried back indoors and reappeared a moment later with one of the pretty paper carriers she used in her shop. Gawaine carefully lowered the tin into it and together they headed for the harbour where the ferry was about to depart.

Once on board, with the ship's wake creaming out behind, Annis began to relax. "We all know that Roddy wants to live on the island," she said. "I can understand that he was disappointed when I wouldn't rent to him. But I didn't think he would go so far as poisoning Merino."

"Oh, I think it began long before this," Gawaine said.

Annis frowned, puzzled. "What do you mean?"

"Spiders."

"What?"

"I thought it was peculiar," Gawaine went on to explain. "Right from that first day when David caught the one in your workroom. Three within one week, and all in… what we might call strategic places. Your workroom, among the wool in your shop, and in your bed."

Annis stared at him. "Are you saying Roddy put them there?"

"Was he in your shop, round about the right time?"

A few moments passed as Annis thought, gazing out at the receding bulk of the Abbey. "He was," she said at last. "He bought some wool and a pattern – said it was for his mother's birthday." She managed a small smile. "He nearly had a fit when I told him what it cost, but he paid up, like the devoted son he is."

"Could he have slipped upstairs without you seeing?"

"I suppose so," Annis replied. "The shop was very busy that day. Some sort of women's outing had come over to see the Abbey, and then they descended on the village for tea and souvenirs. I couldn't keep an eye on everything. But look, this is ridiculous," she went on. "I'd believe it of Roddy – I'd believe anything after today," she went on, glancing through the mesh of the cat carrier to where Merino lay inert. "But how could he know the spiders would stay where he put them?"

"He couldn't, of course," Gawaine agreed. "Though I've noticed they don't move around all that much. Besides, we don't know that there were only three."

Annis stared at him, shocked. "Gawaine, I really wish you hadn't said that."

Gawaine suppressed a shiver. *I really wish I hadn't thought it.* "We could get David to do a sweep," he suggested. "But to get to the point," he continued quickly, "I think you've been the target of a campaign to make you leave, so Roddy could have your cottage. You mentioned a broken window… that might not have been just an innocent bit of vandalism."

Annis took a deep breath. "Gawaine, you really do have the most devious mind!"

"Thank you." Gawaine tilted his head a little. "I try."

"And you could be right," Annis went on. "I thought the window was just trivial, and it never occurred to me that the spiders had been put there. So I never thought that anyone would try… But now," she added fiercely, "I'm going to kill Roddy Chatham."

"A worthy ambition," Gawaine murmured. "But I don't think you'll have to. I don't know what the penalties are for poisoning a cat, but I'm sure they're not pleasant. You'll have your revenge."

"Good." Annis narrowed her eyes, as if she was imagining all the things she might like to do to Roddy Chatham. "And I'll make sure he knows I'm not going anywhere. I worked hard to have my shop."

"How did you come to settle on Morgarrow?" Gawaine asked. "Iris said that you're not local."

"No, I'm from London," Annis replied. "And I never planned to be here. I did my degree in Philosophy, and then when I graduated the only job I could find was part-time in a knitting shop. And I loved it!"

"A far cry from Socrates…" Gawaine murmured.

Annis nodded, smiling. "So when I'd learned my trade, I started looking around for a shop of my own. London was hopeless, of course; I could never afford those prices. It was sheer luck that I saw an advertisement for a cottage to let on Morgarrow. Petroc and I hit it off right away. He gave me a really good deal on the rent, provided I knitted him a woolly hat every winter." She sighed. "I still can't believe he's dead; I'll never stop missing him."

As the ferry manoeuvred into the mainland harbour, Gawaine thought over this latest development. He began to believe that perhaps he had assembled most of the pieces of one of his jigsaws; he was convinced that Roddy Chatham had been trying to drive Annis off the island so there would be a vacant cottage. Then he could move in, become a Trustee of St Cadoc's and make money from the development.

Does that make him a murderer? he asked himself. *Would someone who could kill a cat be able to kill a woman too?* He couldn't answer that, though it was surely obvious that someone who would kill a woman would have no hesitation in killing a cat.

And yet... Gawaine still wasn't happy. With his campaign against Annis in full swing, would Roddy Chatham have gone to the extreme of murder?

Arriving in the town centre, Annis headed for the vet's, while Gawaine climbed the steep street to the police station. Entering, he almost collided with Inspector Bradshaw, who was on the way out.

"Oh, it's you again," the inspector said disagreeably. "What do you want?"

"I've come to report a poisoned cat," Gawaine replied.

Inspector Bradshaw looked down his nose at the bag Gawaine was carrying, almost as if he expected that the moribund feline was lurking inside. "I haven't time for that," he said. Glancing over his shoulder, he added, "Sergeant, you deal with it." He swept out.

Sergeant Godwin, who had been leaning on the desk, looking at some report with the desk sergeant, straightened up and beckoned to Gawaine. "Come through to my office."

"Now," she said, when she was seated behind her desk with Gawaine sitting opposite. "Show me what you've got there."

Gawaine handed over the bag with the doctored tin of sardines and explained how he had come by it.

"Nasty," Sergeant Godwin said. "Is the cat dead?"

"No, Ms Radford has taken her to the vet. We think we know who did it."

The sergeant interlaced her fingers, with a look of satisfaction on her face. "Explain it to me."

"Roddy Chatham. There was a very unpleasant little scene yesterday at the reading of Iris Grant's will."

As Gawaine went on to describe what had happened, Sergeant Godwin looked even more satisfied, like a mouse contemplating a succulent bit of Brie. By the time he had finished, she was smiling.

"So he needs to live on the island…" she said, half to herself. "Then he can become a Trustee and support the development. But Ms Radford has plans for the cottage and refused to co-operate. Yes, this is all very interesting. We'll certainly get your tin examined."

"Do you have Roddy Chatham's fingerprints?" Gawaine asked.

"And his DNA. Don't worry, if he poisoned this cat, we'll nail him. As for nailing him for the murder…" She seemed to wait for Gawaine to ask a question.

Gawaine obliged. "Do you know anything more about that?"

At first, Sergeant Godwin's reply seemed irrelevant. "That poor girl's body has been found," she said, suddenly sobering. "Washed up further down the coast. Given the currents and the tides, it looks as if she went in from Morgarrow, or somewhere not far off."

Gawaine swallowed nausea; the news had been inevitable, and yet he admitted to a faint hope that Bethany's disappearance might have had some other explanation. That hope had vanished now.

"Do you know the cause of death?" he asked, not sure he wanted to hear the answer.

"It's too early for the post mortem results," Sergeant Godwin replied. "But it looks as if the fall killed her before she was swept out to sea."

Remembering the sharp rocks below the cliff beside the Abbey, Gawaine found that all too probable. He could only hope that Bethany had lost consciousness quickly.

"I've some more information for you," Sergeant Godwin continued, shaking off her brief seriousness in favour of a smug smile. "We've managed to access Bethany's phone."

"The selfie?" Gawaine asked, his interest quickening.

The sergeant nodded. "Who do you think it is?" she asked. "Do you want to make a bet?"

Gawaine paused for a moment's consideration. "If I were a betting man," he said at last, "I would bet on there being no one at all."

Sergeant Godwin grinned. "You would lose your money." Reaching out, she touched a key on her computer, then swivelled the screen around so that Gawaine could see it.

The picture in front of him showed a very pretty girl, laughing, her hair blowing in the wind, with the grey bulk of the Abbey looming up behind her. The man with her, a sheepish expression on his face, was Roddy Chatham.

Gawaine looked at it for a long time. There was something about the photograph that disturbed him, as if it was trying to tell him something. *But I don't know what it is.*

"Is there any possibility I could have a copy of that?" he asked.

"Sure." Sergeant Godwin's tone was obliging. "I can send it to your phone, if you like."

While she was working her magic, Gawaine kept on staring at the photo. Even when the sergeant said, "All done," he found it hard to take his eyes off it.

"Well?" Sergeant Godwin said eventually, her voice edged with impatience. "Don't you think that proves he's guilty?"

Blinking, Gawaine looked up. "Oh, no," he said. "It proves that he's almost certainly innocent."

Chapter Twenty

Let guilty men remember, their black deeds
Do lean on crutches made of slender reeds.
                    The White Devil, V.vi

"What do you mean, it proves he's innocent?" David Powers demanded. He couldn't process what Gawaine had just told him, and the sight of his friend, leaning back in his seat in the hotel bar, composedly sipping Prosecco, exasperated him still further. "Are you out of your mind?"

Gawaine seemed completely – infuriatingly – unfazed. "I said 'almost certainly,'" he pointed out. "I'm quite prepared to be proved wrong. But I don't think I am."

David looked around, unsuccessfully, for something to throw at him. "But we thought that Bethany's selfie would show us a photo of the murderer."

"True," Gawaine admitted. "But I was never entirely happy about that, and now I think I know why."

David spoke through gritted teeth. "Enlighten me."

"Certainly, my dear David. For one thing, if the murderer – Roddy Chatham or someone else – came from the mainland, he would hardly advertise the fact by taking a ferry where there were so few passengers. He would aim for a more popular crossing, where he might get lost in the crowd."

David nodded. "Okay…"

"For another thing…" Gawaine paused to take a thoughtful sip of Prosecco. "Now that we know Bethany is dead, I'm beginning to think that the murderer must have killed her, too. A murder and a fatal accident at almost the same time and in the same place is a little too much to believe. Now according to Megan Carter, Bethany was in the vicinity of Iris's cottage at round about the time that the murderer must have arrived. I think she saw him, and I think that's why she died."

"Yes, but what has that to do with—"

"With the selfie? Because if it was the murderer who crossed on that ferry, he would know that there was hard evidence of his presence on Bethany's phone. If he then killed her, he would have grabbed her bag, taken her phone and either thrown it into the sea or at the very least deleted the selfie."

David thought that over. *It's all getting very complicated.* "I think I'm with you," he said cautiously. "Because now we know Roddy Chatham was on the ferry, we also know that he didn't have time to kill Iris and Bethany before he had to show up at Bernard White's meeting."

"Exactly." Gawaine gave him a nod of approval. "I timed it earlier today, and though it's not impossible that he killed Iris, it's very tight. What is quite impossible is that he also killed Bethany."

"So he had no reason to worry about the selfie," David finished.

"Yes. We still have the option that Roddy killed Iris and that Bethany's death was an accident," Gawaine said. "I don't like it, but we can't entirely discount it. And I would love to know what Roddy was doing in that half hour or so between getting off the ferry and arriving at Bernard White's – by which time, if you recall, it was raining."

"We could ask him," David said, "but he's unlikely to tell us."

"I'm not sure…" Gawaine mused, draining the last of his Prosecco. He glanced at his watch and stood up. "I want to try a long shot. Will you come with me? I fear I might need – is 'muscle' the correct term?"

"Good luck with that," David muttered. "Lead on."

As Gawaine led the way towards the village and into the lane that led behind the first row of cottages, storm clouds were once again heaping up in the sky above the mainland. The air had turned close and sticky, and the sea was like a sheet of steel.

"Another storm brewing," David remarked.

The ferry was heading for the harbour; he could make out a crowd of foot passengers on the deck as it manoeuvred towards the slipway.

"The six o'clock ferry," Gawaine said; clearly his mind was on something other than the weather. "Excellent."

Passing Iris's cottage, he let himself into Annis's garden and knocked on her back door.

"What is all this about?" David asked.

"Probably nothing," Gawaine replied. "But it's worth a try."

Before David could ask any more, the back door opened and Annis stepped out. "Gawaine!" she exclaimed. "Merino's going to be okay. The vet is keeping her overnight for observation, but I should be able to pick her up tomorrow."

"That's really good news," Gawaine said.

"Would you like to come in for a drink?"

"No, thank you," Gawaine replied. He indicated a flourishing lilac that grew beside the fence on the far side of the kitchen window. "I should like to borrow your bush for a few minutes."

David was surprised to see that Annis apparently saw nothing peculiar in this request.

"Of course," she said.

As she spoke, David could hear the sound of rapid footsteps approaching. Gawaine grabbed him by the wrist and drew him into the shelter of the lilac as Roddy Chatham rounded the corner, glanced back and forth a couple of times with a furtive air, then entered Iris's garden. He began ferreting around in a clump of lupins, his movements growing faster and more desperate as the seconds ticked by.

Gawaine stepped forward. "It's not there," he said.

Roddy Chatham jerked upright as if someone had peppered him with buckshot. "I don't know what you mean," he said hoarsely.

"I think you do."

Roddy looked taken aback at the accusing tone, like so many other unsuspecting mortals, David reflected, when Gawaine cast off his air of negligent fragility and slid out his claws.

"The tin of sardines," Gawaine continued, "that you doctored with – what? Aspirin? Paracetamol? – is now in the hands of the police. The cat you tried to kill is safely in the hands of the vet. The owner of the cat—" he cast a glance at Annis – "is gunning for you. If you would like her to let you live, you had better answer a few questions."

For a second David wondered whether Roddy was going to launch himself at Gawaine. He might have done so, except for the fence in the way. As it was, he glared at Gawaine, then hunched his shoulders and stared at his feet.

"I don't know what all the fuss is about," he mumbled. "It was only an effing cat."

A small sound came from Annis's throat; David put a hand on her shoulder to hold her back.

"For example," Gawaine went on as if Roddy hadn't spoken, "can you confirm that you have been doing your best to drive Annis off the island, so that you could move into her cottage? If I were to mention spiders, or a broken window, would that mean anything to you?"

Briefly Roddy hesitated, looking truculent, then nodded. "Okay, I did the spiders. But not the broken window. I don't know anything about that."

"And can you confirm that this is where it ends? Because the police will want a chat with you, and I imagine they will take a very dim view of any further incidents. It's a pity they didn't catch you when you were scuffling around in the dark, dropping off the tin."

"What?" Roddy gaped at him. "I wasn't scuffling around in the dark! If you must know, I put the tin there this morning before I caught the eight thirty ferry."

Gawaine looked briefly disconcerted, then shrugged. "A minor point. Once again, can you confirm that there will be no more attempts?"

"Because I can promise you," Annis said, sounding dangerous, "I'm not going anywhere."

"Okay, okay!" Roddy raised his hands, palms outward. "Will you just let me leave?"

"Leave?" Gawaine indicated well-bred surprise. "Certainly not. We have a long way to go yet. Tell me, when you came across to Morgarrow on the morning of the storm, where did you go?"

Roddy stared at him, clearly finding it hard to assimilate the sudden change of subject. "I went to Bernard's," he answered at last. "He'd called a meeting."

"But you didn't go straight to Bernard White's, did you?" Gawaine asked. "The ferry would dock at about eight fifteen, and you didn't arrive at the meeting until after the rain started. Where did you go for that half hour? You didn't call in on Iris, by any chance?"

Roddy's eyes widened, fear replacing the hostility. "Here, are you saying I murdered Iris? I didn't! You can't fit me up for that!"

"Tell me where you were, then."

"I went up to St Morwenna's," Roddy replied, almost over-eager now to answer Gawaine's questions. "I keep a spare laptop up there, and I needed it for the meeting."

David found it easy to believe him; he had seen the laptop there himself, when he went to check St Cadoc's accounts. Roddy kept all the Abbey business there. *Along with the Morgarrow Moor brochure. And his porn.* And the timing would be about right, if he was hurrying on the way back to get out of the rain.

"Did anyone see you?" Gawaine asked.

Roddy shook his head. "I only nipped in and out again. I was in a hurry."

"What a pity." Gawaine examined his fingernails. "A

witness would be so useful. To establish your alibi," he pointed out pleasantly.

"Well, there wasn't anybody about. That's not my fault," Roddy said. "I saw you, though," he added. "When I was running back through the rain. You were ahead of me, and you turned into the hotel."

Gawaine nodded. "That sounds about right. Hold that thought – it might be your salvation."

"Then can I go now?" Roddy repeated.

"One more thing," Gawaine said. "In all that time – from when you left the ferry to when you arrived at Bernard White's – did you see anything of Bethany Fox?"

"Her? Nah," Roddy replied. "Silly bitch. She was all over me on the ferry. But I didn't see anything of her after that."

Again David was inclined to believe him. Bethany had gone to the supermarket; if Roddy had headed straight for St Morwenna's, their paths would not have crossed.

"All right." Glancing back, Gawaine said, "My dear David, have you anything to add?"

David shook his head. "I have," Annis said, sounding even more dangerous. "If you ever come anywhere near me again, you nasty little worm, I'll make you wish you'd never been born. Now get out."

Roddy didn't wait to be told twice.

Annis turned to Gawaine with a beaming smile on her face. "Gawaine, that was—" The distant buzz of a doorbell interrupted her. "That's my front door. I'd better answer it. Don't go away."

"What do you think?" David asked Gawaine when she had gone. "Do you believe him?"

"Oh, undoubtedly, my dear David," Gawaine replied. "There's no way he could have seen me unless he was where he said he was. And if it's true that he went to get his laptop, he wouldn't have been anywhere near Bethany. He had no opportunity to kill her, and no time to kill Iris."

David let out a gusty sigh. "Pity."

"That is a point of view," Gawaine agreed. "But he's in trouble for what he did to Merino. We must make do with that."

Before David could respond, there was an alarmed cry from inside Annis's cottage. "Gawaine!"

"Another spider?" David murmured, following his friend through the back door.

Inside the shop, Annis was standing behind her counter, a defensive look on her face. Inspector Bradshaw stood facing her, with Sergeant Godwin at his shoulder. A uniformed officer was looming in the doorway.

"Gawaine, they're arresting me for Iris's murder," Annis said, distraught. "And I didn't do it! I would never have hurt Iris!"

"What?" Gawaine looked appalled. "You can't do that," he told Inspector Bradshaw. "It's absurd."

"I'll have to ask you not to interfere, sir," the Inspector said. "As for you, miss, you'll have to come with us."

Annis hesitated; David thought she looked too shocked to think straight. "Gawaine, what am I going to do about Merino?" she asked. "I'm supposed to pick her up from the vet tomorrow."

"I'll see to Merino," Gawaine promised. "I'll liaise with the vet." Turning to Inspector Bradshaw, he added, "Have you any idea how long you'll keep Ms Radford?"

"No idea at all, sir," the Inspector replied heavily. "But I doubt she'll be back tonight."

Meanwhile Annis had retrieved her bag from behind the counter and was scrabbling about in it. Eventually she pulled out a bunch of keys and held them out to Gawaine. "You'd better take these."

Gawaine took the keys, while Annis reluctantly followed Inspector Bradshaw out of the shop. Sergeant Godwin paused for a moment in the doorway; David thought she had a particularly smug look.

"You can't win 'em all," she said.

"You know this can't be right." Gawaine sounded suddenly tense. "What evidence—"

"You told me yourself how pleased she was with her legacy. And her DNA is all over Ms Grant's cottage," Sergeant Godwin said, tilting her head in that direction.

"But not on the knitting needle?"

"There's no usable DNA on the knitting needle," Sergeant Godwin admitted. "But that's not really relevant." Her face crinkled into a smile. "I thought you were supposed to be good at this. Don't you realise that this crime must have been committed by a woman?"

Chapter Twenty-one

I have a weighty secret to impart.
> *The Devil's Law Case*, III.iii

"What does she mean, committed by a woman?" David said. "Because of the knitting needle? Surely she's not that stupid? All the men we suspected have access to knitting needles."

He and Gawaine were standing outside Annis's shop; Gawaine locked the door and pocketed the keys. He looked thoroughly disturbed.

"I don't think that's what she meant," he said.

"Then what did she mean?"

Gawaine shook his head. "I need to think it out…" He let his voice trail off and relapsed into reflective silence.

Meanwhile the uniformed officer was removing the police tape from the door of Iris's cottage, and plodded off round the back to do the same there. The police launch still bobbed beside the jetty, as Inspector Bradshaw waited for him to finish. Annis was a small, hunched figure in the stern.

"Okay, let's look at the other women," David persisted, once he was sure that Gawaine had no intention of explaining. "Claudia White is too fragile to strangle anyone. Elaine Chatham has an alibi, cooking breakfast for her students."

"Besides," Gawaine said, drawn in spite of himself out of his abstraction, "Elaine Chatham is a supremely happy woman, up at St Morwenna's, cosseting her students like the mother hen she is. She has no motivation at all to murder anyone."

"Then what about Kate Pengelly?"

"But she didn't want the development," Gawaine pointed out. "It was in her interest for Iris to stay alive. Of course, there's always Bethany."

"*Bethany?*"

"We know she was in the right place at the right time," Gawaine said. "Suppose she had an argument with Iris – maybe about St Morwenna's. She might have blamed Iris because she was so unhappy there."

"And then killed herself out of guilt?"

"It's a theory."

"But you don't believe it, do you?"

Gawaine sighed. "No, my dear David, I don't. For one thing, she's unlikely to have been carrying a convenient knitting needle."

"Then that—" David broke off as the police officer reappeared, headed down to the harbour and boarded the launch.

"Then that only leaves Annis," David continued as the launch pulled away and dwindled into the distance, *en route* for the mainland. "Look at it from the point of view of the police. They wouldn't have arrested her if they weren't fairly sure. She has motive – she obviously liked the idea of having the cottage. She could have gone in and out round the back, without anyone spotting her."

"And Bethany?"

"Bethany was there – she might have seen Annis at some point. Annis might have smiled sweetly, invited her in for coffee, killed her and then disposed of the body after dark when no one would be around."

Gawaine frowned. "Have you tried carrying a dead body? It's some way to the nearest stretch of water where she could have tipped Bethany in."

"Okay, then, Bethany died by accident. That doesn't mean Annis couldn't have murdered Iris."

Gawaine's mouth tightened. "My dear David, think of what we've seen of Annis. Do you really think she has it in her to kill? For a cottage? Iris was her friend."

David sighed. "I know. She's lovely – kind to wandering amateur sleuths and small furry animals. But the police don't see it that way."

"Then we must endeavour to make them see it a different way."

"What way is that, then?"

Gawaine shook his head, clearly confused. "My dear David, if I could answer that question, we could all pack up and go home."

David wondered whether Gawaine was swayed this time by the attractiveness of the cat Merino. Or maybe even – he hid a grin – by the quirky but undeniable attractiveness of the cat Merino's owner. His brief amusement gave way to a pang of anxiety; if they were wrong, and Annis had committed murder, Gawaine was going to be hurt.

"We could go home anyway," he said.

Gawaine's eyes widened, blue and brilliant. "Oh, no," he said. "Not yet. This isn't over. Not by a long way."

He hesitated for a moment, then took the bunch of Annis's keys out of his pocket and examined them. Each one was neatly identified with a plastic tag; Gawaine paused for a long time gazing at a pair of keys clipped together. Looking over his shoulder, David saw that they were labelled 'Petroc'.

"I suppose Annis had those when she used to keep an eye on Great Uncle Petroc," he observed.

Gawaine nodded abstractedly. "Come on," he said after a moment, and led the way around the back of Iris's cottage and into the garden.

By now the sky was dark with bulging cloud, and a hot little breeze was turning back the leaves on Iris's rose bushes. David guessed that the storm would break at any moment.

He followed his friend, alarmed. "You're not thinking of breaking and entering?"

"Breaking, no." Gawaine sounded quite calm. "Entering, maybe. But first I want to tell you a story." He sat down on the bench beside the back door and gestured for David to sit beside him.

"Go ahead, then," David said, when Gawaine did not speak at once.

For a little longer, his friend was silent, fiddling with the keys. Then he looked up, taking a deep breath.

"You remember how the students told us about Iris's art workshop," he began. David nodded, puzzled. *What has that to do with anything?*

"Iris stored the banners in the Abbey crypt, along with some of her art materials," Gawaine continued. "I was down there the other day, fetching vases for Claudia

White. There's an enormous cupboard, stuffed full of votive gifts to the Abbey, mostly Victorian, Mrs White told me. Perfectly frightful thing, full of woodworm and dust and... things with too many legs."

"And this is relevant, why?"

"Let's go back a bit. You remember how Seff told us that Iris had been edgy, ever since she came down here. Uncharacteristically edgy."

"Sure. But she'd just dumped her fiancé, and her great uncle had just died. She had every excuse for being edgy."

Gawaine nodded agreement. "These events may not be unconnected, my dear David. But you'll also remember that she was very keen to get hold of the keys to this cottage, and especially to have a set of keys to the Abbey."

"Yes." David began to have a dim idea of where this was going. "She was in a real state when Bernard White came round and told her she had no right to them because she couldn't be a trustee."

"And the first thing she did was go to see Father Magnus. She said she was going to take him the chess set that Great Uncle Petroc had left him, but I think her real reason was to borrow his keys. They were in her bag when the police found it under the bush the following morning."

"And she used them to get into the Abbey that night!" David exclaimed. "Was there something valuable in that cupboard? Was she going to steal something?"

Gawaine shook his head. "I thought so at first, but no. Because she had to give Father Magnus a good reason for him to lend her the keys."

"I suppose she couldn't say, 'Please, Father, let me have them so I can nick something out of the crypt.'"

"Indeed. In fact, my dear David, her intention was exactly the opposite. She had *already* stolen something. Maybe when she was down in the crypt at Easter, maybe before that. What she wanted to do that night was to put it back."

"Ah…"

"Well may you say, 'Ah…' I believe that her great uncle's death had woken Iris up to what she had done. She was not a woman who would turn naturally to crime, and we must look at her motives for doing so in this case." Now Gawaine sounded at his most pedantic. "But we can leave that aside for the moment. What I believe she did, that night, was to visit Father Magnus and make her confession."

"What?" David asked, surprised. "I didn't think your lot went in for that."

"Oh, we do – or we may – in extreme situations. And I believe that Iris by this time was becoming desperate. She wanted to be free of it – the object, whatever it was, and the guilt. So she confessed to Father Magnus, and he, we can assume, absolved her and lent her the keys so she could put back whatever she had stolen."

"Surely she could just have given it to him?" David protested. "Or done it in the daytime? She didn't have to creep around at night."

"I suspect putting it back herself might have been her penance," Gawaine pointed out. "And remember that the Abbey is never empty while it's open. If no one else, there are the two students on the prayer rota. Iris might have managed to slip down there unseen, and then again she might not."

"So that's why Father Magnus wouldn't talk to you," David said. "Secrecy of the confessional, and all that."

"Yes, he was clearly avoiding me," Gawaine agreed. "Though I believe he gave me the best hint he could, after the reading of Iris's will. Do you remember? 'There's nothing at all that I can tell you.' That didn't mean he *had* nothing to tell me, if he had been allowed."

David remembered the look of enlightenment that had spread over Gawaine's face at the old priest's words. "That's when you realised…"

"Yes, but I had to put it all together. And we still haven't come to what might be the most important point. Because Iris didn't get as far as the crypt. Jenny Morland stopped her when she let herself into the Abbey cloister, and Iris had to go away again. She must have meant to try again on the next night, but…" His voice shook a little. "She was killed before she had the chance."

"So where is it now, this thing? And why won't you tell me what it is?"

"Because I don't know – not for certain." Gawaine turned to glance at the back door of the cottage, and then at the keys in his hand. "Shall we go and find it?" he said.

Chapter Twenty-two

I had a hope… to have gain'd
An infinite mass of treasure by her death.
                The Duchess of Malfi, IV.ii

Gawaine unlocked the back door and disappeared inside. David glanced up and down the back lane, satisfying himself that they were unobserved, before following his friend. He caught Gawaine up in the living room, still in much the same state of chaos as it had been on the day Iris had taken possession.

"This is going to take a while," he observed. "And will we know it when we see it?"

Gawaine nodded slowly. "You have a point, my dear David. At least we know that it must be small enough to fit into Iris's tapestry tote bag. Jenny Morland didn't mention that she was carrying anything else."

David let his gaze travel around the room. There were hundreds of books, any one of which might be a priceless first edition, not to mention smaller things that could be tucked away out of sight. *A piece of jewellery, a rare coin…*

He let out a long sigh. "We'd better get on with it, before we get nicked for breaking and entering."

"Nonsense," Gawaine responded, sounding unusually brisk. "This is Annis's property, and Annis gave us the keys. We are her representatives, as I shall point out to any inconvenient arms of the law. And don't worry," he continued. "We don't have to start here – in fact, we may not have to search here at all."

"Why not?"

"Don't you remember that Iris told us that her great uncle couldn't manage the stairs? She wouldn't want him to know that she had stolen something from the Abbey, so she would probably secrete it up there."

Uncharacteristically energetic, he headed out of the living room and up the stairs. Two doors led out of the landing at the top; Gawaine opened the nearer one to reveal a bathroom, and closed it again.

"Let's hope we're not reduced to looking for oilskin-wrapped parcels in the tank," he murmured.

The second door led into a bedroom. David had been prepared for a version of the chaos down below, but here everything was orderly, even Spartan. The pine bedstead had a brightly coloured patchwork bedcover; the rest of the furniture was similar pine. More of Iris's watercolours were hanging on the white-painted walls, and woven rugs were scattered on bare floorboards.

On one side of the room the ceiling sloped downwards; where it met the wall there was barely enough room to stand upright. Another door was set in this wall. David opened it – it needed a good tug – and peered into darkness.

"What can you see?" Gawaine asked, trying to look over his shoulder.

"Not a lot."

David scrabbled around the door frame until he

located a light switch. A single bare bulb lit up a narrow storage space running the length of the bedroom. A few cardboard boxes were piled up there and a number of canvases and an easel stacked against the wall.

"I think Iris must have stored her art supplies here," David said. "None of it looks very exciting, but we'd better have it out for a proper look."

While David hauled everything out into the bedroom, Gawaine began to investigate the boxes.

"Paints – oils and watercolours – brushes, a couple of palettes…" he murmured. "And those look like blank canvases. I don't think – David! What's *that*?"

As David removed the last of the canvases a package was revealed, tucked into the angle of the roof behind the stack. It was wrapped in what looked like an old red velvet curtain and neatly corded with some kind of braided twine.

"Bingo?" he suggested.

"As you say, my dear David, bingo. Or at the very least, something promising. Let's have it out."

David pulled out the object and handed it to Gawaine, who laid it on the bed and began carefully to pick at the knots.

"I could go down to the kitchen and fetch a knife," David offered.

"Patience, patience," Gawaine said. "Besides, we might want to do it up again."

The object was flat, and had felt quite solid under its squashy velvet wrappings. "Do you think it's a book?" David asked.

"I doubt it," Gawaine replied, still intent on his task.

"Ask yourself, what would Iris recognise that anyone else might miss? I think it's a picture."

As he spoke the last of the knots gave way and Gawaine was able to lay the velvet folds aside. He straightened up with the object in his hands.

David saw that it was a wooden panel, about the size of a large coffee-table book. The painting was dim, overlaid with the grime of years, he supposed, but he could make out a flat gold background with the figures of the Madonna and child, and a flock of haloed angels clustered around them.

"Is that it?" he asked.

At first Gawaine did not reply. David really looked at him for the first time; he had gone bone white, and his hands had started to shake. He leant forward and with exaggerated care laid the painting down on the bed. "Oh, dear Lord…" he whispered.

David was surprised to hear the name of his Creator on Gawaine's lips, until he realised that the words had been a prayer.

"It's a Cimabue," Gawaine continued, his voice hoarse in his throat. "It has to be a Cimabue."

David did not dare to ask, "Who?" After a moment he ventured, "Is that good?"

Gawaine answered the question he had not asked. "An early Italian painter, my dear David. Thirteenth century, if I recall correctly. It will have to be authenticated, of course," he continued. "I'm no expert, but it surely must be… Another one turned up in a kitchen in France, not all that long ago. And this has been sitting in the Abbey crypt for goodness knows how many years." Still shaking, he pointed to a small paper disc glued to the edge of the panel. "Certainly since the Victorians. And no one knew it was there…"

"Is it worth anything, then?"

"The French one sold for twenty million."

As if on cue, a massive clap of thunder crashed out right above, and rain began lashing at the window. Gawaine glanced up, as if to be sure that the roof wasn't leaking onto the precious painting. But the ceiling was unmarked, the roof so solid that the rain didn't even sound all that loud.

"*Twenty million?*"

Gawaine did not reply; he still looked shell-shocked. David nudged him into the basket chair beside the bed, and went downstairs in search of strong drink. He felt he needed it just as much as Gawaine; he couldn't even begin to think what this might mean for Iris's murder.

He found a half-full bottle of Glenfiddich in a kitchen cupboard, and took it, with a couple of glasses, back to the bedroom. Gawaine sat where he had left him, his gaze still fixed on the painting. When David gave him the glass he had to wrap both hands around it to keep it steady.

"Really, twenty million?" David said, sitting on the side of the bed, well away from the precious painting.

Gawaine drew in a deep breath, took a gulp of the whisky, and seemed to come back from whatever distant realm he had been inhabiting. "Oh, yes, my dear David, at least."

"Then why is it still here?" David began to realise that the discovery was raising more questions than it answered.

"Iris must have stolen it at Easter, at the latest. So why leave it wrapped up in her great uncle's cottage, instead of taking it and selling it?"

Gawaine blinked thoughtfully; it was a few moments before he answered. "I should imagine it was a question of provenance. If Iris should take this to an expert, or to a dealer, or make her own approach to a collector, the first question they would ask is, 'Where did you get it?'"

"Oh, I see. She could hardly tell them she had nicked it from St Cadoc's."

"No, but if she tucked it away up here, once Great Uncle Petroc died and she inherited the cottage – and the *contents*, don't forget that – she would have established a provenance for it. Petroc Tremayne was a great traveller when he was younger. He could have picked this painting up anywhere, not realising its real value."

David stared at him. Gawaine's frivolous exterior suggested that he pursued a lifestyle filled with sunshine and kittens – especially kittens – and yet he was capable of confronting the most horrific ideas without flinching.

"That's... cold," he said.

Gawaine tilted his head, considering. "Well, Great Uncle Petroc was ninety-two, with a weak heart."

"Even so... We didn't know Iris all that well, but she never struck me as being the sort of person who would do that. Stealing something so valuable, and from a church, at that. Waiting for your only close relative to die…"

"No, but she probably promised herself she would give some of her loot to St Cadoc's. After all, they wouldn't have had anything if she hadn't discovered the painting. Besides, she was under a lot of pressure at the time."

Gawaine spoke casually, as if David should understand what he meant, but David had no idea. "What pressure?"

"Have you forgotten what Seff told us, right at the start of this affair?" Gawaine asked. "Iris was worried about her relationship with Jake Fletcher. His film was just out, he was about to make another, he was all set for the celebrity lifestyle. Iris didn't think she would be able to keep him."

"I remember now." David reached for the whisky bottle and topped up both their glasses. "Seff said she was afraid Iris would go right off the rails if Jake left her."

Gawaine nodded. "So she offers her *inamorato* riches beyond the dreams of avarice, but when her great uncle actually dies a few months later, what she has done finally hits her. She breaks off her relationship with Jake, and comes down here to make her confession and return the painting whence it came."

"I don't suppose Jake was pleased."

"Nor do I, my dear David. And you do realise we have just given him an excellent motive for murder?"

"Jake the werewolf?" David had to suppress a grin; the thought was just so perfect. "You think he did it?"

"Well, now that the painting has come to light…" Gawaine responded. "I never liked the stalker theory, as you know. But this…" He gestured elegantly towards the painting. "However, we need to ask ourselves how he came to be on Morgarrow when he's supposed to be making a film at the other end of the country."

"Wouldn't he have been recognised?" David said. "Celebrity, film star and all that?"

Gawaine shook his head. "Seff thought not, if you remember. You know, I really wish that he had been the man on the ferry. Or even that the selfie had been deleted, as I expected."

"That would have clinched it," David agreed. "And what about the knitting needle?" he added. "Don't try to tell me that Jake Fletcher knits, because I won't believe you."

Gawaine's mouth quirked into a smile. "No, but it would make excellent publicity," he said. "Can't you picture the werewolf, knitting away between takes? No," he repeated, "but I have an idea about that knitting needle…"

David waited, but Gawaine did not enlighten him. "Then shouldn't we also ask ourselves who else might have known about the painting, other than Iris and Jake?" he continued when he was sure no explanation would be forthcoming. "There's your Annis, for a start."

Gawaine's brows went up. "My dear David, she is not 'my' Annis. And why do you assume she would have known?"

David restrained himself from pointing out that Gawaine was sounding unusually defensive. "She used to come in to look after Petroc," he replied. "She has keys. And somebody has been keeping the place clean – there isn't even much dust in that storage space. In fact," he continued, "I'd put money on Annis knowing the picture was there. She might not have unwrapped it, but she must have seen the parcel."

Gawaine nodded, though he still looked doubtful.

"There's Bernard White, too," David continued. "He had a set of keys. Don't you think he might have come in for a little snoop around?"

"But he has an alibi for Iris's murder," Gawaine pointed

out. "His wife said he was in the garden until it was time for his meeting with Roddy Chatham and George Pengelly."

"But did she actually see him there? He might have had time to pop up the back lane to kill Iris. You told me that his wife said he was wet when he came in," David insisted. "And we mustn't forget Roddy Chatham."

Gawaine shrugged. "My dear David, Roddy Chatham is no more than a low-level cat-poisoner. The timing is too tight, for him or for Bernard White. The only problem I can see is Bethany."

"Bethany?"

"Bethany was here at about the right time, and very soon afterwards, she died." Gawaine shivered slightly and tossed back the last of his whisky. "But no one who killed Iris also had the chance to kill Bethany. It's impossible."

"Unless Bethany killed Iris. Sergeant Godwin said she thought it had to have been a woman."

Gawaine frowned. "I've an idea about what she might have meant by that…" His voice trailed off; he was obviously thinking deeply. "No, I would like it to be Jake Fletcher," he went on after a moment. "If only we could place him on the island. Because he is the only person who would have left the painting in place after killing Iris. Anyone else would have stolen it then and there."

"But why—" David broke off as realisation hit him. "Iris's will!"

"Exactly, my dear David. Iris and Jake had made wills leaving what they had to each other. I must say, I'd love to know whether Jake persuaded Iris to do that before or after she stole the painting. But no matter… The important thing is that Jake believed that once Iris was dead, the cottage and the contents would belong to him. So he could 'discover' the painting once he took possession, and the provenance would remain intact."

"Inspector Bradshaw will say the same thing applies to Annis," David pointed out. "She *knew* she was going to inherit, under the new will. And Jake had an alibi. He was filming at the other end of the country, and if he had been here, someone might have recognised him, whatever Seff says."

Gawaine frowned, shaking his head. "Someone has been trying to get in here. Scuffling around in the early hours of this morning, according to the police officer on duty. I thought at first it was Roddy Chatham, depositing the poisoned sardines. But he says not, and I tend to believe him." He paused, giving David a pointed stare. "And Annis is the one person who doesn't need to break in. Once probate is dealt with, she can take possession legally."

David had to admit that Gawaine had a point, though it didn't prove anything. The mysterious person in the early hours could have been anyone, quite unconnected with Iris or the picture.

"So what do we do now?" he asked after a moment.

"We make something happen." Suddenly energetic, Gawaine sprang up and departed down the stairs. David could hear him moving about; then everything went quiet. David waited, but when Gawaine hadn't returned after several minutes, he took the whisky bottle and the glasses and went down to join him. Gawaine was standing in the middle of the living room, a large book clasped to his chest and an abstracted expression on his face.

"What are you doing?" David asked.

Gawaine started. "Oh – listening to the rain," he replied.

Without any more explanation, he headed back up the stairs. Shaking his head, David followed.

When he reached the bedroom, Gawaine was wrapping the book up in the velvet curtain that had covered the picture, winding the cords tightly around it.

"What are you doing?" David repeated. "What's that for?"

Gawaine looked up at him. "Bait," he said.

Chapter Twenty-three

…their game is all i' th' night.
The Devil's Law Case, III.i

By the time David and Gawaine emerged into the street, the brief squall was over. The air was filled with the sound of water dripping, or gurgling along in the gutters. A stiff breeze was blowing away the last rags of cloud; David was surprised to see the sun still high in the sky, the long summer day still some way from its end. He felt that hours, if not days, must have passed since they entered the cottage.

Gawaine had swathed the Cimabue reverently in a towel, and placed it in one of Iris's market bags, a stout linen affair that closed with a zip.

"What are you going to do with that?" David asked as they headed towards the hotel.

"For the time being, it can go in the hotel safe," Gawaine replied. "Tomorrow I must consult with the Trustees, and I hope that before then we can bring this affair to an end."

"Then you think someone will come for the picture tonight?" David said, nodding towards the bag that held it.

"I believe so. This will be the first night that there has been no police guard on the place. And the murderer will hardly want to hang about and risk someone else getting there first."

"I hope you're not suggesting that we go and lie in wait for him?" David said, alarmed because he guessed that was exactly what Gawaine was suggesting.

"Don't you want to be in at the death?"

"The *death* is what bothers me."

Gawaine reached over and patted his shoulder. "Don't worry, my dear David. I hope that we shall have Sergeant Godwin and her cohort of cops."

"Then you think she'll come?" David asked doubtfully.

"If we offer her the chance of making an arrest – when Inspector Bradshaw has already arrested the wrong person? My dear David, she'll bite my hand off."

"And if you're wrong? If no one turns up? Suppose it was Annis, after all? She's still in police custody."

Gawaine halted at the door of the hotel. "It was not Annis," he said decisively. "Now, David, suppose you find Seff. She'll want to be brought up to date. And once I've deposited this painting, we can have a council of war."

David tracked Seff down in the hotel bar; the barman was just serving her a gin and tonic. Ordering one for himself, and Prosecco for Gawaine, David took the seat opposite her.

"Where have you been?" he asked. "We've a lot to tell you. For a start, Annis Radford—"

"Has been arrested for Iris's murder," Seff interrupted. "I was over there on the mainland when the police brought her in. It will make a very nice scoop. The other nationals think this little murder is beneath them."

And how wrong they are, David thought, reflecting on how much of a scoop the discovery of the Cimabue would make, not to mention the arrest of Iris's murderer – especially if he turned out to be the latest celebrity werewolf.

"Be careful what you say," he warned Seff. "Gawaine doesn't think she did it. Apparently the smart money is on Jake Fletcher."

"Jake? *Really*?" Seff's whole face lit up. "Oh, I wish…" Then the light died and she frowned, shaking her head. "He wasn't even on the island."

David shrugged. "That's the problem. To strangle someone, you have to be on the spot."

"Then I hope whoever it was, Gawaine can make it stick." Seff still sounded dubious. "You'll never make me believe that Jake Fletcher cared enough about Iris to kill her."

"Oh, it wasn't *Iris* he cared about. He—"

David broke off as the barman appeared to serve the drinks. As he retreated, Gawaine appeared at the entrance to the bar and made his way towards their table, already talking on his mobile phone.

"But my dear Sergeant Godwin, I've explained to you that Inspector Bradshaw has arrested the wrong person. Wouldn't you like to arrest the right one?"

He paused, obviously listening to the sergeant on the other end, while he slid into his seat and took a sip of Prosecco with a nod of thanks to David. Seff leaned closer, clearly frustrated at only hearing one side of the conversation.

"The murderer believes there is an extremely valuable

artefact in that cottage," Gawaine continued. "He will come to collect it tonight." A brief pause. "How do I know? Because until now the cottage has been a crime scene, guarded by your highly efficient officers. And the murderer will not risk leaving it any longer in case someone else should find it first."

More silence, and when Gawaine spoke again, there was a faint tinge of impatience in his voice. "Sergeant Godwin, if I'm wrong, and Annis Radford did indeed murder Iris Grant, then no one will come and you will have lost a good night's sleep. But if I'm right, you will make a highly spectacular arrest. Your choice, Sergeant."

The silence was shorter this time, and ended with Gawaine ending the call. "She'll come," he said. "So now, my dear Persephone, take out your notebook and I will a tale unfold."

The last of the daylight had faded from the sky, and cloud had gathered to cover the moon and stars when David, Gawaine and Seff walked down from the hotel to meet Sergeant Godwin at the cottage. David was relieved to see that she had brought with her two large and determined-looking police officers.

"You'd better be right," the sergeant said to Gawaine. "If you're not, Inspector Bradshaw won't like it."

And that bothers you, why? David thought.

"Does he know?" Gawaine asked.

Sergeant Godwin shook her head. "When you rang, he was interrogating Ms Radford. I put my head around the door and said, 'Inspector – ' and he said, 'Not *now*, Sergeant,' so I reckon I'm covered."

"Oh, very neat," Seff murmured.

Sergeant Godwin whipped her head around and glared at her; Seff looked as if she regretted drawing attention to herself. David half expected the sergeant to order her to leave, but after a moment she merely shrugged.

"All three of you, stay out of the way," she said. "I don't want this mucked up."

She turned to give orders to her minions, who rapidly faded into the gloom. Seff vanished a little way down the village street, while David and Gawaine headed into Annis's garden and took cover behind her lilac bush.

"He'll probably come up the back lane," Gawaine whispered.

After his uncharacteristic energy of earlier in the evening, he had lapsed into a fit of nerves; David could feel him quivering as they stood close together in the shelter of the bush.

"Thank goodness it's not full moon," he murmured into Gawaine's ear.

Gawaine stifled a little spurt of laughter. "Not at all," he responded. "A wolf would be quite incapable of entering the cottage and abstracting the parcel. But it's dark enough for all kinds of ghoulies and ghosties and long-leggety beasties."

"And murderers."

David felt a deeper shudder pass through Gawaine. "As you say, my dear David. And murderers."

Time seemed to drag by, but when David glanced at his watch they had only been standing there for about fifteen minutes. And it was still relatively early; the murderer was likely to wait until all the respectable inhabitants of Morgarrow were safely tucked up in bed.

The thought had only just crossed David's mind when he felt Gawaine clutch at his arm. "There..." his friend breathed out.

A dark shape was moving towards them from further down the back lane. The flickering light of a torch announced its coming, but the faint light was directed at the ground ahead of it, showing hardly anything of the figure who held it.

As it drew closer, David thought it was taller and bulkier than he had expected from his sight of Jake Fletcher, and it seemed oddly shapeless. It passed the bottom of Annis's garden with hardly a sound; a moment later David heard the faint creaking of Iris's gate.

"That's not... right," Gawaine murmured.

His voice shook a little; David thought he was becoming thoroughly spooked. He dismissed the idea that some undead creature was stalking up Iris's garden path, yet something was going on that they had not expected.

The next sound was the unmistakable rasp of a key in the lock of the back door. David felt Gawaine give a start.

"He has a *key*?"

"Jake could have got a copy made when he was down here at Easter," David suggested in a whisper.

The sound of the back door opening and closing. Edging forward a little, with Gawaine at his shoulder, David could see the pale light flickering in the kitchen; a moment later it disappeared, to reappear almost at once in the bedroom upstairs.

Sergeant Godwin appeared, flanked by one of her minions, and let herself into the garden. Seff followed, waiting by the garden gate.

They had not long to wait. The torch light appeared again downstairs; the dark figure let itself out; David could just make out something bundled up under its arm.

Sergeant Godwin stepped forward. "Stop right there," she said, turning on a powerful torch.

The beam shone into the face – blinking, bewildered – of Father Magnus.

Chapter Twenty-four

We are engaged in mischief and must on;
As rivers to find out the ocean
Flow with crook bendings beneath forced banks.
The White Devil, I.ii

"I can explain," said Father Magnus.

David's mind was suddenly whirling, wondering if somehow they had got everything wrong. He had once wondered whether Father Magnus might have been Iris's murderer, but he had never taken the idea seriously. Beside him, Gawaine looked equally shocked. He emerged from the shelter of the bush, seemed about to speak, then changed his mind and remained silent.

Sergeant Godwin took a step back, lowering her torch so that the beam no longer shone into the priest's face. "Okay, go ahead," she said.

Father Magnus gestured with the velvet-wrapped book that Gawaine had prepared in place of the painting. "This belongs to St Cadoc's," he said. "Iris was taking care of it temporarily, but I thought it best to remove it, since it isn't covered by the terms of her will."

Sergeant Godwin grunted, clearly unsure whether to believe him. "You have a key?" she asked eventually.

Father Magnus displayed the familiar bunch, with the

chunky Celtic key fob. "If that unfortunate young woman is convicted of Iris's murder, the cottage will revert to the Abbey," he explained. "I am one of the Trustees."

Sergeant Godwin was still eyeing him narrowly, as if she was making up her mind. One of her minions leaned over to his colleague and muttered, "Does she expect us to arrest a bloomin' priest?"

Instead, Sergeant Godwin swung around to confront David and Gawaine, who were still watching over the fence from Annis's garden. "This isn't who you were expecting?" she challenged Gawaine.

"No, it's not," Gawaine responded. "I'm sorry, Sergeant, but—"

"'Sorry' doesn't begin to cover it," Sergeant Godwin snapped. "You're lucky I'm not going to arrest you for wasting police time."

"It could still work," Gawaine protested, beginning to sound desperate. "If we wait a little longer…"

"No way." Sergeant Godwin seemed to be growing angrier with every moment that passed. David guessed she was disappointed that after all she couldn't steal a march on Inspector Bradshaw. "You must think I was born yesterday."

"All right, I admit this went wrong," Gawaine said. "But there's something else I need to tell you. I really think you ought to—"

"That's enough," the sergeant interrupted. "I must have been out of my mind to think that I could co-operate with you. Annis Radford murdered Iris Grant. End of." Jerking her head towards her minions, she added, "Come on. We're done here."

She headed for the garden gate, but before she reached it, she halted. "You," she said, pointing at one of her officers. "Stay on watch. You can come back on the eight thirty ferry."

She might be angry with Gawaine, David thought. *But she's still covering herself in case he was right.*

When she had spat out her final order, Sergeant Godwin stalked off to where the police launch was moored at the jetty, and the remaining officer followed her. The man left behind on watch let out a heavy sigh and plonked himself down on the bench in front of Iris's kitchen window.

Gawaine, David and Father Magnus were left staring at one another, along with Seff, who was scribbling ecstatically in her notebook. Eventually Gawaine met Father Magnus at the gate and reached out for the velvet-wrapped bundle.

"That isn't what you think it is, Father," he said. "If you don't mind, I think I'd better put it back where it came from."

Father Magnus stared at the bundle. "It's not—"

"No, but don't worry." Gawaine flicked a swift glance at the police officer. "I'll explain everything."

The old priest hesitated a moment longer, then handed over the bundle. Gawaine took it and headed inside, switching on the lights as there was no more need for stealth. The police officer opened his mouth as if he was about to protest, then closed it again with another heavy sigh.

"I think I must owe you an apology," Father Magnus said to David after a moment. "Am I right in thinking I have sprung a trap you set for somebody else?"

"Yes," David replied, unsure of what more to say. He still wasn't sure that he trusted Father Magnus; he needed time to consider whether the priest might be a murderer. "It might not have worked anyway," he added feebly.

The light had flicked on in Iris's bedroom, but now all was dark again. But before Gawaine returned, light shone out in Great Uncle Petroc's bathroom, only to vanish a few seconds later.

What is he up to now? David wondered.

Almost at once, Gawaine emerged from the kitchen; he was slipping something small into the inside pocket of his jacket, mystifying David even further.

"All done," Gawaine said, sounding satisfied. "If you would lock up, Father…" Turning to the police officer, he added, "I'm terribly sorry you've been stuck with this. I'll bring you some coffee from the hotel."

"Tea, if you wouldn't mind, sir," the officer said, perking up a little. "Strong tea. Milk. Two sugars."

Father Magnus, having checked that the back door was secure, was shifting impatiently. "This explanation…" he began.

"Of course, Father," Gawaine said. "Shall we walk…?"

"Where is the picture?" Father Magnus demanded as soon as they were out of earshot of the police officer.

"In the hotel safe," Gawaine replied. "David and I found it earlier today."

The old priest frowned. "You knew there was something to find?"

"He worked it out," Seff put in. "It's a very bad habit."

"It wasn't difficult," Gawaine said, self-deprecating. "It made sense of why Iris was creeping around the Abbey the night before she died. And you gave me a hint yourself, Father, after the reading of her will."

Father Magnus looked briefly ashamed of himself. "I thought it best, but that's water under the bridge now. I came down tonight because I wanted to remove the picture and put it back in the crypt, where in the fullness of time I would discover it. I saw no point in ruining Iris's reputation since she had every intention of returning the picture."

By this time they had reached the gate into the hotel garden. Gawaine halted and said, "I could fetch it for you now, Father."

Father Magnus hesitated for a moment, then shook his head. "I suggest you bring it up to St Morwenna's tomorrow. It's our monthly Trustees' meeting, and members of the public are allowed to sit in. I think you might find it interesting."

There was a faint edge to his tone, so that David wondered if he meant 'interesting' as in 'May you live in interesting times'.

Gawaine took a breath. "Very well, Father. We'll do that."

"Then I'll say good night to you." With a general nod, Father Magnus turned and strode off down the road until the glimmer of his torch vanished down the back lane.

Gawaine led the way into the hotel. Everything was dark and quiet except for a dim light over the reception desk and another in the dining room above the coffee machine.

"We never thought about him!" David exclaimed, feeling that he was about to burst with everything he wanted to say. "He could have done it – he could have come by the tracks across the moor. I'm guessing that's what he did tonight."

Gawaine had taken a mug and was persuading the machine to squirt out tea. "Motive?" he asked, raising a brow at David.

"The picture, of course!" David struggled with impatience; he couldn't understand why Gawaine was being so obtuse. "He knew it was there, and he must have known how valuable it is, once Iris had made her confession."

"That's a long way from deciding to commit murder," Gawaine pointed out.

"Then why would he come sneaking down there at night, instead of going to the cottage in daylight, as he had the perfect right to do?"

"He told us," Gawaine responded. "To protect Iris's reputation."

David let out a snort. "Well, he had to think of something, once we caught him."

"I still don't think there's a strong enough motive," Gawaine said. "Once Iris confessed, Father Magnus knew that the picture would be returned to St Cadoc's."

"But that's exactly what I'm trying to tell you! Honestly, Gawaine, are you really as innocent as all that? He didn't want the picture for St Cadoc's. He wanted it for himself."

"He has a point," Seff put in. So far she had been quiet, her gaze flicking from Gawaine to David and back again, like the umpire at a tennis match. "He's getting old. Maybe he's tired of living in some shack up on the moor."

"Seff's right," David said, faintly surprised that he had

even said that. "And to get the picture, he had to kill Iris, because otherwise she would—"

"I believe 'blow the gaff' is the phrase, my dear David," Gawaine said sweetly. "And that is also true of Jake Fletcher or anyone else who wanted to profit from the painting." He neatly fitted a lid on his mug of tea and slid a few wrapped sugar cubes and a couple of packets of biscuits into his pocket. "Besides, you've forgotten about Bethany."

"What about Bethany?"

"Because any theory about Iris's death has to take account of Bethany, and that's something that so far you haven't managed to do."

Still annoyed, David had to admit that was true. "You could at least check out Father Magnus's alibi," he said.

"Barrel, scraping the bottom of…" Gawaine murmured. "And there's something else you've forgotten," he added.

"What?"

"The knitting needle. You'll not convince me that Father Magnus knits, nor does he live with any knitters."

"But he might have—"

"Wait," Seff interrupted. "Gawaine, just now you said to David, *you* haven't managed to account for Bethany's death. Do you mean that you *have*?"

Gawaine's whole demeanour changed; his expression tightened and he seemed to draw into himself. "Oh yes," he said.

"Then who?" David asked. "How?"

At first, Gawaine did not reply, simply looking troubled. Then he said, "I know what happened, but I have no way of proving it."

David wanted to ask him to explain, but he knew there

was no chance of that. Gawaine never explained until he was ready. And much as that annoyed him, he understood.

Gawaine seemed to give himself a mental shake. "I'd better take this tea down to our local gendarme," he said, "before it goes cold."

"You're never going on your own?" David asked, as Gawaine made for the door. "There could be anyone lurking out there."

Gawaine turned to him, his anxiety draining away; he gave David a luminous smile. "My dear David, there's absolutely no danger," he said. "Think how many people know about the picture now. Unless he went on a killing spree…"

David noticed the 'he', in spite of Sergeant Godwin's theory that the crime had been committed by a woman. But he was not going to follow that up now.

"But does he know that we know?" he responded to Gawaine. "I'm coming with you."

Gawaine did not protest. Saying good night to Seff, he and David went out and headed towards the village. The clouds had cleared away and a three-quarter moon floated above the sea.

"Tomorrow…" David began, not quite sure what he wanted to say. "At the Trustees' meeting. Are you going to wrap this up?"

Gawaine sighed. "I wish I could. I really do. But there is a little matter of evidence – which in this case I have not got. No, it will be a while before I can wrap this up… If I ever do."

Chapter Twenty-five

His nature is too honest for such business.
        The Duchess of Malfi, I.i

"I went down to Annis's cottage this morning, and phoned her vet," Gawaine said. "He'll keep Merino for the time being, until we know what's happening to Annis."

David wondered what would happen to the cat Merino if Annis didn't return. He suspected that Gawaine might add a third feline to the two he already possessed.

He, Gawaine and Seff were leaving the hotel on the way to the Trustees' meeting at St Morwenna's. Gawaine had liberated the picture from the hotel safe and was carrying it in its market bag. David suspected he would be happy to hand it over to someone who would take responsibility for it.

"I dropped into Iris's next door, too," Gawaine continued. "Nothing has been disturbed. The package is still there."

"That's just what you would expect, with the police back on watch," Seff pointed out.

"Indeed, my dear Persephone. But—"

Gawaine broke off at the shout of "Seff!" coming from behind them. All three halted and turned to see Jake Fletcher following them up the road, covering the ground with rapid strides.

He caught them up, giving an indiscriminate nod to David and Gawaine. "Hi, Gavin, Dave." Turning to Seff, he continued, "Do you have any idea where I can get a key to Iris's cottage? I left a few things there when I was here at Easter, and I'd like to pick them up before I leave."

David wasn't sure how he managed to stop himself from glancing at Gawaine, or even worse, at the market bag with its precious contents. *Surely he's given himself away?* His remaining suspicions of Annis Radford vanished like morning mist.

"Oh, one of the Trustees can help you," Seff replied. "They're all up at St Morwenna's at the moment, for a meeting. Why don't you come with us?"

"Sure." Jake fell into step beside them as they headed up the road once more.

David bent his head to murmur into Gawaine's ear. "Will you come into my parlour, said the—"

"Don't," Gawaine interrupted. "Just don't."

He looked thoroughly uncomfortable; David guessed it wasn't from the thought of the many-legged, so much as the way Seff was clearly trying to entice a murder suspect to his doom.

David realised that the Trustees' meeting was almost ideally organised for Gawaine to do what Nathan had described as the Poirot thing. All the Trustees would be there, and he was ready to bet that Roddy Chatham would be with them. And since the public were allowed to sit in, there might even be some of Elaine Chatham's students.

Seff and Jake had drawn a little way ahead, enough for David to ask, "Are you going to explain it all now? It was Jake Fletcher, wasn't it?"

Gawaine hesitated, then took a deep breath. When he spoke, he was at his most affected. "Oh, the dramatic moment! How can I possibly resist?" Then, abruptly dropping his affectations, he added, "Yes, of course it was Jake Fletcher. But as I said last night, I can't prove it. I haven't enough evidence."

"There's enough evidence against Annis Radford," David reminded him.

Gawaine looked up at him, his eyes wide and tragic. "I know. That's what's worrying me."

He was looking particularly worn, and David suspected he hadn't slept much the night before. "Are you okay?" he asked.

Gawaine sighed. "I do feel a little frayed around the edges," he confessed. "But I will survive. I spent most of last night writing out an account of what happened," he continued. His lips twisted wryly. "And all I had to show for it in the end was a pounding headache."

"Have you taken anything?" David asked. "I've some paracetamol…"

"No thank you, my dear David." Gawaine managed a wan smile. "I have some stuff my doctor prescribed. It's remarkably efficient, though I confess it does leave me feeling somewhat… limp.

"However," he went on, "*a nos moutons*, I think I've covered all the points that were puzzling us. But I haven't the *evidence*," he repeated. "No cigar ash, no footprints with identifiable mud, no incriminating threads. Honestly, my dear David, I feel like a dog hunting for fleas."

"Somehow I don't see you as a scruffy mongrel

scratching itself," David told him; Gawaine was immaculate as always in spite of his weariness.

"How kind…" Gawaine murmured.

"And you didn't find any?" David said. "Fleas, I mean."

"Not a one. Though there is a fine juicy flea that unfortunately I can't get my hands on," he added. "I tried to tell Sergeant Godwin last night, but she wouldn't listen." He let out another sigh. "If they don't release Annis, I must try again."

The Trustees' meeting was held in a large room at the back of the house, with French windows opening onto an overgrown garden. Large squashy armchairs, upholstered in faded chintzes, were ranged around the sides, while at one end a screen had been set up, with a computer on a table in front of it. Roddy Chatham was fiddling with the computer.

"Oh, we're going to have a presentation!" Seff said brightly as she found a seat for herself. "What fun that will be."

Bernard White was supervising Roddy with his usual air of lemon-sucking disapproval. He looked smart and austere as always, except for the rose – a crimson bud this time – in his buttonhole.

"I suppose we all know what they're going to show us," David said, taking the seat beside Seff. After the shattering discovery of the picture he had almost forgotten about Morgarrow Moor, but he supposed the timeshare development was still high on Bernard White's list of priorities.

Gawaine murmured something indistinct. Instead

of sitting down, he went across the room to where Father Magnus stood talking to Jenny Morland beside the windows, and handed over the market bag with the picture.

Meanwhile, Jake Fletcher had marched straight up to the table, clearly spotting Bernard White as the man in charge. "Hi, I'm Jake Fletcher," he announced. "I need to borrow the key to Iris Grant's cottage."

Bernard White was unimpressed; clearly he had no interest in werewolves. "I remember seeing you at her funeral," he said after a moment's icy silence. "But why do you need to get into the cottage?"

Jake produced his trademark charming smile. "You know Iris and I were together, right? I was down here at Easter, and I left a few things in her cottage. I'm leaving today, and I'd like to pick them up before I go."

"Well, I can't see to it now." Bernard White began to sound irritated. "The meeting is about to start. Why don't you have a seat, and someone will go down with you when we've finished."

Jake's charm began to slip a bit. "You don't need to come with me. Give me the key, and I'll bring it back when I've collected my stuff."

Bernard White drew in air through his nostrils. "Do you imagine I'm going to give the keys to Trust property to any Tom, Dick or Harry who comes waltzing in and asks for them? You can either wait, or do without."

Jake looked about to argue, then thought better of it, and flung himself into a chair at the far side of the room, obviously in a furious sulk.

Seff leaned over and spoke in a low voice to David.

"Trust property? He's jumping the gun a bit, isn't he? That cottage belongs to Annis."

"I suppose he assumes that Annis murdered Iris," David responded. "If she did, she can't profit from her crime. According to Father Magnus, the cottage will revert to the Trust."

Seff gave a little feral grin. "I suppose Jake is working out how he's going to get the picture out under Bernard's nose."

While she was speaking, the door opened to admit Elaine Chatham and the student Nathan, both carrying vast trays of tea, and Grace with a platter of cakes. As they began handing round, David noticed that Grace gave Jake Fletcher a startled look as she offered him a brownie.

"I think Jake has a fan," David murmured. "As far as I know, that's the first person who has recognised him."

Jake, stuck in his frustration, seemed not to notice, though he accepted the brownie and inhaled it in a couple of bites.

A moment later David's amusement faded as Grace intercepted Gawaine as he crossed the room to rejoin David and Seff. "Have one of Elaine's brownies. They're delicious," she said aloud, then added something else too quietly for David to hear, with a sidelong glance at Jake Fletcher.

Gawaine's brows went up, and he signed to Grace for silence, before thanking her for the brownie and taking his own seat beside David.

"What was all that about?" David asked.

"A flea," Gawaine replied. "Or to mix my metaphors, a useful wisp of straw. But I shall need more than that if I'm going to make bricks."

When the tea service was over, everyone began to settle down, and Bernard White rapped the table with a gavel. "Let's come to order, please. Father Magnus, will you start us off with a prayer."

To David's relief, Father Magnus kept it short and sweet, simply asking God's blessing on their deliberations. Jenny Morland passed around copies of the agenda and took a seat at the table with a pad of paper to take minutes.

The first item was the minutes of the previous meeting. While Bernard White droned on, his reading punctuated by the clicking of Elaine's knitting needles – she had a white strip this time – David leaned over to Gawaine.

"Look at that," he murmured, pointing to the next item on the agenda. "'Election of new Trustee.' Can they do that?"

Gawaine's only reply was a shrug. He was looking desperately worried, drawn into himself. He never liked the moment when he had to expose a murderer, but this was the first time David could remember when he had the murderer identified, the interested parties assembled, but little evidence to offer. And Gawaine had already said that wasn't enough.

But if he says nothing, Jake Fletcher will leave. The police won't look any further; they think they've got their murderer. Annis will be charged and convicted. There won't be any more evidence than whatever Gawaine has now.

The minutes over and accepted, Bernard White rapped again with his gavel and rose to expound. "Since the sad death of Petroc Tremayne," he began, "I for one have felt the lack of our fifth Trustee. With only four of us, it becomes much more difficult to embark on any significant work on behalf of St Cadoc's."

"So that's what this is about!" Seff whispered to David. "He wants to sell Morgarrow Moor to the rest of the Trustees, and he's going to need Roddy's vote."

Bernard White paused, having picked up the whisper if not its sense, and glared at Seff, who returned the look calmly, quite unfazed.

"Therefore, I'm going to suggest to my fellow Trustees that we confirm a new Trustee immediately," Bernard continued, "and in my mind there really is no question of who that should be. Roddy Chatham—"

"But Roddy isn't resident on the island," Jenny Morland interrupted.

Roddy Chatham, who had been glancing around the room complacently as Bernard White began to speak, gave a sudden start and gazed at Jenny with an injured expression.

"I'll come to that, Jenny dear," Bernard White said, coldly dismissive. "As I said, there really is no question of who we should choose to join us. Roddy has worked hard for St Cadoc's for a number of years, he knows how we operate, and he is young, with a valuable new perspective, and, I'm willing to guess, lots of new ideas."

"Yeah, that's right," Roddy said.

"He still doesn't live on the island," Jenny repeated.

"Jenny, dear, I know you care very deeply for St Cadoc's, but please don't be difficult." Bernard White's cold tone had given way to condescension that David guessed she would find even more offensive. "We all know that one, if not two cottages will become available in the not too distant future, and it seems unnecessarily nitpicking not to confirm Roddy for the sake of a few weeks."

"A moment, Bernard." Father Magnus's voice was a deep rumble in his chest. "If you're referring to Annis Radford's cottage and the one that used to be Petroc's, we don't know anything of the sort. Miss Radford, to the best of my knowledge, hasn't been charged yet, much less convicted."

"Poor girl!" Elaine Chatham paused in her knitting, her face full of distress. "I'm sure I hope it's all a dreadful mistake."

"Well, we may all hope that, Elaine." Bernard White was still at his most patronising. "But we have to face facts. If Annis Radford didn't kill Iris, then who did?"

There was a stir in the room; David was conscious that some faces at least were turning towards Gawaine. He could sense his friend stiffening.

"I can't do this." Gawaine's voice was no more than a murmur, but it was taut with panic. "I haven't the evidence. It's not going to work."

Before David could respond, there came a loud knock on the door.

"What now?" Bernard White said, exasperated.

The door swung open. Sergeant Godwin stood there, letting her gaze travel slowly and deliberately around the room.

"Really, Sergeant!" Bernard White exclaimed. "We're in the middle of a meeting."

Sergeant Godwin ignored him; her gaze had settled on Roddy Chatham. "Mr Chatham," she said. "I thought I might find you here."

"What do you want?" Roddy asked, sounding truculent.

"Roderick Chatham," the sergeant began, suddenly more formal, "I arrest you on the charge of poisoning the cat belonging to Annis Radford..." The rest of her speech was half drowned by exclamations of surprise, and Elaine Chatham's wail of, "Roddy! You didn't!"

Roddy couldn't even protest, only staring at the sergeant, his face slowly reddening. At least, David thought, he had the sense to see that for this crime at least there was more than enough evidence to convict him.

"You'll need to come with us to the station and make a statement," Sergeant Godwin continued. Her expression was smug and lively; David could almost see her whiskers twitching. "I'm sure we'll be able to arrange bail – eventually."

Roddy cast a hunted glance at the open French windows, but he must have realised there was nowhere he could go. Besides, a large uniformed officer was looming up in the doorway behind Sergeant Godwin.

"That settles your suggestion, Bernard," Jenny said as Roddy trailed across to meet his doom. David detected a certain unpriestly satisfaction in her tone. "The articles of the Trust say that no one may become a Trustee if they have a criminal record. I'm afraid Roddy has made himself ineligible."

Suddenly furious, Bernard White opened his mouth to say something, then clamped it shut again. Seff leaned over to David and said, "Goodbye, Morgarrow Moor."

"And goodbye Roddy," David responded.

On her way out with her prey, Sergeant Godwin turned back. "By the way, I suppose you would like to know," she said. "Inspector Bradshaw has charged Annis Radford with the murder of Iris Grant."

A tingling silence followed her declaration. It was broken by Gawaine, who half rose from his seat. "He can't do that! Annis didn't do it."

Sergeant Godwin directed an unfriendly gaze at him. "And I suppose you know who did?"

Gawaine sank back into his chair. When he spoke, it was as if the words were being wrung out of him. "Yes, I do."

"Really?" Sergeant Godwin came back into the room, shoved Roddy Chatham down into a nearby seat, and took the one beside him. Her officer stayed on guard in the doorway. "Then you'd better enlighten the rest of us. Fire away."

Chapter Twenty-six

I know death hath ten thousand several doors
For men to take their exits.
The Duchess of Malfi, IV.ii

"The main problem in all of this, the *pons asinorum*, as we might say," Gawaine began at his most pedantic, "has always been the death of Bethany Fox." Trapped into this declaration, he was struggling, David could see. "There are three possibilities. One, that Bethany died by accident and her death was completely unconnected with that of Iris Grant. Two, that Bethany killed Iris, then killed herself in a fit of remorse."

"Hey, that can't be right!" Nathan interrupted. "Bethany would never have killed anyone, not in a million years."

Gawaine acknowledged his protest with a nod. "Three," he continued, "that Iris's murderer also killed Bethany. I discount the first possibility because I dislike – intensely dislike – coincidences. Besides, Bethany could not have been swept off the cliff in the storm, because she had ample time to reach St Morwenna's before the storm broke.

"And I discount the second option, because from all that I hear of Bethany, she was not the stuff of which murderers are made. Which leaves possibility three." He paused and took a breath. "Yet it appeared from the timing of Iris's death and the events surrounding it that no one who killed Iris could also have killed Bethany. And for that I partly blame myself."

Sergeant Godwin sighed. "Get on with it. Give me a name."

"All in good time," Gawaine promised.

Now he was fairly launched, David could see, he had set aside his reluctance; he had full command of himself and his material. There would be, of course, a reaction afterwards.

"For a long time," Gawaine continued, "I wondered whether the murderer had crossed to Morgarrow on the eight o'clock ferry from the mainland, which was, of course, the first and only ferry on the morning of the storm. However, the selfie on Bethany's phone proved that the only passenger on the ferry, apart from Bethany herself, was Roddy Chatham."

A horrified gasp came from Roddy's mother. "Roddy – no!"

Gawaine cast her a sympathetic glance. "No, Roddy Chatham was not the murderer. He crossed on the ferry, briefly visited this house to collect his laptop, and then dashed back through the storm to attend the meeting with Bernard White and George Pengelly. His time is accounted for. It is remotely possible that he could have killed Iris, but he had no opportunity of killing Bethany, who headed into the village once she left the ferry."

Seff had slid out a notepad and was discreetly scribbling. Sergeant Godwin wasn't taking notes, but her gaze was riveted on Gawaine, who seemed unaware of either of them.

"Of course, that means," he went on, "that the murderer was already on the island on the day Iris died, which might suggest that he lived on Morgarrow. I considered you, Mr White—"

An explosive noise from Bernard White interrupted him. Jenny Morland, without breaking her attention on Gawaine, said, "Shut up, Bernard," and Gawaine continued.

"Bernard White was supposedly in his garden, and did not come in until after the rain started. Once again, he could possibly have killed Iris, but he had no chance of killing Bethany. The farmer, George Pengelly, also had motive for killing Iris, and we have no knowledge of his movements until he turned up for the meeting at Bernard White's. But like the others, he could not have killed Bethany."

"But what's the point of all this?" Sergeant Godwin interrupted, beginning to sound annoyed. "I told you, this was a woman's crime. Annis Radford—"

Gawaine raised a hand, and to David's astonishment, Sergeant Godwin broke off.

"I think I understand why you believe that, Sergeant," Gawaine said calmly. "I shall come to why you are wrong in a moment. But first let us pick up our murderer when he crossed to the island on the day before. He chose, of course, not the early ferry where someone might have noticed him, but one much later in the day when there were many more passengers and he could be inconspicuous in the crowd.

"His purpose was to speak to Iris – alone, because

if things went wrong for him he had come prepared to kill her. But that day Iris had just moved into her cottage, and either David and I, or Annis, were with her. She also had a brief visit from Bernard White, and immediately afterwards went to see Father Magnus."

"She did," Father Magnus confirmed.

"After that," Gawaine continued, "she spent the evening having supper with Annis, and very late at night she paid a visit to the Abbey, where she was seen by Jenny Morland."

"That's right," Jenny said.

"I can understand how frustrating it must have been for our murderer, but at some point he gave up for the night. I don't know where he stayed, but I doubt that he used the hotel or a B and B, because his purpose was to come and go with no evidence that he had been there at all. I might draw your attention to the covered area behind the supermarket, and the curious incident of the dog in the night-time, when someone knocked the bin over. But that is of minor importance. What is important is that he tried once again to visit Iris very early the next morning, and this time he was successful."

"But—" Sergeant Godwin began, then clamped her lips shut.

"Sergeant Godwin," Gawaine said, "this is why you think a woman murdered Iris. Because Iris was wearing her pyjamas and a dressing gown, and you believe that she would not have let a man into her cottage if she was not dressed. And to some extent I agree with you. She would be unlikely to let in Bernard White and Roddy Chatham, who at the time were quite hostile to her, and even less likely to let in George Pengelly, who was unknown to her, and would be intimidating at the best of times. As for Father Magnus..." Gawaine turned to the old priest. "I'm sorry, Father, but after last night, I had to eliminate you. Of course, you, as a celibate priest, would never dream of paying a visit to a woman unless you could be sure she would be decently clothed."

Father Magnus let out a rusty chuckle. "Indeed."

"But there is one man we have not considered. One man whom Iris would willingly let in – the man she had lived with for some years, and who had seen her in – if I may say so – a greater state of *deshabille* than she was in that morning."

"Here!" Jake Fletcher shot to his feet. "Don't you try putting this on me! I wasn't even on the island."

"That, of course, is what you wanted everyone to think."

David noticed at that moment that the student Grace had suddenly straightened, and leaned over to whisper something in Nathan's ear. But she said nothing out loud.

Jake let out a snort of contempt. "Then explain how I could be down here, killing Iris, when I was filming up in the Lake District."

"For what it's worth," Sergeant Godwin put in, "from the day before the murder to the day after, you had a break from filming. They were shooting scenes with your stunt double."

"You checked up on me!" Jake was outraged.

"Of course." Sergeant Godwin narrowed her eyes as she gazed at Jake: not a mouse any longer, but a leopard who had spotted prey. "We checked up on everybody who had a connection with Iris." Her tone was distinctly more friendly as she turned to Gawaine and said, "Go on."

Jake Fletcher flung himself back into his chair. "Yeah, go on," he said. "I'm on the edge of my effing seat."

Gawaine winced slightly at the vulgarity. "At this point," he began, "it might be useful to go back to Bethany. We know that after she got off the ferry she went to the supermarket. Megan Carter warned her to get back to St Morwenna's quickly, as it was going to rain. Since Bethany knew Iris – she used to be one of Iris's students – I imagine that she might think of taking shelter with her. She rang Iris's doorbell, but she got no answer. And what would she do then?" Gawaine posed the question, but it was purely rhetorical. "She might have fled for St Morwenna's, but what she actually did was go round the back. And with that, she sealed her death warrant. Because she met Jake Fletcher, coming out of Iris's garden gate, and by that time Iris was already dead."

David stared at his friend. "But you—" he began, but Jake Fletcher's louder protest drowned him out.

"That's rubbish! You spoke to her on the phone, after the storm broke."

Gawaine looked at him, blinking. "How do you know that?"

For a moment Jake gaped at him, completely nonplussed. "I – I read it in the paper," he said at last.

"Not in mine, you didn't," Seff said.

"Or in any other," Sergeant Godwin said. "We reserved that piece of information. Ms Brown was the only reporter who knew it, and when I asked her not to publish it, she co-operated."

"Well…" Jake shrugged angrily. "I heard it somewhere."

"Let's keep that in its proper place," Gawaine suggested.

"Sergeant Godwin, I take it there's no forensic reason why Iris couldn't have died earlier?"

"None at all," the sergeant confirmed. "In fact, our pathologist was quite surprised that it was as late as we believed."

Gawaine nodded in acknowledgement. "Then we have Jake Fletcher leaving Iris's cottage at about eight twenty-five. He has already broken the pane in the kitchen door, and hidden Iris's bag under the bushes by her gate. I expect that he intends to catch the eight-thirty ferry – another busy crossing, because that's the one that everyone uses who lives on Morgarrow and works on the mainland.

"However, as he is leaving, he meets Bethany, and Bethany knows him. What did you say to her?" he asked Jake. "Did you tell her that Iris was out, painting, and offer to walk up the cliff path with her to find her? Then on the path by the Abbey, you pushed her over. I heard her cry out; I never did manage to convince myself that all I heard was a seagull."

"Can you believe this guy?" Jake asked, gazing around at the shocked faces all turned on him. "You're making it up as you go along," he told Gawaine.

Gawaine shook his head. "I know that Bethany went round the back of the cottage, because when I found her bag on the cliff there was a rose fastened through the buckle of its strap. A yellow rose. There are yellow roses in Iris's garden. Did you pick it for her, Jake?"

"Did I hell! I wasn't even there."

"I admit, I considered you for a moment, Mr White," Gawaine went on, with a nod to the lawyer. Bernard White by this time looked too shell-shocked to protest. "Because you always wear a rose in your buttonhole, and you have yellow roses in your garden, too. But I find it hard to picture you presenting Bethany with your rose – and besides, at this earlier time I imagine you were still having breakfast."

"She could have got the rose anywhere," Sergeant Godwin commented. "On the mainland, even."

"No, because in the selfie that she took with Roddy Chatham on the ferry, you can see the strap of her shoulder bag and the buckle, but there is no rose. I knew there was something about that photograph that bothered me, but it took me a while to realise what it was. The only place on Morgarrow, between the ferry and the cliff where she died, the only place Bethany could have acquired a yellow rose was from Iris's garden."

Sergeant Godwin nodded slowly. "Okay… So, if you're right, and Jake Fletcher killed her, what did he do next?"

"By this time, Jake has missed the ferry," Gawaine replied. "And the storm is imminent. There's only one place he can go for shelter, and that is the Abbey. He gets there as the storm breaks, and I imagine he lurks in the cloisters, hoping that no one will see him. Now, remember that he stole Iris's phone in his attempt to make her death look like a robbery gone wrong. And at this moment, when the rain is coming down and his escape is cut off, Iris's phone rings."

"Oh, good grief…" Seff breathed out.

"I admit I was somewhat disconcerted when it struck me that I had given an alibi to a murderer," Gawaine said. "The phone rang for quite some time before Iris – as I thought – answered it," he went on. "I imagine Jake's first instinct was to let it ring. But then he realised it presented him with an opportunity. He is an actor, don't forget. And he knew Iris well – quite well enough to imitate her voice. It was a touch of genius," he added, turning to Jake, "to sound annoyed. It meant you could cut the call short. And in any case, the sound of the rain was so loud that I couldn't hear you very well."

"But—" David began,

"Exactly, my dear David. When we were caught in Iris's cottage yesterday, you could hardly hear the rain. That was what made me see that Iris had not been in the cottage when she answered the phone – in fact, that it had not been Iris at all. The sound of the rain came from the Abbey cloister."

"Why there?" Sergeant Godwin asked.

"Because that's where we have our first and only sighting of Jake Fletcher on the island," Gawaine told her. "He still hopes to get away unseen once the ferries are running again, but in case that plan fails, he has another. There's now proof that Iris was still alive after the storm broke, so all he needs is to establish that he was still dry when he reached the Abbey. Grace?"

The student looked up. "Yes, he was spliff guy," she said. "He looked a lot scruffier – he needed a shave, and his jeans were filthy – but it was him, all right."

"Thank you." Gawaine managed a brief smile. "Yes, smoking a… er… spliff in the Abbey, with his feet up on the pew, would make sure he was remembered."

By this time, Sergeant Godwin was looking distinctly interested. "We have DNA samples from the cottage that we haven't found a match for," she said. "Mr Fletcher, I shall have to ask you to come over to the station and be tested."

Jake gave an angry shrug. "Yeah, okay, I was here that day," he admitted. "But I never killed Iris. Why would I? I wanted to get back together with her."

"Yes." Sergeant Godwin turned to Gawaine. "What was his motive?"

"Iris had discovered a valuable picture in the Abbey crypt," Gawaine replied. "Which is now safely in the hands of Father Magnus."

The old priest flourished the market bag, a beaming smile on his face. Jake's head whipped around and he stared, his expression pure fury until he recovered control of himself.

"Jake hoped to sell it," Gawaine continued, "and pocket the – not inconsiderable – loot. But Iris wanted to return it to the Abbey. He couldn't simply steal it, because Iris would have exposed him. So she had to die."

"But he *didn't* steal it," Jenny Morland put in. "He left it there, in the cottage."

"Yes," Gawaine explained, "because Iris had made a will leaving all her possessions to Jake. Which, after Petroc Tremayne died, included the cottage and the contents. He knew nothing about her later will in which she left the cottage to Annis. If he had found the picture there once he inherited, he could establish its provenance as something that Great Uncle Petroc had brought back from his travels."

"So it was Jake you were expecting last night," Sergeant Godwin said.

"It was. Unfortunately, our trap was sprung."

"I'm sorry about that," Father Magnus murmured.

"This is crap," Jake protested. "I never knew about any picture. If Iris stole it, that was on her. And I never made that phone call, either," he added with a venomous look at Gawaine. "Because I never had Iris's phone. And you can't prove I did."

Sergeant Godwin paused for a moment, then heaved a sigh. "I'm sorry," she said to Gawaine. There's a lot in what you tell me, but I don't think it amounts to proof."

"That's what I was afraid of," Gawaine murmured.

"We can place him on the island, and he doesn't deny that now," the sergeant went on, "but as for connecting him to the murder – murders, if you're right—"

"But he knew about the phone call," Seff reminded her. "We're all witnesses to that."

"And a defence counsel would make mincemeat of it," Sergeant Godwin responded. "There's no hard evidence tying him in to Iris's death, and no evidence at all that Bethany's death was anything but an accident. I'll report all this to Inspector Bradshaw, but I honestly don't think he'll go for it."

"Thank you," Jake Fletcher said, heavily sarcastic. "Anyone mind if I go now?"

"Yes, you're free to go." Sergeant Godwin sounded genuinely regretful. "Don't forget to drop in at the station to give us your samples. And leave your contact details in case we need to question you further."

"Sure. No problem." Jake rose and strode towards the door, then halted and glared at Gawaine. "As for you, you'll be hearing from my lawyers."

"Just a moment." Gawaine sat erect, tension thrilling

out of him. His eyes were wide, their blue unnaturally vivid. David reached out to him, suddenly anxious.

"I appreciate what you say, Sergeant Godwin," Gawaine said. "You can't charge Jake for the murders of Iris Grant and Bethany Fox. But what about charging him for the murder of Petroc Tremayne?"

Chapter Twenty-seven

> How came you by this wretched knowledge?
> *The Devil's Law Case*, III.iii

There was an audible gasp from someone in the room. Jenny Morland said, "But Petroc wasn't—" and clapped a hand over her mouth.

David was as shocked as anyone. *I never guessed Gawaine had that up his sleeve!* But he kept enough self-command to watch Jake Fletcher, and saw a flash of alarm cross the actor's face, though he said nothing. The police officer in the doorway seemed to expand to fill the gap.

Eventually it was Jake who broke the silence, with a crack of laughter. "Wow, you should write scripts for the movies," he said. "You want me to put a word in for you?"

No one paid him any attention. "Petroc died of a heart attack," Father Magnus said.

"Yeah, and I wasn't even here at the time," Jake said jeeringly. "You can't put that one on me, either."

Gawaine looked up at him, meeting his hostile gaze calmly. "There is a way you can kill someone without being on the spot," he observed.

"Poison!" Sergeant Godwin sounded half fascinated,

half disgusted. "Don't tell me we have to exhume Petroc Tremayne's body, because I'm not even going to try to get an exhumation order."

"No, sergeant, you won't need to," Gawaine said. "Because you wouldn't find anything. But before we come to that, let's go back for a moment to the picture. Jake, when you were here at Easter, Iris discovered it and you persuaded her to keep it. I imagine it was her idea to store it in the cottage to establish its provenance as one of Petroc Tremayne's travel souvenirs. But for that, of course, Petroc Tremayne had to die. He was an old man with a weak heart, and I believe Iris would have been happy to wait for nature to take its course. But I think you, Jake, were not. In spite of his age and his heart condition, Great Uncle Petroc could have lived for years."

"I admit I was surprised he died when he did," Father Magnus put in.

"Jake had no access to poison here on Morgarrow," Gawaine went on. "Gone are the days when you could drop into the nearest chemist's and ask for a dollop of arsenic to kill your wasps. But Jake had a perfectly adequate substitute."

He slid a hand into his jacket pocket and drew out a small pill bottle. "Great Uncle Petroc regularly took medication for his weak heart," he went on, sitting with his hand curled around the container. "And as they were capsules, they were relatively easy to tamper with. Did you just open up the outer casing and tip out the medication? Or were you a little more subtle: emptying some of the capsules and filling others with an increased dose? So Great Uncle Petroc would either be taking no medication at all, or a wildly irregular amount. Such a fiddly task, though. I'm sure you didn't wear gloves; your DNA should be all over the—"

David had been watching Jake Fletcher closely while Gawaine was speaking. He had begun to look uneasy as soon as Petroc Tremayne's death was mentioned, and his unease deepened as Gawaine explained his plan to steal the picture. His face convulsed with fury as Gawaine produced the pill bottle, and at the mention of DNA his control snapped.

Letting out a roar of rage, Jake Fletcher launched himself at Gawaine, grabbing for the bottle of pills with one hand, and Gawaine's throat with the other. Gawaine was slammed back in his chair; the bottle skittered off across the floor and fetched up underneath the table. By then, David, Nathan and the police officer had dragged Jake off, leaving Gawaine gasping, but at the same time alight with satisfaction.

Jake was spewing out a torrent of obscenities, while Gawaine blinked up at him with a bewildered look, massaging his throat. David realised his friend probably didn't know the meaning of most of the insults that were being hurled at him.

"Are you okay?" he asked.

Gawaine nodded, taking a minute to find his voice.

Meanwhile, Sergeant Godwin was cautioning Jake Fletcher, who had finally run out of profanity and stood limp in the grip of the uniformed officer.

"Two for the price of one," Seff murmured, looking up from her note-taking. "What a good day she's having! Inspector Bradshaw will be *so* pleased."

Nathan looked down at Gawaine from his great height, a wide grin on his face. "That was the most exciting thing I've ever seen," he said.

"It's excitement I could do without," Gawaine responded, his voice weak and rasping.

"It was brilliant, though." Grace came up; she had retrieved the bottle of pills, and held it out to Gawaine.

"Yes, and I need a word with you." Sergeant Godwin's voice was harsh as she broke into the little group. "Are you out of your tiny mind? How dare you remove evidence just for the sake of grandstanding? If you've made it inadmissible—"

"But I haven't," Gawaine said mildly in the face of the sergeant's anger. "These aren't Petroc Tremayne's pills, and I never said they were. They're my painkillers." He held the bottle out to show her; glancing at David, he added, "I brought them with me in case I needed a second dose. No," he continued to the sergeant, "Petroc's pills are still in the bathroom cabinet where he kept them. I would have told you what I suspected last night, but you were too cross with me to listen."

"I had good reason," the sergeant said.

"Oh, undoubtedly. So after that, I admit I took the liberty of locking the cabinet and bringing the key away, just to be on the safe side."

So that's what he was doing in Great Uncle Petroc's bathroom last night! David thought, half admiring and half furious.

Gawaine reached into his inside pocket and brought out the key, which he handed to Sergeant Godwin.

"And you haven't touched them?" she asked.

"I have not. I admit, that was a lucky guess. But I'm convinced that Jake killed two people to get hold of the picture, and if two, why not three? And I could only see one way that he could have done it."

The sergeant grunted, still not totally pleased with him.

"But wait a minute," David said. "If Jake had tampered with the pills, wouldn't he have taken them away after he killed Iris?"

"I doubt it," Gawaine replied. "Maybe he was rattled, and just forgot. But more likely, now that Petroc Tremayne was dead and buried and no one suggested his death was anything but natural, why start disturbing sleeping dogs? With Iris murdered, finding the pills missing might have encouraged someone to ask awkward questions."

Sergeant Godwin shrugged. "That's just a detail now. The pills are hard evidence."

"You might get the Trustees to let you test the picture for DNA, too," Gawaine said. "I'm sure Jake must have handled it."

The sergeant nodded. "Good thought. It's worth a bit, then?" she added.

"If I'm right, and it is by Cimabue," Gawaine replied, "it is indeed worth a bit. The last of his paintings to be discovered was sold for twenty million."

"Twenty—" Sergeant Godwin gaped, the mouse confronted by a mountain of the most succulent cheese in the world. "That's a damn' good motive for murder. I shouldn't wonder if we can nail him for Iris and Bethany too." Pulling herself together, she went on, "You will need to come over to the station this afternoon to make a statement about all this."

"Of course." As Sergeant Godwin turned away to take custody of her prisoners, Gawaine held out a hand to stop her. "A moment, sergeant. What about Annis Radford?"

"I'll need to bring Inspector Bradshaw up to speed," Sergeant Godwin replied, with the hint of a smug smile. "But I think you can assume that Ms Radford will be released."

"Then perhaps you can give her these." Gawaine took out Annis's keys and held them out to the sergeant. "And tell her that the vet still has her cat."

"Sure."

David was disappointed. He could imagine Gawaine as the conquering hero, returning the keys and the cat Merino to a newly released and grateful Annis – and maybe receiving his reward.

On second thoughts, no, I can't. It's just not in Gawaine to behave like that... even if the lady might appreciate it.

Sergeant Godwin collected the market bag and its precious contents from a reluctant Father Magnus, and began chivvying her prey out of the door. But before she left, she halted and turned. "The knitting needle," she said. "You haven't mentioned the knitting needle."

"No more I have," Gawaine said, sounding faintly surprised at himself. "Well, Jake Fletcher clearly came provided with his weapon of choice. It shows he expected all along that he would have to kill Iris. It might be useful," he continued, "to ask around in the Lake District knitting shops. A man buying a knitting needle should be unusual enough to be remembered."

Sergeant Godwin nodded. "Good point."

"But *why* was that his weapon of choice?" Seff asked impatiently.

"Oh, that was a deliberate attempt to frame Annis," Gawaine said. "Remember how she told us she rejected him, when he was here at Easter? Women aren't allowed to do that to Jake Fletcher. And it almost worked."

Sergeant Godwin gave him a brisk nod and left.

David glanced around the room. Bernard White and the two priests were gathered around the table; Bernard looked out of temper and was gesturing at the computer, but it was pretty clear there would be no presentation that day. Elaine Chatham was sitting nearby, quietly weeping, with Grace and Nathan to comfort her.

"And they're left to pick up the pieces…" he said.

Gawaine nodded. He looked white and exhausted, but somehow a world away from the deep depression that sometimes overtook him at the end of a case. "You know, my dear David," he said, "there have been times I've felt sympathetic to a murderer. Someone goaded into violence by unbelievable stress. But this time – I've never encountered a fully-fledged psychopath before." He shuddered. "I hope I never have to again."

Epilogue

We cannot have a cause of any fame,
But you must have scurvy pamphlets, and lewd ballads
Engend'red of it presently.
The Devil's Law Case, IV.ii

Two days after Jake Fletcher's arrest, David was checking out at the hotel reception desk when Seff appeared from the stairs.

"Good, I've caught you," she said. "I wouldn't want you to go without saying goodbye."

David wasn't sure how he felt about that. Normally having Seff out of his life was like finding the source of an irritating dripping noise, and turning it off to achieve blissful silence. But he still couldn't stifle a sneaking suspicion that he would miss her.

"Where's Gawaine?" she asked, glancing around. "Don't tell me he's still packing? You'll miss the ferry."

"No," David replied. "He's gone to say goodbye to the cat Merino."

Seff gave him a sideways grin. "Really? *Just* the cat?"

"Well, Annis too, I suppose. But it's just the cat he's admitting to."

"Pity," Seff said. "Still, I suppose she's here and he's in

Surrey..." She sighed. "If I ever met a man who's crying out for the love of a good woman, it's Gawaine."

David couldn't argue with that.

Seff fell silent while the hotel manager ran David's credit card and he handed over his key. "Are you meeting Gawaine at the ferry?" she asked when he was ready to go.

"Yes, he left his bag in the car," David told her. "You're staying on, then?" he added as he trundled his case out into the car park, with Seff walking alongside.

"Yes, I have a few interviews to chase up. And I *must* get a photo of that painting. You know, David," she went on after a pause, "you ought to get Gawaine to go away somewhere. My story came out this morning, and there'll be press swarming around here like locusts. Celebrity crime, valuable artwork – they'll be all over it. Gawaine will hate it."

David could see that she had a point. Gawaine loathed the attention of the press, and to a certain extent Seff was able to shield him from the worst of it. But a massive news story like this...

"He can't go home... He could stay in my flat, but I suppose that's the next place they'll look," he said.

"Of course. And don't think you'll escape, either."

David groaned. "That's all I need!"

"I had an idea," Seff began. *Well, you're never at a loss for those.* "Where is this conference you have to go to?"

"Venice," David replied. "I was surprised. It's usually somewhere inspiring, like Runcorn."

"There you are, then." Seff's voice was full of satisfaction. "Take Gawaine with you. When you're finished with some idiot lecturer droning on, and all the daft team-building exercises, you can let Gawaine take you round the art galleries. Assimilate a bit of culture."

David had to admit that was not a bad idea, though he would rather assimilate some good food and wine. "Okay, if Gawaine agrees."

"Tell him the press will be on his tail, and he'll agree to anything."

The Arctic Circle? The Amazon rain forest? But Venice, now... "Yes, I expect he will," David said, surprised at being on the same page as Seff for once.

"I'll say goodbye for now," Seff said, giving David a pat on the shoulder. "Take Gawaine to Venice. And for goodness' sake, try to keep him out of trouble."

This book is printed on paper from sustainable sources managed under the Forest Stewardship Council (FSC) scheme.

It has been printed in the UK to reduce transportation miles and their impact upon the environment.

For every new title that Troubador publishes, we plant a tree to offset CO_2, partnering with the More Trees scheme.

For more about how Troubador offsets its environmental impact, see www.troubador.co.uk/sustainability-and-community